"You want to know something about men? . . . A really big secret?" he asked without smiling, all the mirth having left him now.

"Yeah," she replied, looking down at her sticky fingers.

"It doesn't take us years to decide on a woman we want to be with permanently—like a husband. We make that decision in a matter of moments usually, within a meeting or two. We lock on to target, and we know she's the one. We don't intellectualize about it. If it doesn't hit gut level, then we ain't going there. If you see a guy hanging around for a long time, dillydallying about it, he's either not there because his finances are jacked up and he isn't comfortable about that—and no, y'all can't help—or he hasn't locked on target, and she's just not the one."

"You're saying all this to say . . . ?"

He noticed her tone was becoming defensive, and it made him smile. Boy, talking to women was like traveling through a mine field.

"I'm saying all this to say that guys nest when they're ready."

"What?"

"We want a person to be there, to depend on, to trust. If the right woman asks us to do something, we will move heaven and earth for her—if we were raised right, but that's a whole 'nother conversation."

"You're saying all this to say what then?"

She had become so indignant that he feared she might pop up off the sofa. The sight of her feathers being ruffled made him want to chuckle for some odd reason. He was getting to her, and he enjoyed every minute of it.

"I'm saying all this to say that a man doesn't drive to Philly after going to the farmer's market to find crawfish and shrimp, drive back to Jersey, then drive back to Philly, stand in the cold trying to convince a woman who he doesn't care that much about to not kill herself on the slick roads, only to drive her to Jersey and offer her dinner, but not before he gets down on his knees in his mind to thank Jesus for letting her come to his house."

LOVE POTIONS

Leslie Esdaile

ARABESQUE
★BET
BOOKS

BET Publications, LLC
http://www.bet.com
http://www.arabesquebooks.com

ARABESQUE BOOKS are published by

BET Publications, LLC
c/o BET BOOKS
One BET Plaza
1900 W Place NE
Washington, DC 20018-1211

All Kensington Titles, Imprints, and Distributed Lines are available at special quantity discounts for bulk purchases for sales promotions, premiums, fund-raising, and educational or institutional use. Special book excerpts or customized printings can also be created to fit specific needs. For details, write or phone the office of the Kensington special sales manager: Kensington Publishing Corp., 850 Third Avenue, New York, NY 10022, attn: Special Sales Department, Phone: 1-800-221-2647.

First Printing: April 2002
10 9 8 7 6 5 4 3 2 1

Printed in the United States of America

All thanks go to God, first and foremost . . . and for the humor He has added to my life.

Many days I had to laugh to keep from crying: A Black Woman's Anthem. That's why this dedication also goes out to all my crazy home-gurls from back in the day, as well as the new ones that have joined us (they know who they are)! This book is for my partners in crime who sat up late at night with me when we had no dates, who laughed at me, made me angry, who read me, and got me into all sorts of trouble (or agreed to get into trouble with me) . . . telling me madness like, "This is what we can do, see!"

This book is dedicated to friendships—bonds that feel like you were born of the same blood. People who you'll love and fight with till the end of time. Ma, gurls . . . I love y'all!

Special thanks *goes out to Chandra Taylor, my editor, who actually understood the fast-paced, zinging one-liners cast between multiple black women speaking in concert on a page! Thank you for not giving up on this one!*

And I would be totally remiss if I did not offer my very special thanks to Joanne Taylor and her staff at Hair Signatures Salon, Philadelphia . . . for keeping me together, healing me with their professional hair-repair touch, and for the joy and bonding that abounds in their establishment. There ain't nuthin' like a sistah's salon!

Chapter 1

Nicole could only laugh as the lively conversation between her girlfriends hit a crescendo. There was something
about doing hair in the kitchen, with wine, Buffalo wings,
and music blaring in the background from the living room
stereo down the hall that made every conceivable hurt seem
to momentarily dissipate. It reminded her so much of the
gatherings of women in Florida, with kitchen conferences,
pressing hair, laughter, love, and friendly arguments amid
chores and unquestionable support.

Thank goodness her big sister–like girlfriend, Victoria,
always hosted her renowned day-after-disappointing-holidays
fests. It made being away from family during the tough
times so much easier, Nicole noted. And despite finding
herself in Philadelphia after moving there for her husband's
airport job five years ago, she was thankful that at least
she'd been claimed by an adoptive family of girlfriends after

her divorce. Moving from apartment to apartment had made neighbors and friendships rare.

"Not even a card," her friend Delores railed on. "Cheap Negro did not even give me a card, and left the bar early for me to close up so he could go home to his wife. Ain't that nuthin'? Tryin' to play the role on Valentine's Day, and she's too dumb to know what's up. One day, I'ma tell her."

"Maybe his wife does know what's up," Victoria countered. "Just that she ain't stupid enough to throw the baby out with the bathwater 'cause last I saw, his wife was driving a Benz from the bar, and your tired behind was walking to get in a broke-down Toyota. Get my point? And where was he on Valentine's Day? Home. I rest my case."

"Now, see," their friend Gail argued over a glass of wine, as Delores sucked her teeth at Victoria's comment, "that's why I don't even deal with 'em. My baby girl gave me a card and some flowers. What I need a man for? Hmmph!"

"Well," Victoria remarked coolly, "mine called the tax man on me for Valentine's Day, saying I was making more money than I was reporting, all 'cause I wouldn't let that sorry fool borrow two hundred dollars for some trumped-up emergency. Puhleeze! I ain't the one, y'all. You know that. Finance his women? Not Miss Victoria."

"I got the best present ever." Nicole chuckled, pausing for dramatic effect. "My daughter made me a big construction-paper heart card in kindergarten, and presented it to me with the macaroni necklace she made and painted with dozens of kisses and hugs to go with it. It was the sweetest thing. It was all I needed."

"That is a precious age. I remember those days." Gail sighed. "Little bird is five, right?"

"Yup," Nicole said brightly. "Lydia is such a lovebug. She even made one for her sorry father, and I was good, ladies. I mailed it to him. Who needs a guy, right?'' Nicole raised her wineglass and fought back the threat of sudden tears.

"May it drive a stake of guilt through his heart,'' Victoria said in a blasé tone. ''Stop trying to make him into what he's not—a father. You could have used that thirty-four cents' worth of postage to defray that dag-gonned ten thousand dollars' worth of credit card debt that fool left you when he took up residence as a pilot in another country just to avoid child support, girl. How am I going to ever get y'all to focus on the real importance of life—business? Men handle their business, and all nooky and sentimentality is secondary. We should do likewise. Screw Valentine's Day.''

At that moment, all the camaraderie and support seemed to evaporate around Nicole as her emotions expanded and contracted in her lungs, making it difficult to breathe with Victoria's words of truth laid out cold in the room. The card and gift from her daughter were perfect, but something that she would have also liked to share with someone special, someone just for her, who was an adult, and who cherished her. The reality of focusing on the five-digit debt she had to deal with on her paltry salary made her want to wretch. But this was about postholiday triumph today—victory for having survived the night of grieving. Nicole grappled with the sudden gloom that accosted her, and melted it away slowly like the frost now leaving her wineglass.

"Valentine's Day and my birthday are the only days I get like this,'' Nicole admitted in a somber tone. ''Christmas, Easter, Thanksgiving, I'm okay—because those aren't individual holidays; they're family holidays, or mainly for kids. But the ones just for you . . . I don't know. I'm sorry, ladies.''

"Nothin' to apologize for. New Year's does me like that,'' Gail said with a sigh. ''That's why I always offer to work on that holiday. Just reminds me that another year has gone by and my life hasn't changed, and I haven't gone to the islands on vacation to—''

''—Get your groove back.'' Delores laughed sadly. ''I know. I always work on New Year's, too.''

''I go to the islands every holiday after the last head in my salon is done, and the last nail job is finished. Y'all need to treat yourselves better, and get out of this I-ain't-got-no-man funk! Buy your own car, your own jewelry, your own vacations, and your own dinners. Puhleeze! If it's all that bad, send yourself flowers and mail yourself a card. Chocolate just makes you fat and breaks your skin out, anyway.''

''Takes money to do all of that, Miss Vic,'' Gail argued. ''Your kids are grown, damn near. Plus, I hear tell that it's not as much fun alone.''

''No lie,'' Delores chimed in. ''It is not as much fun alone. Ask me how I know.''

''Then take a girlfriend with you, and have a blast.''

Nicole, Delores, and Gail fell silent for a moment, all apparently trying to come up with a rebuttal to Victoria's position.

''It takes extra money to do those things, and that's hard to come by, especially if you have kids,'' Delores finally hedged, obviously trying to find middle ground. ''Not that we expect a guy to do all of those things for us, but it would be nice to know that there was someone special in your life to share both the responsibilities and—''

''Then make some money, gurl. What's your problem?''

Victoria seemed to become indignant at the thought that finances could be the sole reason holding any of them back from anything. It was always her button, and Nicole let out a sad chuckle as she watched Victoria puff up in preparation for hair-salon-via-kitchen-table banter on the subject of money and men.

''All of us ain't got it like that,'' Delores argued with a

wave of one hand while she took a deep swig of wine using the other. "Eddie pays me just enough to keep my bills straight, but there ain't much extra."

"So open up a bar-restaurant down the street from him and make all his clients come to you, then," Victoria argued. "Hell, you can run the bar side, and Gail could cook, right? Why y'all still talkin' about some man who won't let you do something? Are we not in the new millennium?"

"Build all of that with no money, I assume?" Nicole was so incredulous at Victoria's single-minded focus on self-employment that all she could do was laugh as she watched the expressions on Delores's and Gail's faces.

Receiving a pop on her head as Victoria added a glob of hairstyling gel to her natural twists, Nicole laughed even harder.

"Ow! Dag, Miss Vic, you're worse than my grandmom used to be!"

"That's because I'm a professional, and I know how to pop a moving head when I have to. Might knock some sense into it. Now hold still. You're lucky I'm even doing this in the kitchen for free, instead of in my salon, where I have a rep to maintain."

"Miss Victoria," Gail teased as she refilled her plate with spicy chicken wings, "be nice. Just because you want to pop that ex-husband of yours in the head don't mean you can go hittin' on our girl."

"Oh, now, why'd you have to go there?" Delores poured more wine and shook her head with a wide grin when Victoria Jones sucked her teeth as a response. "See, now, we made a pact that we were not gonna talk about dogs in this kitchen."

"That's right," Nicole added. "Just because another Valentine's Day has passed and—"

"And another Christmas, and another New Year's," Victoria huffed. "I didn't bring up the subject, anyway. Dee started it, now I'ma finish it."

"Well, I was working at the hospital on New Year's, myself," Gail Jackson explained again before taking a huge bite of her biscuit, then slathering it with more butter. "Don't know why y'all worry about holidays no way. At forty-three, I'm done. Got my one girl child, and it's me and her on the holidays. Ain't having no more babies, so what I look like runnin' after some man? For what?"

"Whatchu look like is a Holstein cow," Delores crooned, studying her long, multicolored, airbrushed talons as she picked up her cigarette. "Chile, just because you done with making babies don't mean you can't get a little somethin'-somethin' on a holiday."

"Delores Thompson," Victoria warned with good nature. "You need to quit it. You know Miss Gail Jackson don't do nooky, and don't want no nooky. Just because your fast behind is always on the hunt working for Eddie at the bar don't mean that everybody always got sex on the brain."

"My apologies, Saint Victoria." Delores chuckled. "But our girl has to watch her weight for her health too."

"And why are y'all all fired up about me watching my health and my weight, huh?" Gail argued. "You might be skinny and wear that hoochie-momma gear, but I don't smoke or drink, and probably got better chances of comin' out alive than you. Hmmph!"

"All right, all right," Nicole interjected, seeing real hurt easing its way out of hiding on Delores's dark, round face. "We made a pact; no male-bashing today—even if it is the day after Valentine's Day and nobody got so much as a card. So let's not turn on each other, ladies."

"Thank you, Nicole Gordon," Gail added with conviction as she cast a disparaging glance in Delores's direction.

"I'm going to tell you what the problem is, girls," Victoria said with a sigh, picking up her rat-tail comb and using it like a conductor as she spoke to make her point.

"Oh, Lord, have mercy! Here we go, beauty-parlor psychology in the kitchen." Delores groaned, making them all laugh in unison again.

"Here we are," Victoria went on, not allowing their laughter to stop her roll, "all good-looking, intelligent women with good skills, and we are sitting here in the kitchen the morning after Valentine's Day all sad and whatnot—just because we couldn't roll over and get that morning shot. And we have the nerve to be talking about that, instead of *real* issues—like how to become financially independent. Then you can get all the nooky you want. That's the problem. I know what I'm talking about."

The comment drew hoots of laughter and a round of high-fives from every woman sitting in the kitchen. Spurred on by her audience, Victoria Jones hurtled into her normal comedic tirade that always transformed a pity party into a victory celebration.

"See, the reason I'm so cool," Victoria said with mock indignation at her friends' circumstances, "is because I'm already an entrepreneur, and free."

"What?" Delores huffed, obviously trying to bait Victoria into some of her best material. "You don't see no men at your shop like I see at the bar. When's the last time you been laid? Money don't take care of that."

The three spectators doubled over and laughed harder when Victoria Jones set down her rat-tail comb and smoothed the front of her lime-green silk jogging suit over her voluptuous figure. It was a ritual that they all knew too well, and which began in the way that she put a section of her platinum weave behind a diamond-studded earlobe, then flexed her four-inch acrylic-laden fingers. Victoria's hand went to her hip as her laser-beam, almond-colored-contact

gaze locked on them all in a serious, no-nonsense line.
Everyone knew this was what slowed down head jobs at the
shop, but it was why they all came to Victoria's Palace of
Beauty nonetheless—to hear the gospel according to Miss
Vic.

"Aw, sookie sookie." Gail giggled. "You done got her
started, Dee. Watch your scalp now, Nikki. I wouldn't let
her do my hair when she's like this."

"Delores Thompson," Victoria said with dramatic
emphasis, "you are forty-two, work as a barmaid for your
boss-lover, and have two prepubescent girls who are driving
you crazy—and see nothing but married men in there all
day long, including your boss. Now you might be fine, lean,
and bubblin' like brown suga, but when you get your own
bar, then you can tell me something. And you, Miss Gail
Jackson," she added, but in a much nicer tone, "you might
be heavy and all, but you need to be a caterer, stop standing
all night to take care of the sick and the dying, and stop
wearing wigs to cover up what God gave you. Pretty brown
skin just gettin' all messed up with that fried food—and you
in a place where there's MDs, male nurses, and policemen
bringing folks in—chile! Whatchu mean at forty-three you
don't need no nooky and ain't thinkin' about it, and ain't
using the spare time to make no money? I'm older than all
of y'all and I still need some upon occasion—but I handle
my money first. Don't I look good for forty-five?"

Although Miss Victoria had read them, it was with kindness interlaced with the brutal truth. Nicole held her breath
as all eyes turned to her. Even though Victoria's truth was
on target, it could still be delivered with the sting of a
wasp—felt for days afterward.

"You look fantastic, actually," Nicole admitted as the
other women chimed in with nods and sighs of agreement.
"You have the body of life, girl, and the finances to match

it. One day when I grow up, I want to be in your position. But until then, please try to be nice to us."

A sly smile of appreciation etched its way across Victoria's face, and her golden-brown complexion seemed to drink in the compliment from the younger woman the way dry ground soaks in a gentle rain.

"I'll do you one better than being nice to you sorry heifers. I'll tell you my trade secret," Victoria quipped with a chuckle.

"Which is?" Delores taunted, folding her arms over her chest as she spoke.

"Don't worry about the romance until you handle the finance."

Another collective groan echoed in the room from the group.

"She don't have a clue," Delores said, shaking her head. "Give it up, ladies. You can't do nothin' with Miss Vic. She does not know what it's like to be broke, horny, and so angry you could spit, and depressed all at the same time. Forget it. Subject change. More wine, anybody?"

"That's because I focus on the truly important and the here and now—not coulda, woulda, shoulda been. My kids are almost grown, and I don't have any grandbabies yet, knock wood. I'm not still mad at the man who didn't pay me no child support to raise my three. I did it myself. And I'm not waiting on Prince Charming to swoop by my salon and save me from my horrible life. Nicole Gordon—"

"Oops, Nikki, it's your turn," Delores interjected with a flip of her wrist, cutting Victoria off.

"If I had Nikki's thirty-nine-year-old body with those legs, that gorgeous cinnamon brown skin, those perfect curves, beautiful hands, a gorgeous head of hair, a smile to die for, and that sexy West Indian accent . . . girl, I'd have every wife and woman running me out of town on a rail.

And that voice. Oh! Why are you wasting your time as a telemarketer, and why don't you go ahead and go for broke?'' Victoria shook her head and let out a sound of disgust. "Wasted resources.''

Nicole laughed, becoming self-conscious but still appreciating all the nice things her girlfriend just said about her, despite the dig. "That's just it. Got a five-year-old daughter, and if I go for broke, I might really go broke, okaaaay?''

"Fear," Victoria huffed. "Chicken doo doo–based fear. See, your problem is that you ain't from Philly. Had you grown up around here with us, we'da shown you how to deal with fear. Kick its ass! You've been punked down by that no-'count husband who left you stranded, then by a divorce, and by looking at a bunch of bills to pay while raising a child on your own. Just 'cause your momma and daddy live halfway down the country in Florida don't mean you have to be scared. You been punked is all. Hmmph. I can't stand to see sisters afraid of their own potential. You're just scared to step off.''

"Right. And?'' Nicole said with a giggle to dismiss the concept, but allowing her gaze to sweep the room for moral support. "The only thing I can do really well is write. Poetry, if you haven't heard already, doesn't pay the bills. I'm not skilled like you, Dee and Gail. You can do heads, Delores is one hell of a businesswoman and bookkeeper, and keeps all tabs straight in her head. Gail can cook her butt off; plus she's a nurse. All I do is sound good on the telephone, but I'm not trying to go into the one-eight-hundred-phone-sex business.''

"Y'all are knee-deep in rhetoric." Delores chuckled, standing to turn on the small counter television over the music, "and are making me miss my judge shows. Like to see them get wit' those folks on the tube and set them crazies straight. Lord, what I wouldn't do for a little justice to be doled out at the bar." She settled down on a stool directly in front of the screen, and turned up the volume. "Wish I could tell all the wives and girlfriends the truth about the yang their men talk about 'em—and do—when they don't think anybody is listening or looking."

"Move over," Gail complained, working on her fourth biscuit, and sopping up the excess chicken grease and barbecue sauce on her plate with it. "Here come da judge."

"Now, I thought we were supposed to be constructively discussing business opportunities and positive strategies," Victoria fussed, going back to the job of doing Nicole's hair. "See, that's the problem with y'all. You ain't focused."

"I'm focusing on the judge, girl. Ain't he fine?" Gail giggled through a mouthful of potato salad. "Besides, you never did answer the question."

"What question?" Victoria asked with a wave of her hand.

" 'Bout how long it's been," Delores said flatly without turning away from the television.

"Been as long as it's needed to, right, Nikki?" Victoria asked in a casual tone, adding a bit more hair pomade to Nicole's scalp than she had probably intended to, which made Nicole stifle a smile.

"Look," Nicole hedged, trying to wrest peace and civility from the group. "We're all afraid of something, and—"

"The *only* thing I'm scared of," Victoria quipped, "is the IRS gettin' into my pocket."

"Right," Delores concurred in a distant tone. "Told that no-good Eddie that one day the tax man will cometh, and the tax man will taketh away—if he keeps payin' everybody under the table, and skimmin' on what he really makes. Only reason I don't dime him out is 'cause that would probably put a dent in my paycheck, knowing him."

"Eddie's a businessman," Victoria shot back. "Leave

him alone. You just mad because he can't handle you, his wife, and his other girlfriend like he used to. The man drinks too much."

"I'm not hearin' it today, Miss Vic." Delores laughed with a wave of her hand. "I'll be honest. I ain't had no real good rock-the-house in like a year. That mess Eddie delivers ain't even worth my time no more. So, yeah, girl, I got an attitude. And his cheap ass didn't even give me any roses or nothing."

"Well, I gave that all up when my husband left ten years ago," Gail said plainly, then took a big swig of her wine.

"What?" Her eyes darted to each woman in the room when Delores turned around from her stool, Victoria dropped her comb, and Nicole's jaw went slack.

"Ten years?" Nicole whispered. "I've done two years without a date, and thought I'd lose ... I mean ... ten years?"

"Ain't no thang but a chicken wang," Gail said with false bravado, then bit into another piece of chicken. "Got plenty to keep me busy and my mind off of *that.*"

"Now, girl," Delores said sounding concerned, "that ain't healthy."

"If the chile don't want to deal with the species, then the chile don't want to deal with the species," Victoria defended. "I did five, and I ain't no worse for the wear."

This time Gail stopped munching and looked at Victoria hard as all of them momentarily went still.

"You are lying!" Delores exclaimed, jumping from her stool. "Ain't that much bizness in the world!"

"Yeah, there is," Victoria said casually, returning to Nicole's hair and wrenching her body so that she could get to the back section of her scalp. "When is the last time you dealt with one who cracked your rib, gave you a black eye, and almost ruined your business? So leave Gail be."

"My ex just ran women, Vic; he never hit me—so who you talking about? Me or you?" Gail whispered the question as she stood and made the rounds with more wine.

"Yeah, yeah, yeah," Victoria murmured. "They all crazy, which is why I say get self-sufficient and own your own business, in your own name, with your own money; then you can afford to take care of your own kids, and take yourself to the islands for Mother's Day, Valentine's Day, New Year's Eve, whatever. That's why I buy my own diamonds with my own money," she added, flashing her array of expensive jewelry as she spoke, "and I don't have to take no bull from no man but the tax man. Dig?"

Suddenly it seemed like Victoria's reality check had drawn all the mirth from the room, and an emulsion of thick silence, television commercials, and music from the stereo a room away covered them.

"See, I like her," Victoria quipped, blatantly trying to change the subject. "She's got the dream business," she added, pointing toward the television with her comb as the humorous commercial droned on. "We could do that, you know. Sister's got it goin' on. Getting paid for gettin' in people's personal business."

"Oh," Delores scoffed. "So now we're gonna become television psychics, right?"

"Be serious." Gail laughed.

"Why not?" Victoria asked casually. "It's a hustle. None of it's real. Just theater."

"Gurl, puhleeze." Nicole sighed, still thinking about all of their innermost scars.

"We have everything we need." Victoria chuckled with a sly tone. "A location—my shop. A new kid on the block with a sexy voice, exotic island look, and no neighborhood history—Nikki. Plus a person to cook up some placebo greens juice, and put it in test tubes from her job—which

I could sell like a special blend of aphrodisiac elixir after their readings. That would be Gail's department. Food handling, potion creations. Hell, if Chanel made a mint selling perfume, we could make one selling love potions the day after all disappointments days. Dee could even run the elixir through Eddie's bar as an added outlet. Merchandizing. I'll get my receptionist to hook up some designer labels on the computer.''

''She's serious; you know that, right?'' Delores finally said with half shock, half mischief. All activity in the kitchen had stopped, except Victoria's hands working against Nicole's twists.

''You are kidding, right?'' Nicole hedged.

''What's not to be serious about, huh?'' Victoria ceased working for a moment and put her hand on her hip. ''None of us have a man, and all the kids, except Nikki's, can watch themselves one night a week. We can get one of the older ones to watch the baby. You all have bills eating you up alive, and I have tax issues to contend with. You all want a way out of your day-job grind, but can't get a loan from a bank to start a business. This is legal, and it's on television, even. This is something we could do every Wednesday night after quitting time, by appointment, closed to the public without an invitation, and could probably clear—if we did twenty sisters in a party at twenty-five dollars a pop, plus love potion purchases, about five hundred dollars *extra* a week. Hell, it would serve the IRS right for me to make extra ducats under the table to pay off their small business extortion, anyway.

''It's four of us, we do this four weekends in a row, and each of us just increased our monthly income by five hundred a month—each takes the door on their get-paid week. Do it for six months and each one of you've got three grand. Bam. Just like that. Do it for four nights a week, and each one of you just made two thousand dollars a month. By June, say summertime, we'd each have about ten grand. Bam.''

"I told you she was serious," Delores repeated. "When our girl Vic starts doin' head counts with a sticker price, she's serious."

"Now, if we sell each bottle of love potion for, like, three dollars, and each customer gets one each time she comes in, that's another sixty bucks a night—which should cover the expenses of labels and munchies, and will create a little hype. If Dee sells the elixir of love through the bar, well, we just started a microbrewery. Think about it. How much is a beer? Three bucks. How much are the ingredients for some of Gail's thumpin' greens potlikka? Probably less than a quarter, give or take, with the cost of the label. It's a paid advertising strategy."

"First of all," Nicole protested, "is it even ethical, much less legal to do any of this? Don't we need a business license, and don't we have to pass the FDA approval process to sell food in bottles to the public? I mean, really, ladies. We can't do this."

Delores, Victoria, and Gail groaned in unison.

"No, seriously. I don't want to tell people lies that could get them into a worse bind than they are already in. This is nuts." Nicole's gaze swept the room for support, but found none.

"I know everybody's business in this neighborhood, by way of their husbands and girlfriends," Delores soothed. "Wouldn't be telling lies, especially if you just encouraged the wives and girlfriends to check out certain things. You know, being psychic is an art, not a science, so if you're a little off from time to time, they'll give you latitude."

"Are you crazy?" Nicole shrieked, popping up from her

chair, only to be pushed back into it by her shoulders by Victoria.

"Would be justice, actually," Delores pressed on. "Don't you wish somebody had told you that your fiancé had a woman in every city before you married him? Woulda saved you a whole lot of heartbreak. Think of it as justice—no, a public service to other women."

"That's the truth. I know the other half of their beeswax," Gail added. "Just from working in the hospital, you hear everything."

"But isn't this fraud? I mean, don't we have to pay taxes or something? Don't we need a license to distribute food, or this so-called elixir?"

"I pay taxes through the salon at the end of the year; forget quarterly. If you want, I'll give y'all a ten-ninety-nine. I already have a business license on a commercially zoned strip. I can close my shop to the public and hold a nonalcoholic theme party for advertising and client preference, if I want to. No biggie. Besides, churches sell dinners without a license all the time. Plus, I may have a hookup to get L and I to turn the other way. Couple of the brothers down at Licenses and Inspection love some Victoria."

"But we aren't a church!" Nicole let her head fall forward into her hands as her mind raced to make sense of the insane concept. Yeah, she wished that someone had told her about her philandering fiancé before he became her husband. Sure, she wished someone would have given her hope and belief in herself during the period of torment and confusion, and Lord knows she needed the money to get out of debt so that she could really start living. And sure enough, it would take a whole lot of weight off her shoulders to know that she could take care of her baby girl, and send her aging parents much-needed financial support, without a struggle. But . . .

"We can do this, ladies," Victoria pressed with conviction. "We owe it to ourselves to take the bull by the horns and make a way out of no way."

"I'm not trying to go to jail, Victoria," Nicole said in earnest. "I can't send my child to my elderly parents in Florida or, God forbid, down to her father's family in the Bahamas, all because I've done something stupid to get over the hump. Plus, I don't want to hurt anyone. We can't just play with people's lives for profit—that's sacrilege."

"We won't be playing with people's lives," Gail crooned, walking over to Nicole to rest a hand on her shoulder. "Baby, we will stick to the facts. It's their men's karma if they done lied to some poor woman like us and get busted in the salon. Tell her, Vic; don't that happen every day in your shop for free? This is just with a little more flair and mystique."

"Every day," Delores repeated. "You hear about a bunch of drama kickin' off at the bar because the wrong person rolled up at the right time. Girl, puhleeze. At least this way the poor women can hear the truth in the privacy of the psychic's chamber, instead of getting her face pressed in public. Besides, if a psychic tells her, she can always opt not to believe it. The whole thing is about personal choice, right, Vic?"

"But, ladies, we're mothers. We have kids. We can't masquerade as some psychics and sell greens juice as love potion." Nicole looked at them in dismay when they all started laughing.

"Masquerade, thy name is woman," Victoria purred as she chuckled. "You think Gail was born with red nylon hair, or I popped out of my mother's belly with platinum curls and light eyes? And you think Dee ain't had everything lifted, augmented, or tucked? But she looks good, right? My entire beauty industry, the cosmetic industry, and the designer garment industry are built on accepting the illusion, honey. The fabricators of this ruse don't go to jail. You the only one in this kitchen who insists on no acrylic nails, no perm, and barely any makeup. . . . But, alas, you can pull it off. Most of us can't, okay, so few of us are the genuine article, and—''

"I take extreme exception to that," Delores remarked in a fake Southern accent. "My look is naturally effective, darlin'.''

Nicole's gaze ricocheted around the room and the smiling but serious faces. "But if there's one shred of illegality about this, and we were to get caught, or we hurt someone badly, I'd die. We've got kids and—''

"Miss Goody Two-shoes, we've all got kids. Go ask a lawyer, or go to the library, or whatever, and find out what you can and cannot do, if you don't believe us. How else do they have these psychic hot lines, and television psychics, and stuff?" Gail seemed indignant, but was still patient. Her eyes sparkled with mischief and her smile widened when Nicole sighed. "Overhearing information is not against the law, last time I heard.''

"You all are serious . . . no, worse—crazy! I don't want to go to jail. I don't want to get called out into the streets by some woman about her man. I just want to live the quiet life, ladies!''

"The broke life, you mean. Nikki, tell the truth. You haven't had a man or a vacation in two years, and all you do is pay off the bills your ex-husband left you, and then take care of a toddler. When do you get to go out to dinner or have fun?" Delores asked the question in a soft tone, albeit with her hand on her hip.

Nicole looked up at Victoria, then glanced at both Delores and Gail.

"Never," Nicole whispered.

"The last guy you slept with, or went out with, was your ex-husband, right?" Gail asked gently.

"Yeah," Nicole murmured.

"You don't even do poetry slams anymore, and I bet all you write is that sad, he-done-me-wrong mess, right?" Victoria asked the question between sips of wine.

Nicole chuckled. "Yeah."

"And five hundred dollars is about what you make a week, give or take, and after taxes, right?" Delores pressed the question and the mathematics into her brain.

"If we did it four nights a week," Gail said calmly, "you could double your salary and be out of debt from those credit cards your ex ran up in your name in a year. Ain't bad. I could even put something extra away for my baby's college fund."

"Now you're all focused, and thinking like business-women," Victoria said with satisfaction oozing from her high-gloss-frosted lips. "Forget nooky, men, and their incumbent drama. This is freedom."

"But there're still a lot of unanswered questions," Nicole protested, saying it more to bolster her own resolve not to do it, than to convince the others.

"So go check it out quietly, dig into all the legalities, and come back to me in forty-eight hours with an answer," Victoria said coolly. "We could get this operation cranking this week by word of mouth for the first full house. After that, advertising won't be an issue. We'll do a door list, and we'll make sure only a few of the biggest gossips get in to make the others press their noses to the glass."

"I don't know," Nicole hedged. "I need to think about this."

"Either we're all in, or we're out. We need everyone in this room, and the skills you bring to the table to make it work," Delores announced as she went to get herself more wine.

"We keep it safe, by invitation only, and based on salon

female clients and their referrals—which means we keep it in the neighborhood so our information is accurate. Delores and Gail are on info sleuth. My desk girl can book appointments, and my salon will be the hub. No one walks home alone, or takes calls into their homes—strictly business. Nikki, we need your theatrical presence. I'll give you a good disguise, some silk rags, and a veil so people won't be sure who the mystery woman is. Think of it as a temporary, six-month role, just like you had to when you used to do those poetry slams onstage. It's the same thing. You are entertaining people, and you only have to get into character and read from a script for a paid gig." Victoria chuckled as she began doing Nicole's hair again.

"Like I said," Gail quipped, "ain't no thang but a chicken wang."

"Why do I know this is a big mistake, Victoria?" Nicole asked with a sigh. "Why?"

"Because, girl, you're psychic."

Chapter 2

Adam Bastille studied the rim of his beer mug, and watched the foam from the head of it slowly recede. That was his life—roaring to a full head with ambition, only to be forced to recede, and contained by a glass ceiling. Maybe he should have opened up his private-investigations firm in Atlanta, instead of trying the East Coast. But he'd decided that it was far better to get out of the New Orleans Police Department, and far away from that Big Easy scene. However, the choices were slim. On the one hand, he could deal with corruption and rednecks down South, or deal with corruption and the mob out East. *Whatever.* At forty-one, getting in a tight spot didn't worry him much. No wife, no babies to worry about, and his family was all country folks tucked away in the backwaters of Louisiana. *Yeah. Whatever.*

Adam took a swig of the now-calmed brew before him and glanced around the neighborhood establishment. His cousin was late. She was always late. And were it not for his aunt's pleadings, and his mother's urging him to, he wouldn't have taken on this ridiculous domestic case. He hated mixing family business with real business. And he definitely didn't do domestic crap. Insurance fraud was his specialty. Glancing around the terrain one last time, he put down his money hard and polished off his beer. To hell with Cecilia and her nonsense and the superstitions of old women. His cousin was full-grown. There was no such thing as *roots*. And if his cousin was bent on messin' with married men, it would serve her right if some wife killed a chicken on her behalf, or wrung her neck like one, in any event.

"Just one and done?" the barmaid asked as she accepted his bills and he stood.

"Yeah," Adam muttered, as he appraised the smooth, brown sugar-skinned woman with luscious curves and a beautiful smile. He wondered what a fine, tall, sexy woman like that would be doing working at a neighborhood dive, then banished the thought. Everybody had a long story. Tonight that was not his focus—but her presence had slowed him down just a little. "What's your name?" he found himself asking as he went into his wallet to add to her tip.

"Delores Thompson," she replied with a bright smile. "Haven't seen you around here before."

"That's because I'm not from here."

"Where you from, then, Mr. Mysterious?"

"Everywhere."

"Oh." The woman named Delores laughed. "I get it. New bar, new neighborhood, and married as a jaybird."

Adam chuckled when she cut her gaze hard at him and twisted her mouth. But he liked the way she still smiled behind the scowl. A player. Nope. Give her the money and jet.

"Married to my job, is all," he admitted, finding the pull of her hard to resist. Six months focused on the last job and without a little feminine company to take the edge off must be affecting his judgment. Maybe there'd be some redeeming benefit to having to come to Philly on a *pro bono* job for his family. "Looks like yours keeps you busy."

"Sometimes." Delores giggled as an older man moved behind her and began cleaning glasses while steadily eyeing him.

"Well, you have a good one," Adam replied, gauging from the grit the older brother behind the curves gave him that the woman got more than her paycheck from the bar. *Damn. Fine thing, too. Oh, well.* That was life. He wasn't about to get tangled up in some neighborhood drama, or risk getting shot for a woman. "Later."

"I hope so," Delores purred. "Not too much later."

Nicole walked in a tight circle in the back room of the salon. The turquoise silk turban and robe felt ridiculous, and she had never worn a wig in her life! The sheer black veil covering her face—all but her eyes—tickled her nose. Thick plumes of incense in the tight space, combined with the smell of burning candles, made her stomach do flip-flops. *Oh, yeah.* This was a very bad idea.

She should have called her mother, not her crazy aunt down in Florida. But worrying her mom right after her dad had been so ill wasn't something she could do either. Everybody knew Aunt Marlene was out there. Of course she would have said to go for it, and even told her that she'd be helping womenfolk. Her aunt and her old girlfriends dealt with psychics all the time, and her aunties even claimed to be psychic. Two generations in the states, and folks still clung to the old country mess!

"I cannot do this," Nicole said flatly when Victoria and Gail came into the room. "Let's just feed the ladies, give them a complimentary facial, and tell them that the psychic got sick and wouldn't come.'' Nicole looked at the heavy eye makeup that had crusted her lids with sequinlike dust, and heavy Egyptian-type eyeliner. ''I don't even know who I am anymore. Look at me. This is a total farce.''

''It's just a little theatrical jitters. Stage fright,'' Gail soothed with a giggle. ''We've got a full house out there. In fact, this first party is overbooked. I made four flavors of potion, but I think I'll run out.''

''But ladies—''

''Aw, girl. Don't be gettin' cold feet with a full house, and after you said you'd do it. What am I going to tell all of my best clients?'' Victoria had her hands on her hips, but was smiling when she spoke.

''I was under duress, looking at the bills in my house when I said, 'Yeah, maybe.' That was not a definite promise. And in three days you guys did a whisper down the lane and you have twenty-five women in there—''

''Forty,'' Victoria corrected.

''What?''

''At twenty-five dollars a pop, which is a thousand dollars sitting out there—which I've already put in an envelope for you, darlin'. You take the first door, and then it's Gail, then Delores, then me. Just like we agreed, and just like everybody's bill cycle requires—needs-based payout. That's fair.''

Nicole groaned. The competing temptations were making her dizzy. On the one hand, sure, she needed that money to pay the bills on time without effort and without strain for the first time since her separation and divorce, but something about this whole thing, mostly legal or not, still felt wrong. Yet, a thousand dollars for one night of harmless entertainment . . . But then again, that would mean that she'd have to do it at least three additional times, because it wouldn't be fair to get her money, then not reciprocate for Gail, Delores, and Victoria. Nicole let her breath out hard.

"All right. Listen to me. I am not going to tell anyone anything that could hurt her. I'm going to pick out the best qualities of each woman, tell them confidence-building, positive things about themselves, and I'm going to make them feel good about themselves—and I'm not going to focus on any gossip about their love lives. Okay?"

"Yeah, yeah, yeah, Dionne," Gail agreed with a laugh. "But don't forget that I have a hundred bottles of love potion in there. One recipe is for building confidence in love, one is for the courage to tell the truth or to take the truth, one is for finding a new love—I made extra of that—and the last one is what I think will be the top seller . . . an aphrodisiac."

Nicole could only shake her head. "So I'm supposed to write out a prescription, too, for each of these ladies? Oh, Lord!"

"Yeah, chile. Are you crazy? We do it in the salon all the time," Victoria argued. "We do their hair; then they have to buy the products at the counter to keep their 'do right until they return. If each woman buys at least two vials, just like shampoo and conditioner, we'll sell eighty bottles tonight, minimum. That's an additional two hundred and twenty profit, because each bottle only costs, like, twenty-five cents against the three-dollar price tag. If we sell out the whole hundred, then that's a profit of two hundred and seventy-five dollars on top of the grand you pull in from the readings. Hell, the chips, dip, veggies, and all didn't cost but about twenty or thirty bucks."

"What's this stuff made out of? For real, for real?" Nicole set her jaw hard and folded her arms over her chest.

"While I can't tell you *all* of my recipe, since it's based on how I learned to cook from my momma—who came up from Georgia," Gail replied with a wry chuckle, "I'll give you a hint. Confidence might taste like greens—good luck for money, too, just like that old saying about eating greens for New Year's. Courage might taste a lot like black-eyed peas. Thick, strong, with a lotta base, and again, like the New Year's saying, for dealin' with good people. New love . . . well, I thought that should be sweet, so it might have a sweet-potato sorta flavor. And, well, aphrodisiac . . . girl, that's got plenty of cayenne pepper to get the system circulating, garlic to purify the blood, bay leaf . . . you know, you know. Let's just say its contents came off the broth of my award-winning string beans. Thought string beans was appropriate, as they look like little erections, if not overcooked.''

"Help me, Father!" Nicole exclaimed, slapping her forehead and walking in a tight circle again, then peeping out of the door. The crowd of happy, laughing, boisterous women in the next room, who were eating, telling jokes and fellowshipping in fun made her swallow hard. The salon was jampacked worse than on a Saturday before a major holiday! The only saving grace was the fact that Jo Jo, the head stylist and sole male in the room, was butlering hors d'oeuvres and telling jokes to keep the crowd amused. Well, at least they'd get total comic relief if she bailed out now, and he was in his element.

"It's too late to pull out," Victoria warned, as though reading Nicole's thoughts.

"Nothing in the potions will hurt anyone, and I used all turkey products and low salt so as not to hurt anyone's potential medical situation. I am a nurse, and have enough sense to do that, Nikki," Gail argued through another giggle. "Didn't make anything they don't already eat."

"Okay," Nicole said in a shaky voice while trying to steady her nerves. "Only light stuff, since Dee's butt isn't even here, and I can't remember all that mess she told me about everybody."

"She had to work," Victoria said with a flip of her wrist. "Besides, since she fed us most of the info for round one, then not having her in the shop is a good thing. Protects our sources, ya know."

"Yeah, right," Nicole whispered, glancing back at the huge, white, lit candle in the center of the table draped in midnight blue behind her. No tarot cards and no crystal ball, per her insistence on minimal drama that could conflict with her basic religious tenets, but she also had to hand it to Victoria: this was total theater. The salon had indeed been transformed by Jo Jo's decorating flair into a dreamy, mysterious place, all using sheer fabrics, netting, and tiny Christmas tree lights and candles; the entire establishment looked like a sultan's den. "Okay. Right. Delores had to work tonight," she repeated in a murmur, more for herself than for her friends.

"And so do you, chicky-love. You ready? It's showtime," Victoria commanded with a wide grin.

All Nicole could do was nod.

Chapter 3

Nicole discarded the cumbersome veil, then allowed her full body weight to hit the fluorescent-purple salon chair and spin her in a circle. "Two-thirty A.M. I thought we'd never get done." Pure fatigue clawed at her shoulders and lower back, and she tried to rub the dull headache away from her temples with her fingertips.

"Well, honey, let me just say that this event was fab-u-*lous*," Jo Jo confirmed with a snap of his fingers. "We gave them *pure fever*, girl! The buzz-buzz from this will turn the other salons ga-reen, girlfriend. Oh, did Jo Jo give them new flava in here, or what?"

Gail laughed and shook her head. "Yes, Joseph." She sighed patronizingly. "You gave them fever—but keep your buzz-buzz self quiet about our green and our girl, okay?"

"Oh, so now you calling me Joseph and trying to signify. Now listen to Miss Thang over there trying to give directions. *Moi?* Tell the trade secrets from Victoria's? Never." Flouncing away to remove his sky-blue fur coat from the closet, he glanced over his shoulder and made a loud clicking sound with his tongue. "But I must say, your love potions were da bomb. Just the extra drama we needed to compliment my magical re-creation of this post-seventies Greek look that Miss Victoria would not let go of until tonight. Even though I did give her bohemian Genghis Khan caravan à la Asiatic effect amid her ruins in here—now *that* was flava. I love me some Khan, honey . . . oh, chile, what he did with his nasty, warrior self."

"Oh, right, and nobody else in here did any work?"

"Okay, okay, I'll recognize, if that's all you want. You didn't have to fish so hard for a compliment, Miss Gail."

"No," Victoria said without looking up, addressing the group in a monotone don't-bother-me-while-I'm-counting-money voice, "what Gail was telling you is to keep this cool. And what's wrong with my décor?"

"Nothing, doll. It just went out of vogue twenty years ago, and *some* people are too cheap to get it a face-lift. But I just did in here what I do for the clients . . . work with what I've got. Alas."

"Just be cool, Joseph, okay?" Victoria warned. "By the way, we're fully booked at fifty for the next party. The ladies put in reservations with Gail as they were leaving. Not bad."

"Well, you could break off a little somethin'-somethin' for your decorator-stylist who entertained to *the nines* while you were counting money."

Victoria chuckled as she approached Jo Jo and handed him a wad. "Don't be gettin' new on me. Don't I always take care of you?"

"That you do, baby," Jo Jo said with a satisfied grin, pecking Victoria on the forehead. "Because I always take care of you. Right? So fair exchange is no robbery, hon."

"Just be cool."

"Keep this cool?" Jo Jo stopped midfloor as he returned from the closet, and flung his ankle-length coat over his shoulders like a cape while donning a pair of pale cream leather gloves in the process. "How do you keep fire cool, boss lady? I mean, these women were in here all in a big fall-out-on-the-floor when Miss Diva got finished reading each one of them. My only question is, what in the world did you tell them in that back room, honey? Especially Miss Tramp-of-the-neighborhood herself, Cecilia Bastille? Thinking she's all that with her Creole self. Just a ho."

Nicole let her breath out with a low groan. "Jo Jo, I didn't tell anybody anything that they didn't already know. I gave up no names, no tapes. As each one came in, I'd tell her to look more inside of herself and ask why she was allowing herself to be in a toxic situation . . . then, maybe, I'd tell her how to get her finances straight, or work with a wayward child, whatever mother-wit came to mind, the same way my mom would have told me. That's all they really wanted was for a few minutes to be validated, to be heard, and for someone without an agenda to give them some solid advice." Nicole paused as Victoria and Gail shook their heads.

"No, for real," she went on. "I didn't get into names, places, or hurtful types of discoveries. Like, one poor woman came in, and I knew her husband was a cheat, from what Delores had told me. She had three kids, was fifty years old, but it was in her eyes—she still loved that man, and it all began to unravel when she was stressed, he'd lost his job, and her mother was dying. So rather than give up a name, or confirm that he'd had a fling, I told her to look inside herself—and decide what was really important."

"I'm surprised they didn't run you out on a rail, chile," Victoria scoffed.

"That is so sweet, and they all seemed so happy when

they came out . . . go figure. But me''—Gail chuckled—
''I'da wanted a name, okay.''

''Everybody thinks they do, but they really don't,'' Nicole
countered. ''Look, we started talking about how she'd
always wanted to go back to school, now that her kids were
out of the house. Then she told me how he'd always wanted
to go into business for himself, and how they used to dream
together—so all I said was to work as a team, rebuild, and
close out the other woman from a forgiveness strategy. He'd
never cheated before, and if they worked together, whatever
went wrong might be able to go right—stuff like that. No
dirt. If people can save their marriages, well, I figure they're
luckier than I was, and should. Takes communication, love,
both people being able to admit they've erred, and forgiveness on both sides—which is divine.''

''Oh, gurl!'' Jo Jo exclaimed, placing a kid-gloved hand
over his heart. ''No wonder! You had an Oprah thing going
on back there. A positive, just-get-yourself-together-and-
focus-on-you therapy vibration. Oh! Girl. This scene is going
to be off the hook! What else did you tell them?''

Nicole had to laugh. ''Jo Jo, you are a mess. Stop, okay?
I'm only doing a few more until each of us gets a turn to
take the door, and—''

''A few more?'' Jo Jo took off his gloves in slow motion,
then dropped his coat on a salon chair and sashayed over
to Nicole with one hand on his hip. ''Are you mad?''

''We tried to tell her, Jo Jo.'' Gail sighed through a giggle.
''But her mores prohibit fraud.''

''Fa-raud . . . oh, puhleeze!''

''Jo Jo,'' Nicole pleaded as he hovered over her, ''I am
way too tired to go into this tonight.''

''Maybe this will take the edge off,'' Victoria quipped,
dropping a thousand dollars in small bills in Nicole's lap.
''Always does for me.''

"Truth be told," Nicole said quietly, "it only makes me feel worse."

"Baby," Jo Jo said with mock disgust, "I should feel so bad. You keep on like this and I'll wear the blue silk and eye shadow next time."

Nicole giggled in earnest, picturing it all in her mind. "See, that's my way out. Why don't you all let Jo Jo do this?"

"Because," Gail and Victoria said in unison, which made Jo Jo leave Nicole's side to get in their faces.

Victoria walked away from him, doubled over with laughter, and Gail shooed him to back up from her by waving her hands as she laughed hard.

"Could you see it?" Victoria puffed through her bout of chuckles. "Not only would they all *know* who you were, but they would definitely know you'd tell their business in the streets!"

"Jo Jo," Gail said on a heave of air while wiping her eyes, "you'd be in there all in a big three-snaps-and-a-circle, giving advice and telling everybody's business. Not only would we just get one client read per night after you started on a roll, but we'd have to call the police to break up the catfights in the salon after you got through telling people's business. No!"

The appalled look on his face forced Nicole to stifle another giggle.

"Now, I *know* you two are not going to try to talk about me like that. I do not tell all the business; I only absorb it." He made a little lock-turning gesture at his pursed lips, then made a dramatic repose against one of the counters.

"Give it up, Jo Jo," Victoria replied, still laughing as she walked over to him to smooth his ruffled feathers with a hug. "You are so much better at entertaining and decorating, we need you in that role. Do it for me, please, kitten?"

Through a long series of neck motions and an eventual grin, peace had been restored.

"I hate you witches," he huffed with affection. "I just *hate* you, but you do need someone with an eye for design to theme these events out. Okaaay. So stop messin' with me. I'll be here next week to save the day from what would otherwise be a very tired affair."

"Thank you, Jo Jo," Nicole said, swallowing a grin.

"See, for her, I would do anything—not for you old battle-axes. She's the one with potential, and is just a sweet pea. But you all don't appreciate Jo Jo like Miss Nikki does. Thank you, baby."

He waltzed over to Nicole, folded up the money in her lap, and pressed it into her hand.

"You don't have to feel one ounce of guilt about this money, doll," he said in a gentle tone. "See, I know people. And I know you were back there drying people's tears and encouraging them—so what you told them came from a good place in your heart. You don't have a mean bone in your body—I would know. So take this knot that came by way of Victoria's Babylon, fold it up, put it away, and use it to pay bills for you and the baby. Then next week, you just keep being your sweet, listening self, and giving people hope. Okay? You promise to mind Jo Jo?"

"I promise," Nicole said softy, giving him a hug from where she sat. "I love you, too."

"Oh, see, now you are going to make Jo Jo just tear up. You are my favorite girl. Know that."

Nicole caught his hand and gave it a little squeeze. She did know that, and she loved him dearly, like a brother. For all of Jo Jo's high drama, he was good people, and the best anyone could hope for in a friend.

The sound of motion at the front of the salon made everyone go still. They looked at the door, and Nicole put the wad Jo Jo had folded for her in her pocket beneath her silk robe when the locks turned.

"That better be Delores," Victoria murmured, moving toward the door.

"Why y'all sitting around here looking all wide-eyed like you're guilty or something?" Delores asked with a chuckle when they collectively let their breaths out in unison. "Who else has a key to the salon but Jo Jo and Miss Vic—who are also both in here with you?"

"Oh, chile!" Gail exclaimed. "I know, I know, but it was all so good that it was scaring us."

"Got that right," Victoria said with obvious relief. "Girl, it was wall-to-wall in here."

"Dag, y'all decorated the mess out of this place—I know this is Jo Jo's work," Delores said with affection, going to peck him on the cheek.

"Thank you, baby," he crooned. "How's my second-favorite girl?"

"Now I'm taking sloppy seconds?" Delores shot back in mock indignation.

"Maybe second, but nothing coming from me is *ever* sloppy. You know Nikki is my first heart."

"Traitor."

"Realist."

"Oh, forget you, then, Jo Jo. I'm not telling you the scoop just for that."

"Don't be that way, Dee Dee. You like it, don't you— the place is fab; I outdid myself . . . just say it, just once."

They all laughed and began picking up leftover cups and napkins and restoring order to the chaos, while ignoring Jo Jo as he once again went through the ritual of putting on his fur coat.

"Okay. I have done my designer part. I don't do menial cleanup. That's not in my stylist contract, loves."

"Well, I can see this was a smash hit." Delores giggled as she surveyed both the décor and the mess. "But I guess you're in too much of a hurry to hear what they said about the party over at the bar, Jo Jo?"

"Ooooh, girl! Just stop teasing me," he boomed, taking dramatic repose in the salon chair closest to her. "You'd better tell Jo Jo."

"See, Delores," Victoria fussed, "now you gonna have us in here for another two hours with aftermath scoop."

"Market research, honey. Don't act like y'all don't want to hear what Miss Dee Dee got to say. You better recognize," he argued.

"Jo Jo, at least take off the fur and work while we listen," Gail said with a laugh, throwing a kitchen trash bag in his direction.

"Do I look like I work for sanitation, Miss Gail?"

"Well, since you're slumming, you could help," Victoria remarked in a good-natured tone. "I did give you Gail's potion receipts."

"Well, since I'm slumming, and you all don't know how to dress *or* break down a theatrical set . . ."

"How do you put up with him all day, Vic?" Delores groaned, shaking her head as she walked farther into the salon.

"Dee, you might as well tell him"—Victoria sighed—"or we won't get out of here."

"Yeah, by this hour of the night, my Michelle has to crash at Nicole's," Gail pressed on. "Child went over there just to watch the baby for a couple of hours, but now she's going to have to be there in the morning to leave from Nikki's to go to school, all under Nicole's feet, and whatnot."

"It's no bother, really, Gail," Nicole protested. "It's sort of a nice arrangement. We get out for a few hours, and we're just around the corner . . . plus the girls love each other."

"Yeah, and my Michelle gets to help out and learn some responsibilities while being somewhere safe."

"I told you I'd watch her when you worked nights at the hospital, too—and we could say that she's helping me, so she doesn't balk."

"Okay, okay, all of this motherhood logistical stuff is well and good, but let us get back to Miss Dee Dee's story." Jo Jo had folded his arms and was swinging the chair from side to side like an excited child.

"Y'all," Delores said in such a revived, excited, and conspiratorial voice that all cleaning and motion temporarily ceased.

Jo Jo clapped his hands and covered his mouth as though trying desperately to keep himself from interrupting Delores again. The sight of his antics made all the women in the shop burst out laughing.

"I don't know where to begin." Delores sighed.

"Oooooh, too juicy," Jo Jo whispered.

"Shut up; let her tell it," Victoria urged.

"What happened, girl?" Gail pleaded, then plopped her ample frame down in one of the hood-dryer chairs.

"First, this fine, and I do mean *fine,* brother—not from around here—came into the bar around seven or so. Like six-four, two hundred pounds, with buns of steel, deep, dark chocolate, wearing an ankle-length leather and packin' a Glock. Had on this fly silk no-collar shirt, with slip-on leather loafers and pleated wool pants . . . heavy in the crotch. Hung like a Georgia mule, y'all. Bass voice with slightly Southern twang. Oooh, honey!"

"Oh, my God—Shaft!"

"Right, baby." Delores laughed. "Givin' 'em John Shaft,

with Wesley's bod and coloring, Denzel-type eyes . . .
whooo! Drivin' a black Lexus—''

"Just shut up," Gail cut in. "You're killing us!"

"No, all y'all shut up," Victoria fussed. "What has some
fine man got to do—"

"It's part of the backdrop, the drama; come on with it,
Miss Dee Dee." Jo Jo pleaded. "Let her tell the story.
Victoria, shut up. Gail, shut up. Oooh, Miss Dee Dee, tell
me about Shaft in the bar!"

"Well, that was just a little teaser, because whoever he
was waiting for stood him up, and Eddie was sweatin' me,
so he left. Then, about a couple of hours later, who falls in
there with her crew but Cecilia."

"Ho!" Jo Jo exclaimed.

"Right," Delores affirmed. "Girlfriend had an attitude,
and was talkin' loud with her girls about how she didn't
care what the psychic said; she was gonna run whomever
she wanted."

"Whaaaat?" Gail hollered.

"Nikki, what did you say to that hoochie?" Victoria asked
through a chuckle.

Nicole's eyes darted around the room, and she found
herself again walking in a tight circle. "I told her that she
didn't need to run with other people's husbands, and if she
kept it up, someone was going to get hurt—probably, and
first and foremost, her."

"Ooooh . . ." Delores murmured on a low, extended
drawl. "That explains everything."

"What?" Nicole pressed. "Explains what? That's just
common sense."

"No, girl," Delores went on. "See, the Shaft-look-alike
came back. Turns out that he was hired to come up here to
look into who put some chicken guts on Cecilia's steps—

he's some kinda private investigator, which explained the gun. Brother's got a license to pack. He ain't no gangsta."

"No!" Jo Jo gasped, crossing himself. "Somebody did not try to root that vampire, Cecilia. Oh, this is too rich. I'm changing that brother's name from Shaft to Blade, chile, 'cause they might need a day-walker to hunt down the hoo-doo on that hussy."

"Jo Jo, *shut up!*" Victoria yelled. "Please. Oh, my God, shut up!"

"This is too crazy," Gail screamed as she doubled over with giggles. "Ooooooh, y'all!"

"How I know, see," Delores went on, taking center stage in the middle of the shop floor, "heard him and Cecilia fussin', 'cause she was the one who was supposed to meet him earlier, but she got sidetracked over here. Was wondering how her tired ass could pull a brother like that, but it was strictly business—that ain't her man; he's mine if I can shake Eddie."

"Girl, you might have seen him first," Jo Jo argued, "but you have to pull him. I can pull him, now."

"He don't swing like that," Delores offered with a laugh.

"You don't know that man's business," Jo Jo countered. "Chile, you'd be surprised who's in the life, girl."

"Whatever," Victoria interjected. "Get back to the part that affects this salon's new line of business."

"All right," Delores conceded. "He told her that he didn't normally take these kinds of jobs, and somethin' stupid like chicken guts on her steps served her fast butt right. I thought I would die laughing, but I had to be cool and act like I didn't hear nuthin' but drink orders. I'm a pro, you know."

"Okaaay, see Shaft, I mean Blade, got sense, and this was just some woman doo doo—"

"No, but check it out," Delores urged, fussing at Jo Jo in the process. "When Cecilia said that the psychic in the shop foretold that something bad was going to happen to her, the brother took out a piece of paper and copied down the info on the salon. He probably didn't think it was just some rhetoric, or emotional hurt, that our girl, Nikki, was talking about. I'm sure he thinks that she probably knows who threw the guts, since all the folks came here to get a private reading . . . plus, who would be the most likely person to tell someone to put chicken gizzards on another woman's steps, but a woman in the occult? Chile, they think you're the real McCoy.''

''Oh, no, oh, no, oh, no!'' Nicole blurted out, waving her hands and rushing around the shop in a whir. ''See, y'all, I *told* you! I told you, I told you, I told you!''

''Calm down, Nikki,'' Victoria purred with delight. ''This is gonna boost sales.''

''Boost sales! Are you nuts?'' Nicole was incredulous. ''I never in my life told anybody to put chicken guts on some woman's steps—now a private investigator with a gun is looking for me? Are y'all crazy?''

''Girl,'' Delores pressed on, ignoring Nicole, ''they showed him the elixirs—her other friends had bought some—then the men in the bar wanted to know where they could get it when they told them it was an aphrodisiac. Then Eddie's greedy butt wants to run a tray of them in behind the register, for a cut, because he's sure it'll sell as fast as the liquor. I told him he couldn't take no full cut, but—''

''Yeah, we could do that,'' Victoria said immediately. ''Give him seventy-five cents per tube; that way—''

''Wait one minute! No more, ladies. We have a chicken-guts mystery, a private investigator with a Glock nine, a group of people thinking that I do potions and spells—all because of Gail's elixirs, and you are talking franchising? Am I hearing correctly?''

"Isn't this business-expansion opportunity exciting?" Jo Jo exclaimed. "Fine men, unsolved mysteries—"

"Jo Jo, shut up," Nicole snapped. "No way—"

"But that's not the best part, chile," Delores added with a hoot. "Then the man's pager went off, and he said he had to go. So that left Cecilia in there with her crew. Well, her crew loved you, and said that the fact that he was concerned confirmed the fact that your info, at least, was accurate— so they are all planning to bring somebody next week—"

"Next week? Are you crazy? I'm not doing this anymore. Take back the money, you all keep it, and—"

"No, girl, listen. The husband came in the bar, walked up to Cecilia in there, told her he loved his wife and that they'd talked after she'd been to see a psychic, they both toasted their marriage with your potion, and he'd wanted to tell his wife all along, and just wanted her back, and he'd made all these mistakes—but it was over! Do you hear me?" Delores yelled.

"*Shut up!*" Jo Jo hollered, then covered his mouth with his hand.

"Then there was a buzz at the bar from all the brothers in there after he left and Cecilia stormed out. They wanted to know who this psychic was that could change lives for the better and make them want to be with their wives like that—being as how they all think Cecilia is all that and a bag of chips. Never seen anything like it. They all gave Eddie preorders for love potion. How soon can you whip up a big batch, Gail?"

"Tomorrow," Gail shrieked. "Chile!"

"It's a miracle. . . ." Jo Jo sighed. "She has a gift."

"No, I don't," Nicole argued. "Take this money, Gail, since you're next on the door." Nicole put the wad of bills on the counter beside Gail and stepped away from it. "I just dispensed some common sense. The timing of it looks odd, but I'm not—"

"You have to do this," Gail nearly shouted. "Take this money away from me; I don't want it—it would be bad luck for any of us to take this first door except you, because, honey, you just saved a marriage. Oh, no, girl. You got the touch."

"The touch?" Nicole stood in the middle of the floor, gaping at the serious faces around her. "You all are not serious?"

"Naw, girl," Victoria practically whispered. "In all my born days, I've never heard of anything so freaky happening in one night from a little parlor game."

"What did you mix up in them vials, Miss Gail?" Jo Jo asked with genuine concern.

"Just normal good cooking with a lot of love while doing it," Gail whispered. "But me and my aunt always pray over a batch of food we are giving to other people, in case they don't pray. Maybe that had something to do with each type of batch being—"

"This is superstition and bogus," Nicole fussed. "It is late, we all have to go to work tomorrow, and we've got kids at home unattended. Victoria, put this money in the register or in the safe in the back. I'm through."

Chapter 4

Adam Bastille leaned back into the leather seat of his vehicle to avoid being noticed as a car exited the high-rise condominium complex. The posh gated exterior sat above the street level salon. It obviously had an exit into the building. *Note; pretty young woman in a beat-up Ford Taurus with Florida tags just left. Probably one of the stylists. Okay, brother with a sky-blue fur exiting by the front door, locks up, and turns out the light—definitely one of the stylists, if not the head stylist. Candy-red BMW. The fine babe from the bar is in on it somehow, but not by much, judging by her dented Toyota. Heavyset chick rides with her; neither fit the description. Recheck note on younger woman. Either a new stylist or the receptionist, but definitely not the flashy type. Probably not the psychic described. Cecilia said she had long black hair ... a disguise? Possibly. Follow the Florida tags.*

He hated stakeouts in the winter, and despite the comfort

of the sedan, he'd had to leave the motor off. This part of being on the East Coast was his chief complaint, but it had been his choice, he reminded himself while pulling out of the parking space and allowing a discreet block to lapse between his vehicle and the old Ford. He figured the salon owner, more than likely, lived in the condo above and there was no sense in waiting on her car to exit the building. The psychic could be a building resident. In the morning he'd visit the shop as a client. Right now, however, there was the matter of the shy woman who had gotten out of her car and who had a look of innocence like butter could melt in her mouth. Big, doe-brown eyes, short, naturally curly hair, petite but curvaceous frame, and a plain, light brown wool winter coat. She waited hunched against the cold. No purse, wearing jeans and penny loafers. Almost looked like a church girl.

Adam pulled out a licorice stick to chew on. This girl worked on his nerves somehow, and he didn't like it. She made him want a cigarette. That was not a good sign.

He studied the apartment building that she'd entered. Sorta run-down, borderline low-income housing. Wild how the neighborhoods in Philly bordered each other—one turn and you went from the rich to the poor. *Yeah, new stylist or receptionist. Just a sister in there trying to make ends meet.*

Nicole checked on her daughter and Gail's, stroking their hair lightly as she gave them each a kiss and tucked in the edges of their covers. Although the teenager sleeping soundly next to her five-year-old had a lot of bluster for her mother, Nicole could still see the softness of youth in her face as she slept. Tears blurred her vision as she crept out of the room and closed the door quietly behind her. God help her if these antics put any child, or the other mothers, in jeopardy.

Moving into her bedroom, Nicole dropped her coat on the chair, then flopped onto the bed. Three-forty in the morning, and she had to be up at six to get Lydia fed and to school on time, then get herself to work. With effort, she reached across the bed to the nightstand and set her clock. What had she been thinking? "Physician, heal thyself."

The whispered statement in the empty room reverberated off the walls and went through her skull. She peered at the stack of bills on her dresser that was eerily illuminated by the fluorescent streetlight filtering into the bedroom. Maybe it was time to just go home, back to her parents' house, back down to Florida, and give up trying to make it on her own in the big city.

"Miss Gordon, may I have a word with you?" Nicole's supervisor droned the command as she hovered over Nicole's telemarketing station.

"Mrs. Gordon," Nicole corrected as she took off her headset, stood, and followed the older blond shrew to what always felt like a school principal's office.

"You were absent twice this month," her supervisor began, "and were late again today. What are we going to do about this?"

"Like I told you before"—Nicole sighed, feeling knots rise and harden in her shoulders—"my daughter got the flu, she's five, it's winter, and all of the kids are coming down with—"

"But what is your excuse today?"

Nicole could feel her glare harden on the prim, arrogant woman before her.

"I had to work late last night and—"

"Oh, I see. So we are supposed to make do just because another employer got the best part of your efforts? Not acceptable."

"I work another job because I have to, and it won't happen again."

"No, Miss Gordon, it will not. In fact, most of your efforts seem to be waylaid by this other employer."

"I just started yesterday."

"Then help me understand why your sales are so sluggish. Help me understand why you spend three times as long on any one call, which is usually nonproductive, as any of the other reps."

Nicole fell silent. How could she explain that when she got on the telephone with people who were home during the day, they had problems, and for some reason would begin to tell her about them? For what seemed even odder reasons that she could not describe at the moment, she cared. How was she supposed to make some elderly person, who hadn't talked to someone who would listen, buy some useless products? Or how was she supposed to cajole a disabled person, or a poor mother like herself, into buying junk they didn't need so that somebody else could get rich? Sure, she needed a job, but she also had to be able to sleep at night. All right, her supervisor had a point, but she reasoned that, if she knew where the people she called could get the services they needed, wasn't she supposed to tell them? Wasn't that the baseline Christian thing to do?

"Well?" her supervisor asked in a tone so patronizing that Nicole folded her hands in her lap to keep from slapping the glare off the woman's face.

"I'll do better," Nicole murmured.

"We pulled your tapes from your calls. Not one sale in a week, but you've been on our telephone banks providing marriage counseling, giving people advice about where to get medical transport, housing abatements, credit repair, telling people how to handle their utility bills. . . . Miss Gordon, this is not a social services organization.''

All Nicole could do was stare at the woman.

''I think it's best that we terminate this relationship. There are plenty of people out there who need a good job, and who would be glad to do it well. I'm sorry, but given your performance, we cannot continue your employ here.''

''I'm fired? Just like that? Because I've helped people on the telephone, and had to take my child to the doctor?''

''Let's not make this any harder than necessary. Security will see you out.''

''Oh, so now because your wife has been talking to her girlfriends, and they all are working on marriage repair after seeing the psychic, you think it's better for business if I don't work here? Are you crazy, Eddie? How long have we been going out, and she's known about it?''

''She didn't care before, Dee—she said that she had her life and I had mine. But last night when I closed up, she really wanted to talk. I told her I'd meet her halfway, and maybe we'd start again, so, baby—''

''Have you lost your mind, Negro?''

''Now, Dee, we knew this wasn't going nowhere, and it was just somethin' to do for both of us. I'll tighten you up at the end of the month, and you can still bring that potion around for the bar. That can be a little financial help for you—till you find another gig. Cool?''

''Go to hell, Eddie!''

''Girlfriend, we need some more brown gel and some more seven stage-lightener. It's packed in here, love, and the shelf in the back is pitiful, honey," Jo Jo yelled over the hum of blow-dryers and downed hood-dryers.

"Lillian," Victoria ordered, "call over to my beauty supply man and get a dropoff. Tell him the joint is jumpin' today, and they're late with my delivery."

"Miss Vic, can I see you in the office?" Lillian asked in a very discreet voice as she sidled up to a salon chair where Victoria was working on a client.

"Not right now," Victoria snapped. "We've got wall-to-wall clients in here, and the book is full like this all week. Plus, new male clients don't need to be kept—"

"Miss Vic, it's about money," the receptionist whispered.

"Cover my chair, Jo Jo, and get both of these ladies into rinse-out with Debbie and Cheryl."

"Cover your chair? Cover your chair! I've got three in stylistic process right now, and I am not the amazing Kreskin. Do I look like a magician?"

"For real, Joseph," Victoria warned, ignoring him when he kissed his palm and slapped his backside with it.

She followed behind Lillian and closed the door quickly. "What's up?"

"Miss Vic," Lillian whispered, looking at the floor. "Mr. Branch said your check for supplies bounced, and the order was too large to let it ride like that without making arrangements for a payment."

"My check bounced—bullshit! I have fifteen grand in that account," she exclaimed, snatching the cordless telephone from her desk and punching in the number to the bank. "You go back to the front desk, 'cause the phones have been jumpin' all morning. I'll get Branch straight on the delivery this afternoon, and tell Jo Jo that he can also kiss what I twist. All the business I give Branch, and now my credit, even if my check did bounce, ain't good?" Victoria kept her line of vision trained on her receptionist's retreating form. Why was all of this nonsense going on when business was booming in the shop? Of all days!

"Yeah, yeah, this is Victoria Jones calling." After going through the account numbers and security measures with the commercial teller, Victoria launched into a tirade. "How the hell can your bank make a mistake like this? I keep no less than fifteen in checking, and my savings account is attached to that with a knot in there big enough to choke a horse—so even if a check did bounce, overdraft protection should have caught it. What's more, I ought to sue you people for causing a slowdown in my salon, and for causing problems with my number one supplier. Now put a freakin' supervisor on the phone who can give me some answers!"

Victoria tapped her acrylic tips on her desk, which created a clicking sound that annoyed even her at the moment. Finally, when a supervisor identified himself, she opened her mouth to begin a new verbal attack but was silenced by his initial statement.

"I regret to inform you that your accounts have been frozen by the IRS. This is not a bank matter, Ms. Jones. You will have to go down to the Federal Building at Sixth and Arch to resolve it—and until then, we are not at liberty to do anything else."

Victoria put the telephone down slowly in its cradle, then buzzed the front desk as she opened the store safe behind her. "Lillian, I'm going to give you cash for Mr. Branch, if you can ask him, for old times' sake, to make the run. Tell him you will give his driver cash and a receipt. Try to see if you can get another one of the girls to come in early. I have to make a run, and it might take me hours downtown."

"Ms. Jackson, would you open your employee locker for us?"

Gail stood, mouth agape, staring at the hospital supervisor and the security guard who leaned on the desk of her nurses' station. Hot tears rose quickly in her eyes, and she could hear a light ringing in her ears, but catching her breath seemed next to impossible. She'd never done anything illegal in her life, and taking the tubes, at that time, had seemed like fair exchange for the long hours and lack of appreciation she got for her tireless efforts. Oddly, her ex-husband's facial expression jumped into her skull. She wondered if he'd felt remotely the same way when his cheating had been discovered—conflicted, angry, stunned, helpless, ready to bolt, but not knowing where to run. What good would running away have done anyway? *Once the egg is broke the egg is broke,* her mother had always said. Cold busted.

All she could do was nod, then grab her purse and her coat, knowing what stealing medical supplies meant. Immediate termination. No references for fifteen years of hard work. No college funds for her child. No unemployment until she landed on her feet. No respectable way to hold her head up in public . . . all for parlor games.

"No, my friend distinctly said to have . . . uh . . . I can't think of her name. Short girl, about five feet, six inches tall, naturally curly hair, big brown eyes, cinnamon complexion, drives an old Ford Taurus. Her . . . my friend said to have that one work on me." Adam Bastille waited patiently as the receptionist shook her head no.

"Sir, we don't have a stylist here who meets your description. Are you sure this is the right salon?"

"I'm positive," Adam pressed. "Does she do nails, or maybe the facials? But my friend said she was the one I wanted. I don't do salons, so I got a reference from a buddy."

"Lillian," Jo Jo bellowed from the back styling area,

"my seven-stage, doll! What the hell is going on in here today that Miss Thang just up and twists her hips out of here on a dime, our product is late, and we have a full house—and the manicurists are getting backed up. I am not doing waxes, today, either. Heads only. And pedicures are out of the question."

"Wait a minute . . ." Lillian faltered, becoming flustered by Jo Jo's snit while trying to remain customer-service-pleasant to a potentially new, and very good-looking, patron. "Let me check with the head stylist. If the girl you're looking for doesn't work here, he might know what salon she is attached to."

"Thank you," Adam said coolly. The chaos of the establishment—and the fact that the receptionist couldn't place the mystery girl—were details that had not been lost on him.

"Now, in the middle of a color and a perm, I'm supposed to play salon detective," Jo Jo snapped, coming to the front desk in a state of agitation behind Lillian. Instantly, as he spied Adam Bastille, his demeanor changed. "Well, Miss Lilly, I see why you brought me up here. I owe you one, love. Joseph," he crooned to Adam, extending his hand, "but those close to me call me Jo Jo. What can I do to make your life better today?"

Adam shook Joseph's hand, and peered around the shop. "I'm looking for a stylist, perhaps a manicurist, whom a buddy of mine at the bar said to come see here. She's about five-six, petite, pretty, big brown eyes, drives a Taurus—"

"Oh, puhleeze, that's Miss Nikki," Jo Jo said with outright disappointment. "Your friend must have told you about the readings. Well, she won't be back until next Wednesday—if we can get her to come back at all. She's so superstitious, and got all churchified on us last night, but I can get you on the list—even though Miss Victoria said we're supposed to book A-list clients and their guests by invitation only.'' Jo Jo appraised Adam in an unabashed, sweeping gaze. ''But Miss Vic isn't here, and I can definitely vouch that you are A-list material.'' Motioning with one hand and giving Adam still another once-over, he summoned the appointment schedule from Lillian.

''What time is best for you?'' Jo Jo said in a sexy octave.

''The last one for the night,'' Adam said in a flat, no-nonsense tone designed to back Jo Jo up off of him. He knew that the longer he sat in the salon and observed the other invitees that night, the better. ''Yeah, I'll go last.''

''Name?'' Jo Jo lilted, appearing unaffected by Adam's near growl.

''Adam.''

''No last name?''

''Not yet.''

''Well, then, I'll put you down as Mr. Adam. Umph, mysterious works for me, too.''

''Jo Jo, your perm client is burning!'' the shampoo girl fussed. ''We got work to do.''

''Truth!'' Jo Jo said with a snap as he gave the appointment book back to Lillian. ''Much work.''

Chapter 5

Nicole moved through her apartment like a zombie, numbly casting the mail onto the coffee table and going to the telephone in her bedroom without even taking off her coat or setting down her purse. She couldn't remember being home during the day without her child in tow, or without somewhere to be—not since she was single, not since she was free.

The red light on her answering machine bore a hole in her skull. Probably bill collectors, and she had no way to bargain for time, or to tell them that a payment would be forthcoming when her next check came. There would be no next check. Her purse held her severance, and the sum total of what she'd been able to amass was two weeks of work at a low-paying job. Where had all her dreams gone? What happened to becoming a freelance magazine writer? When was she supposed to compose her poetry and books and articles? How was she supposed to create in such a very fickle, artistic field when her gift had been blocked for years? How was she supposed to write through the chaos of a bad marriage, when she needed quiet and peace?

She should have listened to her mother and become a teacher, but the thought of leaving her child in day care as an infant had been appalling, then. How was she supposed to let go of Lydia's smiling face, miss those first steps, and not be there for those tender moments, especially when her daughter's gift of unconditional love was all that she had to claim?

It had taken years to confess that to her mom and dad, and years to be honest about just how hollow the life she was living had been. How did one explain such things to a couple who had lived together and loved each other for nearly forty years? It was hard enough to admit to them that she needed to use her father's old car with the tags on it, when her own hooptie died. The fact that she couldn't pay the insurance rates had not been lost on her parents, and they'd begged her to come home. Why didn't she?

None of that mattered now. She was in a jam, and she'd missed her chance to teach literature or English when the schools were hiring; plus she'd had to wait until she established residency. Now that she had the time during the day with Lydia in kindergarten, she'd have to begin at the bottom as a substitute teacher and go on the long waiting list—and they were hiring now for science and math.

That meant that each day she'd have to wait for the call to tell her which school she'd be placed in, what classroom she'd have, and she'd be working the way she was living— like a vagrant, moving from pillar to post without a home base, really, of her own. And she'd never know how long the commute would be, would never know if she could make it back to Lydia after school to pick her up on time. This was not how she was raised. This was not how she'd ever imagined having to raise a child. What had happened?

Without consulting her brain for permission, her arm stretched out of its own volition and her forefinger depressed the message button on the answering machine as she stared at the little black box. A serious voice that said her full formal name slammed against her eardrum and left an 800-number for her to return the call; then came a voice that was familiar—albeit hysterical. It was a voice that made her sit down slowly, come out of her haze, and replay the message when she heard Gail's sobs.

Stopping the tape, Nicole hit speed-dial on her small console and shot up from the bed to pace. When Gail's machine came on, she grabbed her keys and readjusted her purse on her shoulder. Her return message was brief. "I'll be there, Gail. Open the door when you hear the bell."

"Thanks for letting Michelle spend the night again to take care of Lydia," Gail murmured. Her hands literally shook as she brought the teacup to her mouth, and her eyes were bloodshot from crying hard. "I just called her on her cell phone, and she said she had stuff already there. I don't want my baby to see me like this."

"It's going to be all right," Nicole soothed, not knowing how in the world it would be, but needing to say it for both of them.

"I should be doing this for you." Gail sniffed. "Both of us in the same day, plus Dee."

"Dee?" Nicole could only blink and stare at Gail.

"Yeah. She said she left you a message. She and Eddie split up, and she went to Victoria's apartment to lie down. Jo Jo let her upstairs because the poor chile was a mess, and Vic had to go downtown to handle some serious drama."

"Oh, my God," Nicole whispered, her hand slowly going to her mouth.

"It's like a curse," Gail concurred, staring back at Nicole. "I told you that you should have taken the money, and not blocked that blessing."

"It probably happened because we did something wrong," Nicole whispered. "We brought this on ourselves."

"We should go to Victoria's and all talk about this," Gail reasoned. "We have to all help each other now. And if Victoria left the shop to go to Center City on a tear, that could mean only one thing: the feds finally caught up to her."

"Let's pray," Nicole said in a stricken tone, reaching across the kitchen table to clasp Gail's hands in her own. "Let's stand in agreement in God's name that we don't want to—and hope we didn't—harm anyone. Let's agree that we'll do only His will from this point forward. And most of all, let us ask for forgiveness for what we did wrong in thought, word, and deed. And let us ask for His mercy and abundance to help us as single mothers."

"Amen," Gail whispered, closing her eyes. "Amen."

"She hasn't said a word to anybody since she came up here," Jo Jo said in a low tone, while brewing some chamomile tea in Victoria's kitchen.

Victoria, Gail, and Nicole shot nervous glances toward the pass-through between the kitchen and the living room, and all returned their gazes to each other. It was as though Delores's prone body on the sofa were each of their bodies, and they all had been there too often not to know where she resided now.

Jo Jo's shoulders slumped as he worked, and his voice remained calm and tender as he spoke. "That girl has been through a lot of tough times, but this one, I think, could break her back. She might be the sassy one, but trust me, I know. Everybody has a last-straw point.''

"Yeah, I know," Nicole murmured, accepting tea from Jo Jo as he offered each of them a china cup. "Me and Gail prayed about it today before we came over."

"I say we pray again, all holding hands," Gail whispered.

"I say we do it in there," Jo Jo concurred, motioning toward the living room with a nod.

"We all could sure use a miracle," Victoria said in a low tone. "They froze everything liquid I owned. So the good news is, I'm out of debt. The bad news is, I have no operating capital to run the salon—only the receipts I bring in on a daily basis. Busted. Just like starting all over from scratch."

"Why don't we go into the other room and put Dee in the center of our prayer circle," Nicole suggested. "I don't know what else to do, y'all. My momma and aunties and folk down home used to do that when someone was in trouble. They said prayer was powerful, and things seemed to change in people's lives. . . ."

Without further discussion, everyone moved in unison and gathered around Delores's limp form. Her face was toward the cushions on the sofa and her fist was clenched around a wad of wet tissues. Jo Jo squatted next to her and began rubbing her back, and soon all parties in the room were touching some part of Delores, trying to stroke away the hurt.

"Dee," Nicole said gently. "We're gonna pray for all this pain to go away—for all of us."

"You can't take this case to God; it was all my fault," Delores rasped. "He ain't tryin' to hear nothin' from or about me."

"Last I heard," Jo Jo whispered, "we're all His children,

and even when we're dead wrong, if we admit it and try to do better, He forgives us. Isn't that right, ladies?''

"That's right, girl," Gail said tenderly, brushing damp strands of stray hair away from Delores's forehead.

Delores opened her eyes, and her gaze searched their faces as though she were a bewildered child. "I knew he was married. I knew I was wrong. And I knew it wouldn't last . . . and God forgive me if I made his wife feel like this, even once. But where am I going to go? How am I going to take care of my two kids? They're almost eighteen, but not ready to be on their own. I just wanted someone stable, who I could . . .''

Her voice had trailed off into a soft sob, and Nicole found her own vision blurring as she stared at her friend's body that now harbored a broken spirit. All of the women whom she'd heard about in the streets, all of the affairs that her husband had had, and all of the hang-up calls that had made her nearly lose her mind, now had a face. And it was a sad, lonely, tortured face—not that of a haughty home-wrecker. It was the face of a woman who had fears, and children to care for, and who was vulnerable, and who just wanted love and a home of her own, but had just gone about materializing that dream in the wrong way.

Nicole bent and kissed the crown of Delores's head, and that gesture seemed to make her friend cry harder.

"I am so ashamed." She wept.

"We gonna pray. Right now," Victoria said with sudden authority. "We've all done things we wished God couldn't see."

To Nicole's surprise, all of her friends, even Delores, were staring at her. Why her? It was Victoria's condo, Gail went to church with regularity, and she didn't . . . Jo Jo was the one who knew scripture backward and forward, and could quote it like Shakespeare if he had to argue theology. . . . But they were staring at her.

Nicole took a deep breath and she could feel hands slip into hers and grip them tightly as she closed her eyes and prayed hard in her heart. Words formed on her tongue and parted her lips, and air filled and refilled her lungs as she began praying out loud. Her voice became strong, she could feel tears run from the corners of her eyes, and she heard the word *Amen* murmured from those who stood near. And as she told the truth, her body swayed with conviction. Help and heal them all, Father God.

Yes, they had all done things that were wrong. Yes, they had all held onto grudges, and pain, and hurts. But yes, they all believed that with the faith of the mustard seed, they could be covered by the protection of God's grace, and could be forgiven. Yes, they all wanted love, and laughter, and family around them. Yes, they all wanted the best for their children, and yes, they all wanted to have someone special in their lives. Yes, they all wanted to have a way to pay their bills, and to cancel their debts. Yes, they could all forgive those who had hurt them, and would agree to let go and let God. And, by agreement, all praying and standing there of one mind and of one spirit, they would do the good works as they were directed.

When she opened her eyes, Nicole looked at the friends around her. She was truly blessed to have them in her life. Tears were streaming down everyone's faces, and each person slowly sat down either on the sofa or on the floor near Delores.

"Dag," Gail said, as the first person to speak. "Ain't been to church like that in a long time."

"Something miraculous just happened here," Jo Jo murmured, his tone totally serious. "That's why the people were coming to her. She's a healer, and didn't even know it."

"I feel a lot better, is all I know," Delores said with a sniff. "Like something just lifted."

"It did," Victoria whispered. "I can't explain it."

"Neither can I," Jo Jo agreed. "Never should have had her in a turban and getup. Should have given that girl a Bible, and let her just straight-up pray with people in that back room."

"Jo Jo," Nicole whispered, shaking her head slowly. "Listen to yourself. In one day we all lost our jobs, and Victoria's shop is in jeopardy, all because we were playing around. Now I'm no fool, and not about to tempt the Lord to strike us all down for giving false prophecies. Lightning can strike twice."

"That's the thing of it," he said in a very quiet tone, almost as though speaking to himself. "I don't think you told anyone anything that was wrong. In fact, you gave people hope. I think what we did wrong was, first, we didn't give any of it back to the church, and second, we billed you as a psychic. That's what was wrong."

"What are you saying?" Victoria asked in an unusually quiet voice.

"I'm saying that perhaps this is the leap of faith, or push, each person needed to go out and do the real work that's supposed to be done. Awful coincidental that this all went down in one day . . . you can either look at it as a punishment, or a sign of opportunity."

All eyes were on Jo Jo, and then he shook his head, stood, and found a chair across the room.

As she watched him move away from the group, an inexplicable thought popped into Nicole's brain. It was a knowing, somewhat like a feeling, and she found her line of vision trained on Joseph.

"Jo Jo is right," Nicole found herself whispering. "He and Dee and Gail are supposed to work together."

"What?" they all said in unison.

"Gail, the people loved your potions. But you are supposed to be catering. That's what you have to do ... you prayed over those batches, didn't you?"

"Yeah, but how am I supposed to open up a catering company when I don't have any money; I don't even have a commercial kitchen? I have no money, no way to advertise, and—"

"Your church has a commercial kitchen," Nicole interrupted. "Give them a cut of the proceeds to allow you to cook during off-peak hours there, and they have insurance. Delores is an excellent saleswoman—"

"Get a separate line with your severance, Gail," Victoria murmured. "Will only cost like thirty bucks a month, and add on voice mail for another ten, and you've got a way to get client calls. Use your full name, and then you can open a checking account without fictitious name registration, and the licenses are only a couple of hundred bucks. Worth the investment to start your own thing. You and Dee now have a job—you're self-employed."

"I know people in the business, and can get you borrowed serving trays and equipment on loan from my friends," Jo Jo murmured, his gaze locked on Nicole's. "I can get them a few A-list parties to start them off with a good reputation."

"But to even do the first job would take money that—"

"Ask for a fifty percent down payment, which covers your cost and your hired serving staff up front," Victoria added.

"I have a buddy who works for a graphics-design house. Some labels, business cards, and a brochure would do you fine, and I know he'd do it for me, gratis. I know some people who know some people. I'll buy your paper for the first run. Staples won't break me," Jo Jo offered.

"Where did that come from?" Delores whispered. "I've

never seen Nikki just pop up with something like this, business-wise ... that was always Victoria's department.''

"Go back to the IRS," Nicole whispered, now looking in Victoria's direction. "Go with a tax attorney. There's still something unresolved there. But this man, the attorney, be honest with him—he was sent to help you."

"What?" Victoria whispered while slowly standing and walking toward the bright orange leather chair where Jo Jo sat. "You're scaring me, Nikki. I still have a bunch of city-wage tax stuff to deal with, and *nobody* knew that."

"He came into the shop today. Find him."

Joseph reached up and clasped Victoria's hand. "Fifty, divorcee. Silver sideburns. Two-o'clock manicure. Said his sister said Victoria's shop was the place to be. He'd tried the aphrodisiac elixir and wanted to know if we had interest in a venture capitalist arrangement. Lillian helped him because we were backed up ... he said he was a lawyer."

"I feel so tired now," Nicole whispered. Her body began giving way to the floor from where she was sitting. As she moved to lie outstretched on the white-carpeted floor, the pale colors of the Oriental rug covering the thick pile began to create chiffon ribbons behind her closed lids. Intermittently she felt a cool, damp towel being applied to her forehead, and heard people gently calling her name, and as her eyes opened to slits the bright colored leathers from Victoria's furniture made her shut her eyes again. "I just need to go to sleep for a little bit," she murmured, feeling more relaxed and at peace than she'd felt in a very long time. "Tell that tall guy in the leather that I'm really not so bad."

Chapter 6

Adam walked around his cousin's car while she stood on the sidewalk gaping at him as he tried to pick up clues from the damage. This was definitely an act of revenge. The tires were slashed, the driver's- and passenger's-side windows were cracked, and the front windshield was smeared with a substance he did not want to guess at, but the stereo unit hadn't been touched.

"Look at how they keyed it," Cecilia wailed. "The windows and tires alone will cost a fortune, not to mention the paint job!"

"The paint job and cosmetic work are the least of your worries," Adam said as he appraised the gas tank. "Sugar."

"What! Those bitches!"

"You're finally gonna give me a list of who you've been running with so I can begin to piece this together, or you gonna wait until they damage some more of your property?"

What he didn't tell her was that now this wasn't just some

little rift between her and one of her lovers' women. From the looks of things, it had escalated to ugly, therefore to dangerous. Whoever was behind this latest act against her had taken the warning to a new level. Trouble was that he couldn't understand why. In the last twenty-four hours, unless Cecilia was lying, she hadn't argued about anything with anyone, or done anything to anyone, or slept with anyone. In fact, she'd spent a lot of time with him. A person holding on to a deadly, seething rage that didn't require immediate provocation probably committed this act of vandalism.

Despite his reluctance to take on the case, his mother's and aunt's fears now had a basis that he could see, feel, and touch. Now he definitely had to ride this one out. Being stuck in Philly on a domestic case was not on his agenda, and his other paying clients were losing patience.

Adam let out his breath hard and ran his fingers through his hair. "Dammit, Cecilia!"

His cousin looked at the ground and folded her arms around herself. "I want client privilege."

"You've got family privilege," he warned. "I'm up here *for free,* losing time and good clients, probably, on your mom and my mom's prayer-line requests after they had visions! I'm also going to be up here a lot longer than I had intended. This ain't just about chicken guts anymore."

"I don't want Mom or Aunt Zelda knowing about every little indiscretion."

"I'll spare 'em the details," Adam said with a wave of disgust. "Go in the house and call the police, and don't tell them anybody looked at your car first. After they get here, call your insurance company and put in a claim." As he paced away from her, he turned again quickly to address her. Fury uncoiled and recoiled in his gut. He hated this sort of mess, and it was precisely why he didn't do love, marriage, or women who got attached and went fatal. "Don't be on the telephone blabbing this to your girlfriends, either. Give me a head start on the action, for once."

"Are you sure you're okay?" Gail whispered, still fanning Nicole with a magazine as Jo Jo helped her sit up.

"Get her some water, Dee," Victoria ordered.

"I don't think she should be alone tonight," Jo Jo added with authority. "You just sit right here—when's the last time you ate something, love?"

"I haven't eaten all day," Nicole murmured, still feeling disoriented. "But I can't stay out all night. Who's going to take Lydia to school, and check on Michelle?"

"My twenty-three-year-old daughter," Victoria scoffed, "whom I already called, who is already at your apartment, and who has everything under control. The girls are having a blast."

"But—"

"I think we should all spend the night together," Delores yelled into the pass-through as she returned to bring Nicole some water.

"I have enough room," Victoria added in an extra gentle tone. "It would be fun. Haven't done that in a long while." Her gaze became tender as it swept over toward Jo Jo's downcast expression. "Now, you know, we have to put Jo Jo in my son's old room so his long feet don't hang off the bed."

"I'm invited?" Tears swelled in his eyes and he looked away with a slow smile.

"You're *family,*" Victoria said with conviction. "You are loved here, safe here, and a part of all of us—*here*. So stop being so crazy. You know that."

"I'd take a bullet for any one of y'all," he murmured thickly.

"Stop being so melodramatic." Victoria chuckled with affection as she went to hug him.

"But that's why we love you so, Jo Jo," Delores said softly, "because you are so alive with drama . . . and you're the best true friend any of us has had, right?"

"Yup, you tell us off, cuss us out, criticize and signify, but love us madly," Gail said with a tender laugh as she went to him to pet his face with a stroke of her hand.

"You brought me into this fold all those years ago," Nicole reminded him. "I was sitting in your chair, you were all in my business, made me tell you my life story, and then you grabbed Miss Vic by her elbow and brought her over— telling her, 'This chile needs some mothering, not to mention a full makeover!' "

They all joined in companionable laughter as Nicole added to the circle around Jo Jo and kissed his forehead.

"You know what"—Jo Jo sniffed—"we should do a makeover party."

"What?" Victoria fussed in good nature. "Ain't you tired of the shop yet?"

"No," he said with a laugh. "We all just got reborn here, right? Well, I say that calls for making our new business-women into new women."

"You know," Nicole agreed, "he does have a point."

"Miss Gail should finally let that red wig go. You have beautiful tresses under that nylon, and gorgeous eyes . . . with a few highlights, new nails, your feet buffed, and your eyebrows lightened and waxed, you'll feel like the new owner and CEO of Gail Jackson's Curious Southern Cuisine."

"Aw, go on, Jo Jo," Gail said with a self-conscious

chuckle. "You'd have to do an overhaul, not a makeover, to get me looking like a CEO."

The circle shifted focus onto Gail's smiling face, each friend seeming to appraise the years of inner hurt and damaged self-esteem contained within it.

"Jo Jo's right," Nicole argued. "You are a *very* pretty woman, Gail Jackson."

"No, I'm just a good cook." Gail sighed with a sad laugh. "Delores is the pretty one; so are Nicole and Vikki. Work with them—"

"You doubt my skills?" Jo Jo gasped in mock offense. "I know good raw material when I see it, darling. We'll give you an angular, sweeping front line on the hair, and lift the back of it to balance the hips; we do the eyes, and matte-finish the face, beat lovely . . . oh, it's on now. Don't tell me what I can't do."

"Anyway, if I got one of those highfalutin parties," Gail said quietly, "what will my wide behind wear, hospital scrubs or a sweat suit?"

"Your husband was foolish," Jo Jo shot back as he stood and walked away from her, then spun on Gail to face her. "You loved him. You had children for him. You worked like a slave for him. And you cooked, cleaned, and cared for him. Do not let his lack of appreciation keep you down for the rest of your life. My father did it to me, and my family turned their backs on me. I know how hard it is to shake off hurtful words and disrespect, or to be the one who has to laugh all the time to keep from crying—but Gail, sweetie, you are so pretty and so talented and so smart. Let me try, just once, to show you, please." Jo Jo was sucking in large sips of air as his voice faltered.

"You know Jo Jo wouldn't lie to you about that," Victoria confirmed. "If you didn't have it going on, he'd just straight-up tell you. Jo Jo would say," she added, while mocking

Jo Jo to obviously break the tension, "'Doll, I can't do nuthin' with that. I'm not a magician; I'm a stylist.'"

"Don't you know it," he added with a snap of his fingers, seeming to revive his spirits during the emotional rest-break Victoria's humor had provided. "Besides, Bibbidi-Bobbidi-Boo, I do have a few friends in fashion that could turn you into a plus-size model, as long as you bring the clothes back after the jobs. Modern spin on Cinderella, but I could pass as a fairy godfather. Might even be able to get Miss Dee Dee to go classic on us, and to give up her hoochie-momma gear. Elegance is back in vogue for women over forty, you know."

"No, you did not!" Delores laughed. "Okay, it's on now!"

"Might get you to give up that press-'n'-curl, glue-add-on ponytail, and go for a classic black bob, long black dress to show off your curves with style, slit up one side, no back, and ropes of pearls to go with a little number I know my buddy, Shawn, is dying to put on a natural clotheshorse like you. But since I don't know what I'm talking about . . ."

"No, no, I was just playin'," Delores fussed. "Oooh, please, can't you hook a sister up?"

"Lose the orange talons."

"My nails?" Delores said aghast as the rest of the group roared with laughter.

"Listen, I don't do retro on the over-forty. Short, tapered American manicure. The kind that will pull and stroke a well-heeled businessman who's into the refined look. I do have the advantage of knowing what men like."

"We don't even have the first gig yet."

"That's because I haven't had a chance to work the phones . . . might call a few people in the film and video community, see what shoots are coming to Philly—must have wrap parties, set parties, plenty of—"

"You'd do that for us?" Gail covered her mouth with her hand as her eyes welled with tears.

"Pish-posh, mish-mosh," Jo Jo exclaimed, flouncing into the kitchen. "When you don't have family, you make family. My sisters need help, so my brothers will help out. Life is about a series of favors and barters. Sometimes cash obstructs justice."

Nicole knew that he needed distance, just as she could feel herself wanting to weep from the joy of having people around her who cared so much. And at the same time, the emotional overload made her want to go home to her baby, hold her little girl in her arms, and be in that smaller circle of love. She missed her parents, her large extended family. Florida seemed so far away.

"What about me?" Victoria yelled as they hurried to follow Jo Jo into the kitchen to rummage for food.

"I told you to lose that platinum a *long* time ago, doll. But I just work here."

"Seriously," Victoria asked with a chuckle, "if I allowed you to have your way with me, what would you do?"

Jo Jo leaned against the refrigerator and furrowed his brow, then rubbed his chin with his long, manicured fingers. Delores, Gail, and Nicole stifled giggles as they took seats around the kitchen table and waited for his pronouncement. Victoria stood in the middle of the floor facing him with her arms folded in a challenging stance. They nearly held their breaths as the two professionals began the stylist showdown.

"Deep, honey blond—monochrome effect. Hair the same color as your skin, darkened brows . . . your hands are good, but I like natural enamels on you better than the frosted. Taupe silk duster tunic, with matching pants, peau d'soie shoes, in that same honey brown, and a copper choker—no jewelry save that. The truly wealthy don't have to show all their money in one sitting; they serve you dramatic in hors d'oeuvre-sized portions. Less is more. Each time they meet you they show you a different piece, like fine art with focused lighting against a bare wall. So flaunt that long, beautiful swan neck and your Indian-mixed African blood with a tribal conversation piece.

"Yes. Minimalistic, IKEA for the body, class. Barely-there makeup; mouth, instead of Cherokee bright reds, toned down to a bronze matte. Give them Paris in Philly. The attorney will love it, and I'm glad he didn't see you in full platinum, between you and me."

"Damn, Jo Jo, you are awesome," Delores whispered.

"Yeah, you are," Victoria murmured when Gail and Nicole nodded in agreement with Delores.

"I know," he replied with a casual smile that made them giggle.

But all laughter ceased in the room when his expression became serious and his line of vision went to Nicole.

"Before you went down for a few moments, you said to tell the guy in the leather that you weren't that bad," he murmured, looking at her steadily. "I never told you that a man who fit that description came into the salon."

"I was just exhausted," Nicole stammered. "I hadn't eaten all day, was upset about everything going on, may have remembered that stuff Dee said about the fine guy in the bar and got it jumbled into my consciousness. Was probably just fatigued and talking out of my head when I said—"

"His name is Adam—the name of the first man made by God. Deep," Jo Jo whispered. "You saw him in your head, didn't you?"

"Fruits of the spirit," Gail interjected. "The gift of prophecy."

"We are *not* back to that again, are we?" Nicole tried to

laugh, but sudden fatigue claimed her. She set down her tumbler of water and her fingers found her temples as her shoulders slumped.

"Get the girl something to eat," Victoria warned. "I don't know what's in here, as my kids swoop by all the time and raid the box even though they're grown, but at least pull out some cheese and crackers or something."

"Gail, people were swarming the shop all day, telling all of us about how the aphrodisiac worked, or how they met a new love just after tasting your connection elixir, and how they got a boost of confidence, whatever," Jo Jo pressed on, while rummaging for food. "You've both got something going on here that helps people."

"It's placebo." Gail shrugged. "The juice off of stuff I would normally cook."

"But you and your aunt prayed over each batch," Delores reminded her.

"Bottle it and give it away as a freebie at your catering functions," Jo Jo urged. "That's the curiosity of your Southern cuisine; hence the new name I've selected for your enterprise—Gail Jackson's Curious Southern Cuisine. Okaaay. Need I say more? If you cook it, they will come." He laughed. "Seriously, me and my crew will show you how to present your delectable spread like it's haute cuisine. It's all in the presentation. But there *is* something mysterious going on—so serve that, too, as a conversation piece. We can get vials from the beauty-supply distributor. Easy."

They all stared a Jo Jo for a moment before Victoria cut in.

"We should give it away for free in the shop when people come in to get read. Nicole can tell them which one they need, like a prescription."

"Wait," Delores interrupted before Nicole could form the words to do so herself. "Didn't we all learn our lessons?"

"I couldn't have said it any plainer," Nicole concurred.

"No gaudy theater this time," Jo Jo said with a soft voice. "We drape the salon in elegance, play smooth, relaxing jazz, and offer comfort dessert foods displayed with the utmost care and style. No. The psychic is gone, and there is no more love goddess. Instead, when they step behind the curtain into the back room, they will meet with the love healer. She will be wearing a simplistic Asian tunic with dolman sleeves and slits up both sides to show off her gorgeous legs—raw silk of midnight blue, natural. Everything about Nikki must be natural, real, palpably from the good Earth. Her tendrils of unprocessed hair will be upswept and held with chopsticks to show off the beautiful nape of her fragile neck, with an invisible necklace around it that hosts a single pearl. Her tapered hands should be manicured with one coat of clear polish and white stick under her nails only—no color, no additives. Her eyes will be the sole focus on her face ... smoky, caring, deeply riveting, and she will—"

"Not do it. I am not going to tempt fate; I told you all that." Nicole could feel a low buzzing in her ears, and her stomach churned with a mixture of emotions that she couldn't describe either to herself or to her friends. "We can't set a price and take money for something I cannot guarantee, or do. I don't have any special gift that I can charge for!"

"You're right," Jo Jo hedged. "We shouldn't set a price, even though you are gifted with discernment. We should let people contribute whatever they think her advice has been worth to them." His gaze swept the group and he paused as though to allow the concept to settle in before he went on.

"Let their conscience be their guides. Then we give one-tenth of it to a worthy cause each week that will help someone less fortunate.''

''We tie the catering to the salon and the advice to redesign the shop into a makeover studio for the mind, body, and spirit,'' Victoria added quickly, picking up on Jo Jo's line of reasoning. ''Each designer from whom we borrow our new outfits should also have their cards at the end of the buffet, as we can be walking signboards to return their favors. If we look as good as Jo Jo says we will, then that ought to bring them some upscale clientele—especially at the film parties.''

''See, now you're thinking like a family, by making sure that one hand washes the other, and everyone's talents are recognized,'' he agreed.

''I get it,'' Gail said with excitement. ''We debut the catering at the shop at this full-house event, and put the business cards out on the table, after we dress it to the nines in elegance and class. Then, when we get our first cast party through Jo Jo's contacts at the film office, we set out tasteful little embossed cards for the mind, body, spirit experience at the salon . . . touting *total* makeovers.''

Delores clapped her hands and popped out of her chair, whirling around in the kitchen as she spoke. ''We can do this, y'all—without scamming anyone, without hurting anyone, and helping people to see their own inner beauty. Every private session would open with a prayer for clarity, wisdom, and guidance, and close on the same note . . . wishing the person well and Godspeed. People would leave feeling good about themselves, uplifted—''

''We could add scented candles and light incense to help soothe the minds through aromatherapy, and tell people to lay their burdens down for just an hour or two,'' Victoria urged. ''Jo Jo could give makeover prescriptions that the people could book appointments to follow up on during salon hours. He was right. I do need to redecorate and turn this into a day spa. We'll get rid of the harsh chemical stuff and go with a full line of natural products for the skin, face, feet—do massages, hydrotherapy—I'm gonna need an investor if we keep this up. But the sisters need a transition, Jo Jo; gotta keep my weave and perm business going, too, now, let's not be crazy . . . that's the bread and butter. Acrylic nails keep the lights on.''

"Do that at the back stations, then; put the glamour up front," he reassured Victoria. "I mean, we can do rice-paper screen dividers, and get some hoods to suck up the fumes."

"But—" Nicole tried to get a word in, but was cut off by Gail.

"Look at how we all came in here. We were all depressed, hopeless, and feeling like we didn't have a chance. Nikki uplifted us in prayer, and gave us just a few tidbits of advice after God spoke through her. And Jo Jo made us feel pretty, and Victoria gave us direction and confidence . . . and now look at how good everyone is feeling after two or more of us stood in agreement in the Father's name. I say we ask God, through prayer, if this is all right, and try it. Let's also ask Him, if we aren't supposed to do this, to *gently* show us that we are going down the wrong road, and to open up other glorious options for us. If He doesn't think this is a good idea, then He'll shut us down before we have a chance to go wrong—because He knows in our hearts that we are asking for guidance and for Him to help us make a way out of no way. Amen."

"Amen," Jo Jo echoed. "But I still want to know how girlfriend knew about the guy in the leather, and what she meant by her not being that bad?"

"Order some Chinese food, y'all." Victoria interjected with a laugh. "We've got less than a week to make us all over, make the shop over, and we've gotta do it with practically no money and a *lot* of panache."

"It's just set, doll. I've got a hookup for dressing set. Some of us are unemployed and have all day to go buy fabric—some of which will come by way of donations—make screens after I show them how, and pick up set items from my friends in the business. Some of us need to be going down to the Municipal Services Building to get their licenses in order, and go have a talk with their minister about what days they can cook in the church, then go to the restaurant-supply store to buy in bulk at a savings."

"Amen," Gail said with a chuckle, slapping Delores five. "Necessity is the motherhood of invention. The dollar store has candles."

"And the Muslim brothers got the incense," Delores nearly shouted.

"And we got style, ladies!" Jo Jo piped in.

"True dat!" Victoria boomed as they made their way down to the salon.

Arguing with her friends, now that the concept had earned a life of its own, seemed pointless. As long as Nicole prayed for guidance first before she spoke, with the caveat that they'd all ask the Lord to be gentle with them, she'd feel better. After all, it was easy to see the good in people, and if her telling a person about that goodness healed their spirit, then that couldn't be bad, could it? None of them wanted to hurt anyone, she reasoned and repeated in her head. Besides, if prayer, fellowship, good food, genuine caring, a makeover, plus some placebo-confidence-in-a-bottle, and a little hope could transform people from a state of depression to one of euphoria for a few hours in the same way it had been an antidote to pain for her friends, then perhaps that was indeed a miracle. What could be so wrong with that? Plus, people could pay or not pay.

Nicole heard her friends talking in the back of her mind, and she thought for sure that she'd ordered something from the Chinese food menu that Victoria had passed around, but couldn't remember what it was. Her mind's eye was focused on something that disturbed her in a way that she hadn't been affected in a long time. A man. *Silly. Why now?*

As they entered the salon and waited on their food, she moved as though not attached to her own body while they fussed about ways to improve the shop décor and traffic flow. In her head she pictured glimpses of a deep-ebony face that she didn't know. His mouth was what she could best make out. He had a brilliant smile, flawless white teeth that held what looked like a piece of bark or a stick between them, and his mouth was lush in the way that it curved up on one side more than the other. Her stomach gurgled.

"Is anybody in here eating licorice? I smell it everywhere. I'm starved."

Chapter 7

"He cut off all of my hair," Gail lamented as she spun around in the chair and looked in the handheld mirror to see the back of her head in the wider salon mirror. Running her palm against the tapered, clean nape of her neck, she sighed. "He cut it off."

"And you look like a million bucks," Victoria said with a grin, smacking Gail's hand away from her hairline to spin her to gaze at her own reflection in full frontal view. "Look at that sweep he put in the front, going over one eye all dramatic."

"I got rid of that doo-doo ball of naps she kept stuck up under that filthy wig," Jo Jo snapped, becoming peevish.

"You look fabulous," Delores soothed. "Wait till Miss Vic does those brows, and we get your feet into shape. You've gotta see the whole look with the clothes and everything. Right, Nikki?"

"Huh?"

"Girl, where are you?"

"Just thinking, Dee," Nicole murmured. "Going through a lot of what-ifs in my head, I suppose."

"Chile, puhleeze," Jo Jo fussed as he thrust Victoria into a chair. "Everything is gonna be all right."

All she could do was nod and smile at them as the reverie continued. Her thoughts were now held hostage in her head, and there was no way that she could explain that her body was coming alive again as the excitement and fun escalated in the salon. She stared at the glass of zinfandel, the pink liquid pulling memories from her depths. For the first time in years she missed the touch of a man. For the first time in years she didn't ache for that touch to come from her husband. That frightened her, and felt too perilous to consider. New hopes dawned in her belly like hundreds of butterflies being set free all at once.

It was almost midnight, yet she felt a sense of restless anticipation that wouldn't allow her to doze off under the dryer when it had been her turn in Jo Jo's chair. The pampering given to her hands and feet made her remember that her heart was connected to her body. The warm wax on her legs and brows made her feel feminine and pretty as Victoria had leaned over her . . . as though she were getting ready to go on a date. That was it! The entire experience of preparation reminded her of getting ready for a date.

And just as quickly as the errant thought had popped into her head, a sudden rush of sadness followed it. There was no one coming to her door. There was no one special to get excited for. There was no one to endure the stripping off of hot wax for, much less get dressed up to attract. She was a single mom in a big city, with no job. She had to be careful, lest she break her little girl's heart by introducing her to a string of liars, or worse. There was no room for such feelings or needs.

But she had good friends. However, the combination of

laughter and wine and a full belly made her want to curl up in one of the salon chairs and go to sleep—but each time she did close her eyes, a frightening level of physical hunger overtook her.

How in the world were they each going to go upstairs after the royal treatment in Jo Jo's throne, then have a nice bubble bath in Victoria's luxury condo while decadently eating in the tub Häagen-Dazs purchased at 7-Eleven, without feeling this way? This was body-and-soul torture that Victoria proposed. Right. She was crazy. *Treat yourselves like queens,* Jo Jo had said. Just slip on one of her sexy silk nightgowns, watch tearjerker movies on cable until they were zombies, then sleep in one of her sumptuous beds, and get treated to waking up to the smell of breakfast. She needed to go home. The mere thought of indulging in such luxuries was making her remember freedom and lovemaking, unvarnished adult time. Gooseflesh rose on her arms, and she became suddenly aware of moisture forming in a place on her body that she'd ignored for two years.

"I can't do this," Gail whispered in a conspiratorial voice as she sat down in a chair next to Nicole.

Starting at Gail's sudden intrusion to her thoughts, Nicole stared at her friend.

"I need to say this to you while they are in the back waxing Dee and doing her feet. I'm not used to this, and . . . I need to go *home.*" Gail's eyes searched Nicole's face with a level of urgency, and her expression seemed pained. "I'm not used to all this attention on me . . . or treating myself like this. It's not that I'm ungrateful, or that I don't love them, and I know it would hurt their feelings to the bone if I left, but—"

"I know how you feel," Nicole confided, chuckling, letting out a sigh of relief in the process. "I thought it was just me."

Gail leaned closer to Nicole from her position in the next chair. Her voice dropped to a barely audible whisper, and her eyes were glassy from unshed tears. "It just hit me like a ton of bricks all of a sudden. I felt pretty . . . and it just sneaked up on me, after all these years of not feeling it. After being able to just think it away, and tuck it away . . . I had a kid to raise by myself, and I'd convinced myself . . . But I feel too alive. The worst part is, I'm so out of shape, and let my behind spread that, even if I wanted to, it would take years before anybody would want . . . well, I shouldn't feel this way if there is no way, because that's a sure recipe to lose your mind. Do you know what I'm saying? I know you don't have this problem, because you stayed slim, at least, but . . . I'm not making sense."

"You're making perfect sense, Gail," Nicole whispered in a hard rasp, then took a deep swig from her glass. "My hands were trembling before you sat down and I could barely hold on to my wineglass."

"For real?" Gail whispered back while gaping at her. "You?"

"Yeah." Nicole sighed.

"I was scared to become like Dee, so angry about my own circumstances that I didn't care if I hurt anybody else. Then, too, I knew how easy it was to give in to the temptation . . . so I keep tucking it away, trying to forget about that part of my life till my baby grows up, or it just withers away. Been so long, I thought my girlfriend had dried up like a raisin and might just fall off."

They both giggled and slapped each other on the arms. What Gail had confessed was beyond profound, and Nicole could only nod in agreement for a moment.

"We can't leave, though," Nicole murmured. "It would break Jo Jo's and Victoria's hearts . . . not to mention make Dee just spiral again."

"I know, girl," Gail whispered, growing serious again.

"But it didn't dry up; it plumped up and I wet my panties listening to Luther while I was getting a facial."

This time they both burst out laughing, and Nicole shook her head.

"I was sitting on the vibrating, bubbling pedicure throne with my feet in the warm water, leaning back with a glass of wine in my hand, and a soothing mint mud pack on my face. The music was filtering into my bones, and I was thinking about slipping into a hot tub of bathwater, naked; then I was done for."

"Girl, I'm just afraid that it might slip up on me at night." Gail giggled in a low voice. "What if I leave a wet spot in Miss Vic's pretty robe? What if I have to take this demon in hand and deal with it while I'm there? I haven't even had to go there in over a year . . . and the last thing I want to do is get busted at Miss Vic's with Jo Jo there, too."

"Look at my arms." Nicole sighed. "I've got goose bumps just from thinking about being with a man." The confession sent a slight shiver through Nicole's belly, and she shut her eyes briefly to ward off the renewed arousal.

"I think we've got more than goose bumps." Gail chuckled sadly, looking down at her own blouse.

Immediately Nicole looked down at her sweater, horrified by the tiny pebbles that stood erect beneath it. "Oh, no . . ."

"Oh, yes," Gail corrected. "This will look worse under silk. It's what I was afraid of. Can you see my wide behind sashaying around the apartment in one of Victoria's one-size-fits-all getups; then I sit down to watch the movie, the movie gets hot and steamy, I have to stand up—"

"Don't say it." Nicole laughed, waving Gail away with her hand.

"Colossal wet spot. I can only imagine what Jo Jo will say . . . I'd never hear the end of it. The salon would be buzzing about it until the end of time!"

"I say we make a pact to try to put this mess out of our minds tonight, once and for all. I don't have prospects, you don't have prospects, and it can take months, if not years, to find one, date him for a period of time, court, check him out, do a security clearance, then get a free night away from the little ones for prediscussed, preplanned interaction—with latex. Focus on the difficulties of the logistics."

"Thanks for the sanity check." Gail giggled as Jo Jo flounced back into the room with Delores in tow, and Victoria on her heels.

The stricken look on Delores's face and the way Victoria seemed to struggle to keep their banter going made Nicole and Gail both laugh even harder.

He needed to go home, go back to Jersey. Time was wearing a hole in his brain as he drove around the streets of Philadelphia. Cecilia had his pager number, and one of her girlfriends had agreed to stay with her. Tonight he couldn't. He needed space. He'd been around women all day. Checked out every one of them, and all of them had an alibi that matched up. Not one of them had been by Cecilia's car during the window of time when it had been damaged, even though any of those barracudas could have thrown chicken gizzards on Cecilia's steps.

The sound of their voices was starting to make him lose focus and was getting on his nerves. None of them seemed like they'd go to the lengths to hire somebody—Cecilia was messing with the sort of brothers who had women who would deal with you directly, loudly, and in the streets. He'd been past that raggedy apartment building fifty times if he'd been by it once. The salon lights had gone out by eight P.M., then went back up an hour later, but the grates were down. Probably doing inventory, the books, whatever, because there was no client street traffic from the outside going in.

*Doe eyes, pretty face, long legs, beautiful ringlets of curls
all over her head . . . and that mouth.*

He had to stop it. So what if she was drop-dead fine? So
what? She was the key to who had wrecked his cousin's
car. She was a fraud, too—a scam artist, just like the rest
of the women he'd investigated so far. Maybe he'd just roll
up on her, ask her a few direct questions, check out her
body language, and warn her to warn whomever her client
was who was doing this crap to chill. It would be almost a
week before he'd have a chance to sit in a room with her
alone and ask her some questions. The dull ache between
his legs became acute as he began to wonder what she
smelled like. Where the hell was her car?

"I can't hang any longer," Victoria confessed. "I'm the
old doll in the group. Gotta get my beauty rest, and the salon
won't wait for me in the morning."

"I hear you." Jo Jo yawned. "Some of us are still
employed."

"I'm right behind you." Dee sighed. "This was a wild
day. Thanks so much for making me whole, big brother."

"Yeah, thanks, sweetie," Gail murmured, and kissed him
when he came to her for a good-night hug.

"I love you, big brother," Nicole said, yawning, "and
thank you for making us feel like a million dollars." She
hugged him hard when he came over to her side and gave
her a kiss.

"Sleep tight and don't let the bedbugs bite," he whispered, blowing them a kiss as he clicked off the movie with
the remote. "If I have enough energy tomorrow night, I'll cut
off Miss Vic's platinum atrocity—but I didn't trust myself to
do a color reversal after all that food, wine, and three heads.
I know my limits."

"I know mine, too," Victoria fussed. "Go to bed, y'all!"

"G'nite, Miss Vic!" Delores, Nicole, and Gail yelled back in singsong unison, then laughed.

"I'm not getting up first." Gail snickered. "Nope."

All three of the remaining couch potatoes looked at each other, and quickly covered their mouths to keep the riotous giggles down and out of earshot of Jo Jo and Victoria, who had gone to bed.

"This don't make no sense." Dee wheezed while huffing air and wiping her eyes.

"No, it most certainly does not," Nicole concurred before another wave of giggles made her lean over and almost fall off the sofa.

"Turn off the light, Dee. It's closest to you; that way you don't have to get up," Gail pleaded.

"We'll kill ourselves in the dark, fool," Delores argued.

"Or break one of Miss Vic's crystal pieces; then it'll be over," Nicole added through her giggles.

Delores snapped off the light, which started a new round of hysteria.

"I'm going blind," Gail wailed, nearly screaming from merriment.

"Tomorrow morning you'll go blind," Dee said between hard giggles. "It happens after you do it, not before."

Nicole's foot collided with something hard as she tried to stand, which made her fall back onto the sofa. "Ow! Stop, y'all," she pleaded, laughing and rubbing her big toe and catching her breath in short pants. "This don't make no sense!"

When Victoria hollered at them again to go to bed, they each hopped up and ran down the hall laughing and bumping into one another to avoid being the last person in the room.

Chapter 8

Adam stood in front of his open closet carefully considering the options. He was going in. He needed to look like the regulars who visited the salon. A suit was a requirement. He didn't need to look like Five-0, a cop, or a detective, or put on anything that would make the patrons freeze up. No. He needed to blend in, be able to infiltrate the small talk in the place, and act like he was just another pampered, well-to-do client.

He let out his breath slowly. Upscale was in order, but not too upscale. Maybe midway, professorlike? Wearing a shoulder harness was, however, out of order. He'd have to stow his weapon on a leg belt. Tension curled itself around the base of his spine. This was just a stakeout, he reminded himself, not a date. What did it matter how she thought he looked?

* * *

Nicole smoothed the front of her midnight-blue tunic dress and allowed her hands to revel in the sensuous feel of raw silk. "I'm almost afraid to drink a glass of water in this," she admitted to Gail, who was transfixed in front of the mirror.

"I know what you mean," Gail murmured, turning to look at how her matte-gold satin suit-dress looked from behind. "All of these sequins and seed pearls on the lapels . . . This is so pretty, Nicole; I can't replace it if I drop some cobbler on it, or something stupid like that."

"But you look like a million bucks in it," Delores crooned, studying her own reflection and openly approving of what she saw. "Jo Jo worked miracles on us."

"Yeah, I'd have to say he did," Victoria admitted, giving her own reflection the once-over lightly. "I love this monochrome effect. . . . But what all of you did to this salon . . . It's a totally different place."

The foursome fell quiet as their gazes scanned the newly screened-off sections of the salon. Sinks were hidden away, hoods had been removed from the dryers to open up more practical seating, and tiny wrought-iron chairs with colorful cushions had been scattered about so that people could sit in little conversational groupings. All salon implements had been stored in the cabinets below, which allowed more space for candles, small water sculptures, and incense pots. Small tables had been set up with board games of chess and checkers, and each tiny table affixed with a full-length linen tablecloth along with a small vase of fresh flowers, and tea-light candles. The walls had been draped with sheer netting and tiny white lights, and the atmosphere was brought together with smooth, relaxing jazz.

"Your dessert buffet is the showstopper, though, Gail,"

Nicole said with appreciation as she moved toward the long, elegantly appointed table against the far wall. "You've got such a wild mixture of choices ... chocolate soufflé, chocolate-cherry cheesecake, chocolate mousse in the gourmet section, then peach cobbler, bread pudding, and sweet-potato pie in the Southern section, and all this beautiful fresh fruit, berries, cheeses, and vegetables. ... Oh, girl, I might have to risk spilling something on this outfit tonight."

Gail beamed with pride as she surveyed her silver-laden table that had been draped in midnight-blue velvet and strips of wired gold lamé. "I *love* the way Jo Jo laid it out, and showed me how to trim each platter with fabric, kale, and flowers to make a statement. And the way he tied gold ribbons around each vial and arranged the potions in a silver decanter with a linen napkin draping out the front ... looks like the elixirs are being poured from a Grecian urn of water. I'd give my eyeteeth to one day be able to buy one of those ornate silver coffeepots with the gold handles, and those white-on-white embossed cards look so pretty in the tiny gold holders, don't you think?"

"I think if folks don't hurry up and get here that I'm going to have to sample a little somethin'-somethin' and mess your spread up," Delores said with a chuckle as Gail slapped her hand away from a chocolate-covered strawberry. "I mean, where did you all come up with all these fancy-schmancy ideas, huh? Silver spoons dipped in white chocolate, then dipped in colored sugars for the coffee?"

"Look at how Jo Jo did the wineglasses," Victoria purred. "He even hand-painted the catering company's name on each one, and tied a gold silk ribbon around the stems."

"Makes the dollar-store buy look like Gail's operation is off the hook," Delores noted with admiration in her voice. "This can work, ladies. This can work."

"Well, it had better work," Jo Jo exclaimed as he breezed through the door, stood, and slowly spun to give them all the full effect of his ankle-length Blackgamma mink.

"Oh, my God." Nicole gasped in awe as Jo Jo modeled for them.

"You are sharp as new nails," Delores boomed. "Look at you. . . . *You go, boy!*"

"Whoooo, man!" Gail exclaimed with total appreciation. "Go 'head wit' your fine self, Jo Jo."

"Got it goin' on," Victoria added, coming to his side, and turning him slowly for the group to inspect.

"Y'all better recognize," Jo Jo said in a playful tone, thrusting his chin up higher as their compliments poured over him.

"Black fedora with pheasant feather, classic Humphrey Bogart brim, broke down over one eye, so fly . . . full-length black mink," Victoria announced like a fashion show host, grabbing Jo Jo's sleeve and flipping the lush fur back to peek at his wrist. "Rolex, gold. Leather gloves, da butter," she added with a laugh. "But let me help this gentleman off with his coat."

Jo Jo stood in front of Victoria like a king, not looking at her as she played his valet and the other women scurried around to accept his gloves and hat. Once his coat was removed, they all stood back, and hoots of approval rang out.

"Black raw silk, Nino Cerruti with Nehru-collar cream silk shirt, slip-ons by Bally, belt by Gucci, one-carat diamond ear stud, and *fine* by Jo Jo—recognize, ladies. Just recognize."

The four women clapped as Jo Jo took a little bow. They could tell that he was beyond pleased by the way that little crinkles formed at the corners of his eyes just before he gave them a full belly laugh.

"I outdid myself, true, but I thought the occasion warranted it. This is a coming-out party, after all." He chuckled when they offered him puzzled glances. "All of us are coming out of our various states of closetry tonight. Right?"

"That's true," Gail admitted with a chuckle. "Do you like it?" She spun around and waited for Jo Jo's approval, and her eyes held the quality of excited expectation that children's eyes offer when they are awaiting parental praise.

"Look at you," he said with a sweeping gesture. "Oh, Gail . . . fabulous, honey. Fabulous. Look at how that hair balances and slims you down, and I told you Shawn would find something divine for you—but your face," he crooned, going over to her and lifting her chin with his forefinger, "is absolutely gorgeous. Beat lovely."

The way Gail beamed at him made Nicole tear up. All of them let out their collective breaths, and warm smiles radiated in the small spaces between them. Each one of them knew how important feeling pretty was to Gail, and Jo Jo had made her feel absolutely stunning simply by, for once, fawning over only her as his favorite girl. Tonight this was really Gail's ball, and it had been decided without discussion or forethought or planning. They all just knew. And they all basked in the pleasure and gentle spirit of kindness offered to their girlfriend.

And in return, each one of them had also known how important it was for Jo Jo to feel included and appreciated for all that he'd contributed, and without words they had stood in agreement to express that to their beloved friend in manifold thanks and returned acts of kindness. They were indeed a family.

"I think we should say a prayer of gratitude, and ask that this event tonight be blessed, and that everyone's dreams come true," Nicole murmured as the warmth surrounding her entered her soul.

Without speaking, they all held hands. Unafraid to lead the group this time, Nicole knitted them together in prayer. Murmurs of assent rippled through the room and fused with the mellow music and sweet-smelling foods and scents from the candles and incense.

"You know," Victoria said in a quiet voice when Nicole had concluded, "for once in my life, I don't care how much we've invested in this, or that we may not cover the investment with what we bring in at the door. I know it sounds foolish, but this is just nice. I'm not worried about the money, and for me, that's deep."

"No, that's *profound,* Miss Vic," Jo Jo said in a serious tone. "I told you something miraculous was happening to all of us."

"I know I feel different," Gail added shyly. "I feel like for the first time in my life, there's nothing I can't do."

"I feel so relaxed, but so excited . . . like a schoolgirl," Delores admitted. "Crazy, but I don't care if nobody comes. This is *our party,* you know—and I haven't felt at such peace in a long, long time."

They all nodded, and a companionable silence fell between them. But as the doorbell rang, they all glanced at one another, chuckled, and began scurrying again.

Nicole was immediately ushered to the back room where her advice would be dispensed, and as Jo Jo blew her a kiss, the butterflies returned. What would she tell the people who came to the salon gala tonight? Slowly she sat down at the round table, which had been covered in midnight-blue velvet. In the center of it stood a seven-wick, short, fat, vanilla-scented candle, and the tall, slim candles that had been lit around the room created a dreamy effect.

Off to the side of the table, a low crystal vase filled with tiny violets blended with the scent of the candle, and the gurgling sound from the tabletop water sculpture and piped-in jazz began to chase the fear from her bones. Although she was still somewhat nervous, a sense of calm started to replace the edginess. She reasoned that as long as she stayed positive in her approach, and as long as she continued to pray, and with all the good food and good vibes, no one should leave there disappointed. That was her main concern. Everybody had such high hopes, and her friends had worked so hard at transforming the salon into a retreat, if not a sanctuary. She just hoped that she wouldn't spoil those dreams.

Each time the front salon doorbell rang, she nearly jumped out of her skin. She could feel her curiosity getting the better of her, and after a while even the water harmony and jazz couldn't keep her from moving to the back room door and peeking out of it. The fact that people were milling around, laughing, talking, and having fun didn't calm her in the least. Her nerves started to fray and pop more when she realized how many of them had returned—to see her!

Finally she could make out Victoria's form heading toward the room where she'd been sequestered, and Nicole quickly slipped back into her seat. When the back-room door opened, she searched her friend Victoria's face with anticipation.

"It's un-be-lievable out there," Victoria whispered in an excited rush. "I'm at capacity, and folks are still coming. People who got an appointment brought friends with them, and even though they don't expect a reading, they're hoping for one—and the ones with appointments wanted their friends to be there when they came out. This is not a party, this is an *event!*"

A new knot of worry gathered in the pit of Nicole's stomach. "But they all came back to see the love goddess. She's no longer here."

"Well, Jo Jo spread the word, and told people as they

came in that the psychic couldn't come back due to her religious convictions,'' Victoria said with a chuckle. ''But they said they'd try the love adviser . . . and they didn't care who was in the back; the love potions, they swear, work. Go figure,'' Victoria added with a shrug. ''The fact that we changed the set is blowing people away. They were coming expecting one thing, and we served them elegant on a silver platter, literally. They have decimated Gail's desserts, and the people are vibing . . . what can I say? You ready for your first client?''

Nicole was momentarily speechless, but she nodded anyway. When Victoria slipped out of the door and closed it behind her, Nicole shut her eyes tight, said a silent prayer to be able to do the right thing, and almost fell out of her chair when the door opened again. Garnering a facade of calmness, she peered at the young woman in front of her, smiled, opened her hands for the person to grasp them, and bowed her head.

Father God help her!

''What are you doing to them in here, girl?'' Delores asked in an urgent whisper as she brought in another box of tissues for Nicole's table in between clients. ''Folks are coming out crying, laughing, looking stunned, and telling the others who are waiting that you are *deep.*''

''Is that good or bad?'' Nicole asked quickly. ''Are they upset?''

''No, no, no,'' Delores cut in. ''They are blown away. Plus, Gail is upstairs now refilling trays and trying to defrost some pot liquor from her greens batches to fill some more potion vials—we sold out.''

''What?''

''You heard me,'' Delores confirmed. ''We sold out, and

we've got eight events to cater, and folks are still coming in. I met this fine brother who wants to discuss doing a full catering job for his bank, and another slim-goody is talking about a publisher's party for his new magazine. Chile, I've got more play in here than in two years working at the bar—plus we'll be getting paid! They not only want us to cater, but they want us to also decorate and set the tone. We are in the events business, honey."

"Are you serious?" Nicole was dumbfounded.

"Victoria had to open the book up to do this more than one night a week, because of the volume. I don't know how we're gonna keep up. And Gail met this cute contractor who almost ate a whole pie by himself. Girl, it's mobbed out there, but folks are being cool and patient, because nobody wants to be kept from coming back to the place to be. Are you hearing me?"

"How many more?" Nicole whispered, her shoulders slumping. Fatigue tugged at every muscle in her body, and she felt as though she could just lay her head down on the table and pass out. "I am so wiped, and I don't know why. What time is it?"

"It's only ten o'clock."

"I feel like I've been here all night."

"Well, you've got a whole bunch more people trying to see you, and the ones who don't have an appointment are angling to be seen—if somebody on the list doesn't show up."

"I can't," Nicole whispered, stifling a yawn.

"I'ma bring you some coffee, kiddo. Stand up, stretch, then give me the signal when you're ready to rock 'n' roll."

"I don't know how much longer I can keep this up."

"You'll be okay. We made you a plate of chocolate-covered strawberries, and saved you some cheesecake. All you need is a little sugar hit to get your circulation going, and some air. I used to fade fast when I first started working at Eddie's . . . people siphon energy from your battery; that's why working with the public is so draining until you build up your reserves. Ask me how I know—I did what you're doing now, only with a bar between me and a barfly instead of a table with candles and flowers between you and a patron. Same diffy. Advice is advice.''

"I suppose it is,'' Nicole replied with a yawn. "Yeah, some coffee would be good.''

"You got it. Take ten. And, oh, by the way, did I tell you the men out there are fine? Do you hear me? Fine! Don't know where they all came from. Shop has never been loaded like this.''

Nicole stood as Delores dashed out of the room, and she once again approached the cracked door. Peeping out, she was awestruck by the fact that the twenty clients she'd already seen were still there. Everyone was gabbing, eating, with some patrons engaged in what appeared to be heated but friendly debates on current topics, or general rhetoric. Some were playing chess or checkers, and some were linking up and making either business connections or love connections.

A few people were quietly sipping wine and leafing through Victoria's plush array of magazines. Others were at the front desk getting consultations and making appointments for follow-up treatments with Jo Jo. The sight of it all made Nicole's head spin. It was good energy, but Delores was right; it felt like someone had hooked up a set of jumper cables to her and drained her battery.

But as the doorbell sounded again, an electric current ran through her. Nicole's gaze from her hiding place was trained on the door. As Victoria opened it and stepped aside to accept another guest, Nicole found herself unable to move. She'd seen that handsome, dark-chocolate face before . . .

that mouth . . . chewing a stick. Her eyes appraised the wide
shoulders and height that was swathed in a camel-hair coat.
His countenance dwarfed Victoria's, and she was no tiny
woman. . . . *Dear God.* Unable to leave the doorway, Nicole
watched him as he offered his coat to Victoria with a warm
smile. Her gaze traveled over his brown-and-black-flecked
herringbone jacket and black turtleneck sweater that did not
hide the expanse of what appeared to be cinder blocks in
his chest. She stopped herself as he slipped past Victoria
and approached the buffet table, not sure whether it was the
sight of his long strides across the room that had taken her
breath, or the intensity of his eyes when he flashed Delores
a polite smile.

Closing the door quickly and quietly, Nicole fanned her
face with her hands and sat down . . . then grabbed a tissue
to blot her makeup in the mirror behind her. If he wasn't
on the list, she'd be sure to save enough energy for one add-
in guest tonight.

"Here's your coffee," Delores said brightly as she entered
the room. "You awake enough to start in about ten minutes?
The natives are getting restless, but Jo Jo said that making
them wait a little bit is part of the whole mystique vibe.
Everybody is falling through here tonight—even out-of-
towners."

"I-I'm awake," Nicole stammered, taking the coffee,
slurping it fast, and setting down the china cup.

"You look flushed, girlfriend. You sure you don't want
to go out and get some air first, or eat something?"

"No. It's just a bit warm back here with all the candles.
Like you said, let's rock and roll."

Chapter 9

"You okay?" Gail asked in a quick whisper as she slipped through the back-room door with the water that Nicole had requested. Glimpsing around the room, her gaze settled on the half-eaten plate of desserts, and she immediately issued Nicole a soft ticking noise of admonishment. "See, now, you are going to make me put all these folks on serious hold . . . don't make no sense. You have to eat something, sweetie, or fall out. You can't keep treating your body like it can run on fumes forever."

Nicole responded with a weak chuckle as she accepted the water from Gail. "It's not your cooking. I just lost my appetite. Each time I'd start working with somebody, I just wasn't that hungry. But I'm feeling it now." Nicole sipped her water and reached for a semimelted chocolate-covered strawberry, more to satisfy Gail's concern than to quench her own need for food.

The rich flavor of the dark confection at the end of the

fruit immediately melted in her mouth and covered her tongue. The taste of it made her close her eyes, and she moaned her delight while allowing the creamy substance to roll around on her taste buds before chewing the fruit. When she bit into it, a burst of tart flavor created a luscious quandary for her senses to absorb.

"Oh, Gail, this is *so* good," she confessed. "I was hungry, and just didn't realize how much."

"Well, I would think so," Gail teased. "It's almost one o'clock in the morning, and you haven't had a thing since I fixed y'all lunch."

"I know, I know. But with all the last-minute running around, making sure that the kids had pizza money or could order cheese steaks, then having to get the finishing touches on the salon, then get ourselves dressed," Nicole mumbled through another bite, this time stopping to suck the chocolate off her forefinger and thumb, "I simply forgot about it."

"I hear you. There was a lot to do, I'ma tell you, but at least I did sit down and have a small plate before I got dressed. Otherwise, I would have passed out in here."

"I was feeling like that until you brought me in this water. Thanks, lady."

"You're welcome, hon. We gotta take care of each other," Gail said with an easy smile. "Besides, you only have one more appointment; the rest of the people who are waiting know that they have to go on the books for the next event. Victoria figured you were wiping out, and told them that you'd be better once fresh. Nobody in there seemed to have a problem with the concept of being invited back to do this again."

An odd sense of disappointment suddenly gripped her, even though Gail's words made perfect sense. There was one add-on client that she did want to see. But it didn't appear to be in the Master's plan.

"I was hoping to get to everyone who came out tonight, since they went to all the trouble to come out, and whatnot." Nicole sighed. "Well, I guess you might as well show the last booked guest in; then we'll call it a night."

"Now you're making sense," Gail agreed. "Victoria wants to know if you can do this on Friday night. That gives me and Dee a day to shop and cook, and all of us a day to rest. Plus, we need the day to clean and return our clothes to the designers in between gigs. Jo Jo might have to touch my hair up, though."

Nicole looked at the way Gail was beaming at her, and an odd knowing came over her. "Delores told me that you met some construction guy out there who loved your pies."

Gail giggled and waved her hand at Nicole. "Yeah, miss busybody. Also met this guy who's the head of his Masonic lodge, and guess where he works?"

"Where?" Nicole asked with a chuckle, thoroughly enjoying her friend's Cinderella moment.

"Licenses and Inspections."

"Get out!" Nicole lowered her head and covered her mouth with her hand as they both laughed hard.

"I know, I know," Gail went on through a giggle. "He's a deacon in his church, too. And a widower."

"You're serious, aren't you?" Nicole looked up, her eyes wide, and another giggle erupted as she looked at Gail's elated, mischievous grin. She loved the way her friend's entire demeanor seemed to broadcast a new confidence that Nicole had never seen in her before.

"Both of them have been sweatin' me all night, and fighting over portions at the buffet," Gail quipped. "So," she said with a broader grin, "like Jo Jo told me, let the best man win. They should pursue me a little bit, and court me. I am *not* desperate."

"Well, you go, girl!" Nicole sat back in her chair and laughed, and offered her palm to Gail for a high-five.

"Victoria has been hemmed in all night by this attorney who has expansion plans on his mind, but I don't think it's just business expansion, though, chile."

"Get out . . ."

"Yup," Gail cooed. "And Miss Dee Dee has been flitting through the place like Madame Butterfly. Chile, the brothers fell through here tonight, and my aphrodisiac is sold out with back orders. If they keep this up, I'ma put the Viagra people out of business."

All Nicole could do was laugh. The brief levity and refreshment that Gail provided had begun to restore her. "Okay, Friday night it is. Let's do this last client and call it a night."

"You got it, lady. I'll check the book and send them in, and I'll let Victoria know that Friday is a go."

As Gail slipped beyond her sight, Nicole chose another fat strawberry from the neglected plate, closed her eyes, and licked at the melting chocolate. Leaning over the table and holding the fruit away from her dress, she carefully bit into the treat and moaned again with delight, but almost dropped it when she heard the door close and she looked up.

"I'm sorry," her last client murmured as their gazes met. "I thought they said you were ready for me. I didn't mean to startle you."

He had not been able to breathe for a moment as he'd watched the gorgeous woman before him decimate the chocolate at the tip of a strawberry with her tongue.

Nothing could have prepared him for the sight of her sitting there in a midnight-blue sheath that matched the surrounding drapes, with her pretty face lit by soft candle-light, her mouth pouting, and her long, tapered fingers gently cradling the berry. . . . But it was the deep, sensuous moan that she emitted from the base of her throat that had entered his skeleton and shook it. Then those big smoky-brown eyes opened and captured him. No wonder the first Adam couldn't say no to a woman eating fruit in the middle of paradise. Who born of flesh could blame the man? The wild thought made him chuckle. Yep, his mom was right: the devil sure knew how to tempt a man away from his senses.

Flustered, Nicole gulped the strawberry and almost choked, then quickly sucked her fingers.

Dear God in heaven, why did she do that? He watched her as she put each finger in her mouth and quickly pulled them out wet.

This could not be happening to her! Gail said that she was sending in the last appointment schedule, not an add-on client. This was a terrible mix-up. She wasn't ready to deal with this guy.

Realizing how ridiculous she must have appeared to him, she grabbed a tissue to remove the chocolate from her hands, but a whole wad of them came out of the box when she pulled.

"Oh, I'm sorry." She knew she was babbling, and she had to get it together. Nicole looked at her hands while trying to dip a tissue in her water glass and wipe off the sticky goo. "Sit down, sit down. Where are my manners? I just hadn't eaten all night, and was getting light-headed. I don't want to get any of this on you."

"You can," he said with an easy smile. "And you don't have to apologize."

His response seemed to make her hands work faster at the task than necessary, and for some odd reason, that pleased him. This could not be the charlatan his cousin had described. She didn't look anything like the blue-turbaned, veiled woman with long, black hair from the Middle East that Cecilia was ranting about. Yet, at the same time, he'd been around the streets long enough to not take anything for granted.

What was she doing? Nicole silently berated herself, and summoned discipline. She didn't know this man from Adam, and as they all were, this one was here because he had baggage. Slapping herself with that reality, she calmed down.

"Wait." Nicole finally chuckled, becoming more steady. "This is so tacky. I have to hold your hands, and after what you just saw, I wouldn't blame you if you got up and left." She turned quickly without waiting for his response, reached behind her under one of the cabinets, and pulled out a plastic tub of wet antiseptic towelettes. Thoroughly cleansing her hands with them, she finally garnered enough courage to return her gaze to the absolutely breathtaking man before her. "Okay. Now I'm ready."

"Your hands were fine before," he said in an easy tone.

His eyes twinkled with a brand of delight that unnerved her. It was as though he actually enjoyed seeing her become so discomfited. Why that sent a quiver through her didn't make sense.

"Well, at least let them air-dry for a second, and let me put some lotion on them before I put cold, clammy hands in yours. That's no way to begin."

He thoroughly enjoyed watching this woman and all of her antics. Although, at the moment, she was the one who seemed temporarily undone, the effect it had on every male that had come out of the room was nothing short of disarming. Her slight Caribbean accent, coupled with those deep brown eyes, set in an innocent face . . . *Wow*. And he imagined that her homespun brand of self-deprecating humor and lack of a show of ego had probably relaxed the womenfolk enough to make them let their hair down. She smelled so good, too. She was wearing something intoxicating that interwove itself between the incense, candles, and chocolate scents in the room.

"Since we are pulling ourselves together," he added with an octave drop of his voice that he hadn't planned, unable to withstand watching her place a dot of lotion in the center of her palms and work it into her skin with long strokes, "may I?" Without waiting for her response, he pulled out a piece of licorice bark and began chewing on it. He needed a cigarette.

It was as though watching something occur in slow motion. She saw his head tilt down, watched his hand reach into his inner jacket pocket and come away with a stick, that same stick she'd seen before, in that same mouth—and the sight of it locked her gaze to his smile like an adhesive. Soon the delicious scent of licorice filled her nostrils, and she could feel her eyelids becoming heavy as the effect began to awaken something more disturbing than nervous jitters within her: desire. God this man was fine.

"Let's pray," she said quickly, extending her palms to his.

Yeah, it was time to pray, he thought. Right about the time that her nostrils flared and her eyes went half-mast, he knew that the only thing keeping him from making a complete fool of himself had to be the good Lord. But touching her would require a miracle to keep him focused. Slim, tapered hands softer than the velvet on the table slid into his, and with them went an electric current through his system. He tried to push lustful impulses out of his mind, especially since she was getting ready to talk to God. He and God were already on poor terms, and he suspected that this little incident wouldn't help their relationship.

"Heavenly Father," she began in a reverent voice, "please let only positive discourse happen here, that is for the good of all concerned. Please allow me to give only good advice, and only advice that You feel would help the person before me. Please let this person's deepest hopes, dreams, and desires come true, if it be Your will ... and let nothing I have to tell this person hurt or disturb him. Amen.''

He'd watched her as she prayed, her voice soft, caring, and gentle. Her spirit felt so good, so honest. ... But he'd been fooled before, too many times. And since God wasn't speaking to him, it was best to push foolish hopes out of his head. He wasn't the kind of guy to get attached or to settle down, and this woman had the marrying kind of effect on a man's brain—that sort of effect that turns lust into love, and he was not ever going there again.

''My name is Nicole, and you don't have to tell me yours, unless you are comfortable with that. Whatever we discuss stays here in this room. So let me begin by telling you that I am not a psychic. All I do is pray for people to get help with whatever is bothering them, or whatever worries they have in their heart. Where would you like to begin?''

Deep. She had taken his first one-line zinger out of his head and turned it on him. He was all prepared to ask her how she came to think of herself as a psychic before he set to seriously grilling her.

''Um ...'' he stammered. ''I'm actually here on behalf of somebody else.'' What was on his mind? That sounded so cliché and so lame!

''Okay,'' Nicole said with a calm smile. ''What problem is your *friend* having that you are worried about?'' Nicole tried to steady her breathing and to get the burning sensation that his hands had left in her palms to stop.

''I quit smoking,'' the man before her said with a self-conscious chuckle. ''Licorice root. Some brothers down in Geechie country gave it to me, said it's also good for your teeth—so I figured, Why not? Then when I came up north,

I saw the African brothers selling it on the tables, so, like my momma always says, everybody can't be wrong.''

Mortified at the fact that she'd probably been looking at his mouth so intently that he'd felt the need to explain, Nicole lowered her gaze.

"I am so sorry," she murmured. "I didn't mean to make you feel uncomfortable."

"You didn't," he replied with a good-natured chuckle. "I think you had a right to know why a grown man was sitting in front of you eating bark. Must see a lot of interesting people in here . . . didn't want you to think I was crazy or something."

His warm response made her chuckle with him, and for a moment no conversation passed between them as they reset the meeting and began again.

He studied the dark eyes that stared back at him and the even cinnamon complexion that appeared to be fired with gold from the candle. He noticed the soft curve of her cheek and the gentleness of the way her mouth bent into a smile, and wisps that had fallen away from natural, lush hair swept up high to reveal a long, graceful neck. The packaging on this one would be his downfall, if he didn't watch his step.

"Been trying to find out who would throw chicken gizzards on a person's steps. Gave me the creeps," he finally said, needing to get to the point, get the information he needed, and get out of there.

She said nothing for a moment, and he could have sworn her pupils opened wider. Nah, he was spooking himself.

"Don't see a lot of that up here. That's from down home," she said without breaking eye contact. "Whatever you all are running from comes from home."

She'd pulled her hands from his and wrapped them around herself.

"I don't like this," she quickly added.

"What's the matter?"

"I don't know. Everybody else I had a session with had light issues, domestic affairs. This gives me the creeps."

Adam Bastille sat back in his chair and continued to study the woman who had gone from serene to nervous before him. "I thought you wanted to help people."

"Yeah," Nicole whispered. "But this is out of my league. I just give basic love advice. I don't deal with crime."

"Crime?" Now he was intrigued, because he hadn't said a word about any crime, and his cousin swore to him that she hadn't said anything about the chicken guts to the psychic last week.

"A woman didn't do this," Nicole murmured in a faraway voice. "It's a man."

"A man?"

"Who was in a fire?"

Adam stood slowly as the woman before him covered her mouth and dry-heaved.

"Look, miss, I don't know what type of game you're playing, but—"

"Sir," she said excitedly, "do you have small children . . . a wife . . . a brother? There's a fire. I don't know . . . a house. I'm so sorry. God forgive me, but I don't know why I'm saying these things to you—I must be tired. Something's wrong. I am so sorry."

The tears in her eyes glistened in the candlelight, and the way her eyes searched his face for answers drew him back to his chair. He hadn't had to think of those things for a long time, and he had tried to bury it with his partner and his partner's wife and kids. Yet there was something in her countenance that dredged his soul. His mother and aunt had told him of such things, people with this sort of gift, and the department even used a woman to help them locate the missing—but he'd never believed in it. Steadying his voice, he spoke to her in a low murmur.

"You don't know me, and nobody who knows me is out there," he said, motioning to the door. "My partner's family, wife and kids, were trapped in a suspicious house fire several years ago, and didn't make it out. When he got there, he blew his brains out. Yeah ... it was ugly ... and if you have the gift of second sight and saw that, well, I can't blame you for reacting the way you did. I had a similar reaction to yours, but it wasn't as pretty. Then I left the force, and went independent. I investigate things for people who need answers ... so right now, I need answers about who might want to hurt—"

"Why is there glass everywhere?"

Her question had cut off his flow of words, and her line of vision went past him out into nothingness.

"Someone bashed in my client's car windows," he said in a casual tone, "if that's what you're referring to. That's why I'm a little concerned. Things are escalating, and if you can help—"

"Innards from the chicken were for you. Message that it was from down home, and—"

"They'd rip out my chicken guts." Adam sighed, looking past her, then dropping his head and running his hands through his hair. "Thanks. I should have known."

"Men did this," Nicole found herself whispering.

"Yeah, they did," Adam admitted, standing and going into his wallet.

"No," she said fast. "I don't know if I've helped you or hurt you, but I don't want any money for this."

"I'll give it to the house, then," he replied calmly. "You're no fraud, lady. You're the genuine article. Seen a lot of scammers in my day, and you aren't one of them. You helped. Immensely." Then he was gone.

* * *

He could feel his heart trying to find a way to slam itself out of his chest as he made his way through the dwindling crowd, collected his coat, and dropped a hundred-dollar bill in the hand of the brother who had put him on the list. His ears were ringing with rage as he opened the salon door and a bitter blast of cold air cut into his face. It still wasn't over. After all of these years! It wasn't enough to just leave the department and get out of the Big Easy. No. This was hanging around like a vexed haint. And this was no life he was living.

He'd trusted one woman, the one he'd loved and who'd set him up for money. It had cost his partner his family and his life. For what? And it was the thing that had kept him from getting too close to anyone else again, practically living like a monk, afraid to make a family . . . living in exile from the basic pleasures of life, the truest desires of his heart . . . the way he grew up.

With this trailing him, he'd never know a day without fear. There was no way he was going to risk taking a wife, or starting a family—only to have kids to worry about, or summer barbecues where they could be sniped, and family get-togethers at his home that could one day be burned down. No. He'd distanced himself from everything precious to him and had vowed not to invest his heart in anything or anyone that could make him put his own gun to his head and blow his brains out. When his needs got the better of him, he indulged in quick, no-strings-attached fixes. That was the only practical way to live until this was over.

As he approached his sedan and hit the alarm on his key ring, images cascaded in his mind with the sound of the disarm tone. He could almost hear his voice pleading with Fred as he got out of his police cruiser slowly, and all Fred did was repeat two words over and over with a revolver to his temple. "My family . . . my family." Then it was done.

Adam sat in his car for a moment, and rested his head on his steering wheel. He'd been warned that it was maybe time to push on, and he did. They'd asked him to drop the investigation effort into the trucking scam, and he did. And they'd left him alone without incident for years, so why now?

Wresting back his clarity and logic, his mind began to dissect the facts. Okay, they'd sent a message that this was clearly from down home—that they'd pull out his chicken guts. Why hadn't he seen that before? Then they let him know they were serious. But why on Cecilia's steps, and not his? Why her sedan, and not his? Adam looked at the remaining bills in his wallet, then got out of the car. Friday, he'd find out.

"Gurl, we took in over three thousand dollars!" Victoria boomed after turning the locks on the door.

"What!" Jo Jo hollered, rushing behind her to the back part of the salon. "It only took six hundred to pull all of this together, and that came out of the balance left from the first night—and next time it won't even cost that much, since we have all the primary pieces."

"I know. Folks were dropping anywhere between thirty-five and fifty a head, plus the potion sales," Victoria said with glee. "And tomorrow I have lunch with a person who wants to talk location expansion."

"What!" Jo Jo shouted again. "You work it, Lady Macbeth."

"I'm just going to lunch to check it out, and maybe get into a little somethin'-somethin', but trust me, I'm not about to have any man I just met push up on this, or my salon. Momma wasn't born yesterday.''

Gail and Delores were jumping up and down and spinning each other around.

"Eight jobs!" Delores yelled. "Eight!"

"And da brothers!" Gail exclaimed as she threw one hand on her hip. "Aphrodisiac, y'all. I've got a date for Saturday night and a brunch date after church on Sunday. I'm being taken to Bluezette's first, then to the Zanzibar Sunday brunch, okaaaay. They both said that since I spend so much time cooking for other people, I needed a break. Can you get to that? Brothers are cookin' for Momma, in high-class style. I ain't seen that much action in over twenty years—all in the same night!"

"Friday, we do a winter-white-and-gold theme," Jo Jo commanded with a snap of his fingers. "All of this set goes back, and we work on a new thematic presentation. And let me tell you, Shawn made out like a bandit, too. The women *and* the men in here all came to me for a custom prescription to rescue their images after seeing our stunning fashion presentations, and he's only taking custom clients who have an RX with my signature. So you have to be in the circle to get into his exclusive design house, okaaay. Brother's going to have his phones ringing off the hook with the who's who in Philly—next stop for him is New York. This is big, ladies, and so well done. Victoria's is booked solid for the next month, and we may have to bring in another manicurist, colorist, and somebody to give full-body massages and facials just to keep pace—or stay open for another four hours a night."

"It was da bomb," Delores said with a laugh, rushing over to Nicole and giving her a kiss. "What were you telling those folks back there? And what did you tell Cecilia

Bastille's cousin that made that fine man run out of here like his house was on fire?''

The last part of Delores's statement made Nicole taste bile in her throat and want to retch.

"Cecilia Bastille's cousin?" Gail's gaze darted between the friends in the room.

Nicole blanched and looked up from her slumped position in a salon chair. Her tongue felt like it was swollen in her throat for a moment, and she could feel hot tears rise in her eyes.

"Mr. Adam is that heifer's cousin? Go figure," Jo Jo fussed.

"I told you about Adam Bastille, PI . . . Shaft . . . Blade . . . Remember? Leather coat."

"I didn't put it together," Nicole whispered. "I am so sorry." Stunned, she stared at the people staring at her.

"Oh, girl," Delores scoffed, "I know I saw him first and all, but when I found out Cecilia was his cousin I knew *that* wouldn't work—we'd be out in the street fighting like banshees, with me snatching the weave out of her hair. And Jo Jo ain't pressed, neither. He found out at the front desk that the brother ain't in the life, like I told him before, and wasn't about to change his way of life, so nobody here is mad at you for sitting with him for over a half hour . . . and probably pulling him. I met a few good prospects tonight, and I'm going to check out every one of them—especially the guy with the cast-party gig . . . and he said he might turn us on to a music-scene party as a catering job, too."

"Hey, hey, sweetie," Gail soothed as two big tears spilled over the edges of Nicole's lashes and ran down her face. "It's all right. Everyone left here happy, and Adam Bastille came back to see you, specifically, and gave Victoria two hundred dollars. A C-note when he left, and another one to get on the list for Friday night after he doubled back before you came out of the room. The man digs you and wants a private consultation again. Dee was just teasing you.''

"I don't want to do this again so fast, if ever," Nicole shrieked as she shot up from her chair. "I got lucky tonight—lucky that I didn't hurt anybody, or say something that could mess somebody up. Go with the party, sans adviser. They love the food, the clothes, the music, the vibration, the potions . . . you don't need me.''

"She's tired; can't you all see that?" Jo Jo warned. "All those people, all night long, with no food. I get like that when my nerves have been frayed. Creative people are sensitive to overload. The child just needs some rest and some personal space.''

"Yeah, baby," Victoria said in a gentle voice. "Jo Jo, you see her home, and me and the girls will handle this mess. You both have outdone yourselves.''

"I'm just so tired," Nicole whispered. "Maybe you're right. After eight hours and a good breakfast, I'll be fine.''

She kissed her girlfriends good-bye, and let Jo Jo help her on with her coat and walk her to her car. Stunned numb, she leaned against him as he kept his arm about her shoulders and opened the car door for her to climb in, and she waited patiently as he entered the driver's side and put her key in the ignition.

"Baby, I'm going to say this once; then I'll let it rest," he murmured. "You know you have the gift, right?"

She couldn't look at Jo Jo as her vision blurred from unshed tears, and a quick nod was all that she could summon.

"It's scaring you to death, isn't it?"

Another quick nod; then her hands covered her face.

"You know you aren't a fraud, don't you?"

This time she could only shrug her shoulders.

"You saw him before he'd been described to you, and you asked us that same night who was eating licorice. Nobody in the shop was or does ... then, after an hour of waiting tonight, brother pulls out a stick and chews it. I roll up on him to refresh his wine, all because I am not ashamed to be that nosy, and what do I smell? Licorice. I ask him about the stick; he tells me it was because he used to smoke. We shoot a little small talk, and he asks me about the psychic who was in there last week. Wants to know, for real, for real, if the chick was a fake and whatnot. If she scams people, et cetera, or is the real McCoy. I tell him what you asked me to tell him.''

Jo Jo paused, and the silence forced Nicole to look at her friend.

''What did I ask you to tell him?''

''That, quote, 'I'm really not that bad.' That's what I said, and he looked at me funny, then smiled. After your session, he dropped a C-note, then said I was right—you were the genuine article. Then he bolted. Then after about five minutes, he was back, gave us another hundred, and asked to be put on the list last again. So whatever you said obviously helped him.''

''Can we pray on that?'' Nicole whispered. ''I mean, right here in the car? I'm scared. This guy is in some sort of trouble, and I may have inadvertently seen a part of it. I don't want to have that type of gift. So can we pray together, Jo Jo?''

''Yeah, baby,'' he murmured, pulling her head against his chest. ''And if you want me to, I'll sleep on your sofa under my fur. Told you a long time ago, I'd take a bullet for you.''

''Let's also pray that it doesn't come to that.''

Chapter 10

The sounds of movement and water going on and off had filtered into her dreams as she dozed. But it was the smell of pancakes and fried eggs that finally made Nicole drag herself out of the coma she'd been trapped in, sit up, and stagger down the hall toward her kitchen.

Lydia and Michelle were munching away when she approached, and Jo Jo was fussing at them and pouring juice.

"Mommy!" Lydia yelled. "Uncle Jo Jo made pancakes and is going to take us to school in his pretty red car."

"No offense, Aunt Nicole," Michelle mumbled through a mouthful of breakfast, "but it wouldn't hurt my image none to have Uncle Jo Jo drop me off in front of the building, ya know what I mean?"

"Good morning to you all, too," Nicole said with tears of gratitude in her eyes, going to Jo Jo first for a hug and kiss, then moving toward the children.

"Good morning, sweetie," he said in a very tired voice. "You mothers got this. Every day, too?"

Nicole responded with a weary chuckle. "Every day. And thank you so much."

Offering her a warm smile in return, Jo Jo began fixing Nicole a plate.

"I had to get up at six o'clock when the little bird bounced out of bed. Figured you could use the rest. Got Michelle up so I could walk back around to the salon and get my car, then stopped at the market to put some real breakfast food in here. I can't do cereal and milk. Goes against my religion in the morning."

Nicole looked at his exhausted face and went to him again to touch his cheek.

"No, girl," he said with a chuckle as she brushed her fingertips against his five-o'clock shadow. "My alter ego is showing, so you know I must be tired. Wasn't enough time to properly groom this morning, but as soon as I get them to school, Jo Jo is going home for a hot shower, and then going to bed until eleven. Miss Vic's stylist is going to be late today."

"I am so sorry," she whispered, and hugged him.

"Now don't be getting all teary-eyed and sentimental. Eat," he murmured with love in his voice. "I was glad to do it, and now I know why all mothers who do the full monty are saints." He set a plate in front of Nicole, and poured her a glass of juice. "Oooh, girl! Six o'clock in the morning. Kids'll make you change your lifestyle—can't be out all night like Dracula when you have them, 'cause when the sun comes up, they'll open the shades, let the sun in, and jump right in the middle of your chest."

Nicole laughed hard as she filled her mouth with warm pancakes. "No lie . . ." she mumbled. "Keeps a lot of activities down, if you know what I mean."

She and Jo Jo exchanged an adult understanding, and their secret made them laugh hard and receive quizzical looks from the children.

"Saints and martyrs," Jo Jo exclaimed while shaking his head. "Every man and child alive ought to throw palms at y'all's feet."

She didn't protest when Jo Jo corralled the children and took them out with him. Nor did she tell him that her child at age five would not be able to eat an entire hoagie for lunch, along with five different snacks and a big bottle of soda. And there was no way to explain that dungarees and a sweatshirt would be more fitting for kindergarten than a church dress and Easter shoes. And she didn't feel it necessary to comment on the fact that all the ribbons he'd put in Lydia's hair would be missing by the time she rough-and-tumbled her way through a kid's day. Nor did she interject as he fussed with Gail's daughter about the appropriate fashions for a young lady. But she did note how Michelle hung on every word as he restyled her hair in the kitchen.

Nicole just chuckled and kissed them all good-bye as Uncle Jo Jo lavished her child and Gail's child with pure affection. The bed called to her from the other room, and she made her way down the long hall toward it, feeling safe, and happy, and content.

Freedom coursed through her bones as she allowed Lydia to pull her to one exhibit after the next in the Please Touch Museum. She couldn't remember when she'd not been on a schedule, or a deadline, to hurry home after work. Just a week ago she was picking up her baby from the after-school program, getting in the house with her tired child in the dark, rummaging for a quick dinner, then giving her daughter a bath, reading a bedtime story, and tucking her into bed. The weekends hadn't been much better, fraught with errands, going to the supermarket, and trying to squeeze in all the things that couldn't get done during the week by a working mom.

Today she was able to get her child as soon as school ended, and they had time to simply play and enjoy each other's company. The change in pace was soul-rejuvenating, and as Lydia laughed and enjoyed the exhibits, or stared wide-eyed at something that had caught her attention, Nicole realized how long it had been since she'd felt that same way. At peace. Whole. Filled.

The sensation was foreign. When she'd first married, everything was a rush of ambition. Her husband was trying to work his way up in the commercial-pilot ranks, and she was trying to get a foothold as a columnist for the local newspaper. Everything was about money and building assets and buying that first home. Then she got pregnant, and everything was about preparation for the baby. Then the baby came, and everything was a whirl of activity around the baby and juggling jobs. Interspersed through that entire frenetic scramble were power struggles about whose responsibility this or that was. There was no time just to be.

And with the power struggles came the arguments, and with the arguments, her writing ebbed, and with that loss of identity came the erosion of friendship and trust to the point where each party simply walked away from all that was trying to be built. Although his exit was less graceful than hers, they both, at different points, had walked away and stopped trying.

The sad reality made her stop and look at her child, who was happily engaged in the moment. That was a gift—to be able to be innocently, happily engaged in the moment.

And in that moment of watching Lydia, she knew: today
was the turning point. She'd write to Duane. There was
no sense in harboring old hurts, nursing old angers, and
remembering every single detail of every offense. Today it
was time to let it go. Because for the first time it really sank
in for her that he was not the one held hostage by her
indignity: she was.

She had to practically carry Lydia up the stairs by four
o'clock, and she wondered how children still got up at six
A.M. every day, even with a little nap. Her child had missed
her normal noon nap and was now a limp bundle of arms
and legs. Managing the locks with a sleepy youngster in
tow, Nicole got them through the door and swept Lydia up
to strip the child and put her in a comfortable pair of pajamas.
She'd already decided that, if they were both sleepy in the
morning, then Lydia could stay home from school with her.
In fact, perhaps she'd just keep her home, unless her baby
really wanted to go.

Limp and peacefully sucking her thumb, Lydia sprawled
on the bed where Nicole had placed her, and she allowed
Nicole to move her little arms and legs into and out of
clothes.

After turning on a night-light and closing the bedroom
door, Nicole paced to the kitchen to busy herself with preparing dinner. She understood why Gail stood at the stove
for hours. There was something therapeutic about doing
something with one's hands for others, while also having
brief chats with God and solving one's problems.

She'd pulled out enough red fish to feed a few extra
mouths, and now she also understood her mother's custom
of adding extra into the pot—just in case. Strange, but when
she'd lived with her husband, in their insular, upper-middle-

class environment, people just didn't fall by. Dinners were prepared only for the inhabitants of the home, if at all. But there was something about the interdependence of the neighborhood, the small village that she found herself surrounded by. Other people's children were always in and out of your home, and that kindness was reciprocated without it even being viewed as a favor. The same held true for adult friends. Folks might happen by on their way to and from a destination, and they'd stop to chat at your table, sharing a light meal before they pushed on.

She readied the pan with peanut oil and began dicing tomatoes, onions, and bell peppers. She missed home. She missed the humid summer nights on the screened-in porch, sipping peppermint-spiked iced tea, the smell of good foods coming from her mother's kitchen, and the lively guests that drowned out the crickets and the sound of bullfrogs. Here, the sound of sirens, loud music, and traffic drowned out the sounds of conversations, making people need to shout to be heard.

The sound of her doorbell chiming broke her reverie, and she turned down the flame under the pan and wiped her hands on a dish towel as she reached for the intercom. Thoroughly expecting to hear Jo Jo's voice, she was startled by the deliveryman's dry response.

Flowers?

Then a warm feeling permeated her bones. Jo Jo was so thoughtful . . . or maybe the girls had put in together to cheer her up, as they all normally did for one another. Hitting the buzzer to let the man enter, she waited by the peephole in her door until she could see the uniformed person with flowers standing in the hallway, his face and body distorted by the fishbowl effect of the hole.

Upon opening the door, she could only gape at him for a moment before accepting the tall, cellophane-wrapped vase.

She thanked him quickly, offered him a dollar for his trouble, then shut the door, taking the two dozen long-stemmed white roses into the kitchen. This was definitely a Jo Jo touch, she thought, gently peeling the paper away from the delicate petals and noticing the big gold ribbon around the vase.

"He'd said winter white and gold," she murmured. "Oh, Jo Jo, you have done too much. . . ." But the card she opened made her sit down slowly when she read its simple message.

I'm sorry that I upset you. I had no right. You are the genuine article. Thank you for helping me. Adam Bastille.

An eerie combination of excitement mixed with dread threaded its way through her bones. Immediately she popped up, turned off the flame under the frying pan, and headed for the telephone. How did this person know where she lived? What right did he have to invade her personal space? By what right did he presume that a token of appreciation like this wouldn't have caused a domestic problem for a husband or lover that she might have? It was arrogant, out of line, and definitely not acceptable!

"Gail," Nicole boomed as she connected with her friend.

"Hey, girl, what's—"

"This fool sent roses to my house! I am not having this mess!"

"Wait, chile, who? Your husband?"

"No, no, no, Duane doesn't care if I'm dead or alive."

"Don't say that. That's not true. He's just angry that you initiated the divorce after you caught him—"

"It was from that client, and I can't have people from our sessions invading my personal—"

"That one who Delores was talking about?"

"Yeah. Him!" Nicole had spat out the response with so much fury that she thought she'd levitate from the exhale.

"Ooooh, girl!"

"No, 'oooh, girl,' Gail," she fussed, finding herself walking in a tight circle. "I have a child. I don't know him from a can of paint. Plus, I don't deal with men in mysterious, dangerous professions. Not with a child—and how did he know that I was in here by myself?"

"Maybe he didn't know, but was hoping that you were."

Nicole was taking in air in short pants, and Gail's unusually chipper response just increased the torque of her indignation. "You're in an extra good mood today," she snapped against her will.

"Honey, I just got back from my late-afternoon luncheon date. Was gonna do dinner, but didn't want to leave Michelle home by herself to be out with no man, so I asked him to change it to earlier in the day. Almost lost my virginity," Gail said with a deep chuckle. "Oh, chile, he pushed up on me so hard all through the meal, and then when he brought me home, had Michelle not been here, I might have invited him in. This is crazy . . . my daughter has become my chaperon, and I was the one standing on the front steps all trembly and hot, and waiting for the next date. Ain't life funny?"

"Hysterical," Nicole said in a grudging tone. Gail was not getting it, nor was she going to understand it with her panties wet and in a state of pure euphoria.

"You know he's on the list for the Friday event," Gail said with a giggle. "I'll watch Lydia over here that night if you spot me with Michelle over the next few days, because, girl, after a ten-year drought, one of these brothers is gonna get lucky. I can't help it."

"Sure, sure, sure," Nicole said flatly, ignoring the beauty of the roses on her kitchen counter, and trying to banish the fragrance from her nose. "Just let me know what days, and I'll be sure to watch your back."

"What do the flowers look like?"

"White roses, long stem, gold ribbon on the vase. Period."

"He sent you a dozen white roses. . . . Nicole!"

"Two dozen, and the SOB had no right."

"What? Are you crazy, chile?"

The sheer outrage in Gail's voice forced a begrudging chuckle from Nicole.

"Okay, so he sent some flowers to apologize. Big deal."

"Big deal? What was he so sorry for?"

Nicole hedged and remembered what she said about things staying in the room between her and a client. "He was sorry that he had a messy situation and had brought it to me to advise him on."

"He's married . . . oh, girl, I'm sorry. . . ."

"No, well, I don't think he's married," Nicole said haltingly. But, truth be told, she wasn't sure.

"Then?"

"Then he needs to understand the boundaries between the events at the salon and my house."

"Okay. I see your point on that one," Gail offered as a compromise.

"Well, at least now you're seeing my point. Thank you."

"I say, if you still feel strongly about it by tomorrow, then tell him to his face not to ever do that again—or, if he wants to see you that way, then he needs to do it on the up-and-up, with your permission, and when you say so. Now, you do have to train some of these brothers, and not let them think they own your space just because they took you out or something."

"That's right," Nicole concurred. "That's all I'm saying."

"Okay. So enjoy the roses, put them somewhere nice, and even though you don't like how they came, let them remind you that you messed some brother up enough, without even sleeping with him, to make him drop a knot at the florist, as well as have to think up something to put on the card. Now, as we know, girlfriend, that just doesn't happen every day."

Mollified considerably by Gail's words, Nicole turned the burner on under the pan as she glimpsed the offending flowers. "He was kinda cute," she said with a soft giggle.

"Kinda cute? Understatement if ever I heard one."

"He's got a lot of drama with him, though," Nicole countered. *"Fine* doesn't change that."

"All men have a lot of drama with them. It just depends on what type of drama you can deal with."

"He's in a dangerous profession," Nicole pressed. "He's a private investigator and an ex-cop. . . . Delores told us that, so I'm not breaching any confidentiality by saying that."

She could hear Gail letting out her breath hard.

"Chile, being a fireman is a dangerous profession; truthfully, being a lawyer is a dangerous profession. Being a pilot is a dangerous profession. If you get cut, and have the wrong client in your chair or on your operating table, hell, being a dentist or a doctor is a dangerous profession. Even being a teacher is a dangerous profession, these days. But he is not a criminal, has an honest profession . . . so?"

"So, just 'cause he's a PI doesn't mean he can tail me to my building to find out where I live to deliver some flowers. Feels weird, and I don't like it. What if he were a stalker?"

"You've been watching too much TV, Lord have mercy," Gail exclaimed with a laugh. "Every brother uses the wiles of his profession to woo a girl. Don't you know that?"

"What, Gail?" Nicole puffed. "Are you crazy?" The idea was ludicrous.

"Didn't you tell me your husband used to take you up in those little propeller jobs when you were dating and before he got a big commercial-airline job? He was showing off, and was trying to court you with what he knew best, flying. And didn't that professor you went out with used to recite sonnets to you, and try to show off his intellectual prowess, huh? Be honest."

Nicole became still for a moment, then dropped her fish in the pan with a crackling splash.

"Oh, so now you in there cooking on me and ignoring me, right?"

Nicole felt a chuckle coming up from her belly despite her resolve to remain peevish. "I'm not trying to hear no roundabout logic."

"That attorney who has the hots for Miss Vic did it, too. First thing he did was flex his bankroll and business acumen for her. Then that guy who was digging hard on Delores kept her hemmed up all night telling her about his platinum Rolodex of contacts in the various entertainment industries he's affiliated with."

"That is so transparent, and so tired."

"Oh, well, that construction guy I went out with today did a good job of driving me past some of his building projects, and implying that if he had the right woman he'd build a home from scratch. Tell me that ain't showin' off. Now we done sat in my kitchen plenty of nights callin' men dogs, and I'd say a big rottweiler just came up and sniffed you—and the only problem is, you liked it."

"Gail, shut up!" Nicole laughed hard with her friend as she tended her fish.

"It's nature. All the animals do it . . . drives the females wild, so we might as well admit it. Nothing wrong with what's natural, didn't you tell me that? This is just the primal part of life in the city. We like it when the peacock spreads his tail and struts, and when the rams butt horns to prove which one has the hardest head and biggest horns, and when the gorilla beats his chest, and—"

"Okay, okay. I get the point. So now I'm supposed to accept that this one wants to show me how cool he is and how sly he is by just sending flowers without my having to give him an address? What's he gonna do next, show me his gun? Men are such kids."

"True." Gail giggled. "But you must admit that there is something sorta nice about having a tall, fine brother recognize that he's gotta do a little strutting to get your attention—even if we are moms."

Silence fell between them for a moment, and all that could be heard was the crackling of the frying fish.

"You don't have to act on the gesture," Gail pressed on after the brief pause. "You don't have to go out with him, or accept anything else from him . . . but, take it from me, after being ignored and thought of as a throwaway woman for all these years, I find it pretty nice to be paid a little courtin' attention."

"Yeah," Nicole said slowly. "I guess it does feel kinda nice—even though I'm going to tell him not to do something like that again."

"You just haven't had a man strut for you in so long that you're out of practice, and he startled you when he came out of the bushes beating his chest."

This time they both laughed hard together.

"Okay, okay, you win. He scared the bejeebers out of me."

"Right," Gail huffed, still laughing hard. "And he made your heart beat fast, and your eyes bug wide, and your palms get sweaty . . . and you haven't felt like that in so long that you didn't know what to do with yourself."

"No," Nicole replied with a giggle, "I didn't. Oh, girl, what am I going to do?"

"Oh, I thought you were just going to tell his no-right-to-be-sending-roses-to-your-door self off, and be done with it."

"I am."

"Then if that's what you want to do, that's what you should do."

"That's right. Yes. You're right and making sense."

"Only problem is . . ."

"What?" Nicole asked quickly, trying to turn her fish while keeping the telephone firmly cradled in the crook of her neck.

"That now you have a face to place with the ache."

"What?"

"You know what I mean."

"I most certainly do not."

"You have a face to think about when you're lonely . . . and you have a face to think of when you want a little somethin'-somethin'—and his is going to be a hard one to shake. Might have to take you to a detox clinic."

"Oh, shut up, girl!"

"Wait till Lydia is in bed, and all the chores are done, and you're lying in bed with the radio on, trying to fall asleep, and that throb starts between your legs. When you don't have a face, you can roll over and think about the bills and cry yourself to sleep. But when you have a face, you'll be tossing and turning all night. Ask me how I know."

"We are not having this discussion anymore," Nicole said with a forced chuckle. "You are making me burn up my dinner."

"I love you, too, chicky. Think of something nice we can do for Jo Jo."

Nicole let her breath out in relief, glad that Gail had finally changed the subject. "Yeah, we have to do something really special for big brother."

"Uhmmm-hmmm. And before I get off this phone, remember you called me. Sweet dreams!"

Chapter 11

What on Earth had possessed him to send the woman two dozen roses?

Adam sat in his study looking through all of his client files, trying to see if any of the insurance jobs he'd done had any links to the trucking scam from his past. The major conglomerates that hired him were all blue-chip firms—firms that wanted to know why their clients' rates of accidents, injury, or theft were going up. Most were simple gigs. Go in, find out if someone was beating the company, and get out and get paid a pretty penny. He didn't have to cart anybody to jail, or worry about what the judges or juries had to say. He'd done his part clean and simple.

He wondered if she'd liked them. Wondered if they had gotten his note right with the flowers. Maybe the gesture was a little over the top—but she deserved them. It had been a long time since he was moved to send a woman flowers ... but he didn't have time to think about that right now. In fact, the flowers were a nice way to show appreciation and to let her know he wouldn't be bothering her again. Yeah, he'd just go by the salon and take his name off the list. No sense in even contemplating getting to know her better.

Trucks and insurance rates. *Hmmm.* Adam let the linkages tumble around in his brain. None of his clients directly underwrote the trucking company fleets that had caused him so much grief down home. What the hell was it? The scam down there had been moving narcotics in the fleet, and allowing things to fall off the back of those trucks. Hot electronics ... big-screen TVs, stereos, and cell phones, then claiming over a million dollars in merchandise shrinkage while his captain and a few other dirty cops looked the other way, and got paid. The insurance carriers had to eat the cost—but after the sting went bad, only a few low-level thugs got hit with stolen-property charges, and, coincidentally, on the day of the bust, no drugs were found. Inside job all the way around. No cops were ever implicated. So why were people still on his case ... unless he'd sniffed too close to something big again?

Adam switched off the light and moved from the study into the bathroom, and cut on the shower. He hated this business, even though he'd traveled halfway across the country to establish it. He peeled off his sweater and dropped his jeans and briefs after kicking off his sneakers. All day and night in the streets, then sitting in places he didn't care to frequent. The worst part of it all was never being able to turn off his mind and relax. His brain was always going, fitting together pieces of information and evidence like a jigsaw puzzle. If he ever wanted to change professions, what would he do to bring in the kind of cash that this one afforded him? According to his boys, he had it all going on. Big house all to himself, with every accouterment a bachelor

could ever want. Nice ride. Plus he had his freedom. No
wife and kids to bog him down.

Stepping into the hot spray, he tried to allow the water
to wash away his thoughts.

Hell, he couldn't even enjoy the Super Bowl last month.
He'd been working, so he was watching the game in a bar
as a cover, and not getting to enjoy it. Where were all his
boys from the old neighborhood now, anyway? Probably in
good, comfortable jobs with wives and kids, and able to
barbecue on their back porches and have a few laughs and
a brew with real friends. That was living, he told himself
as he thrust his head under the spray and lolled his neck to
work out the tension.

Playing pickup hoops, going to a concert, having dinner
with a fine woman . . . that was living. Making love to a
fine woman who you could bring home to your family . . .
that must be priceless.

And all those guys did was sit around complaining about
having to do the basics like take out the trash, or watch their
own kids, or fix something broken around the house. *Fools*.
He'd give his eyeteeth to have somebody to wake up to
every day, and who would worry about him, and care if he
had on an extra sweater or not . . . or kids to take to the
zoo. And what he wouldn't do to have a woman in his arms
who had vowed to go through thick and thin with him . . .
somebody who loved him enough to allow his seed to be
planted in her body and to care for that life. The brothers
didn't understand. He'd tried to tell them that the fine women
he'd rolled in the hay with occasionally gave up good sex,
not good loving, and until you've had both, you don't know
the difference.

A face edged its way into his mind as he soaped his body
and turned around in the hard spray. The way it beat down
on his back made his shoulders relax as the water pummeled

his aching muscles. Shy eyes opened wide in his memory, becoming startled like a deer in the headlights; then she licked her fingers.

A visceral tremor coursed through his body as he pictured her. The image became a central focus in his mind and swiftly turned to a dull ache that just as soon became an acute central throb in his groin. Her hands felt like velvet . . . no, satin. And the way she'd licked that chocolate off the strawberry with her eyes closed and then moaned . . . The ache had turned into pure pain, and he faced the spray to try to rinse it out of his system. But as the water thrashed against him, all he could imagine was being her chocolate. The tiny jet streams became her tongue and his soap-laden hand became her satin-smooth touch, and he held on to the tiled wall as her moan soon became his own.

She was going to be harder to give up than the smokes.

She was going to cuss Gail out the next time she saw her. Eleven o'clock at night, and she was still tossing and turning. It was just the power of Gail's crazy suggestion. All that silly business about a face being hard to shake. She'd seen lots of faces before . . . even movie-star faces when she and the girls rented movies or watched cable, in fact. But this was ridiculous!

The fragrance of the roses on her dresser was the problem. That was all it was. Sitting up quickly, Nicole popped out of bed, grabbed the vase, and took it to the coffee table in the next room.

"There. Out of sight, out of mind!"

She stomped back into her bedroom and flung herself onto the bed. No man she just met was going to awaken that side of her. She was a mother, and was in dubious financial circumstances. Besides, she didn't know him. If she were so inclined, it would take months to get to know him. It would take a lot of interactions and a lot of finding out about his life, his past, his family, his intentions, his integrity . . . and all of that would have to happen before she even allowed him to meet her daughter. Yes. He'd have to first pass *her* security clearance, then Lydia's, then prove himself to be honorable—way before he could even get a whiff.

Where did these brothers get off thinking that they could just send some flowers, or take a woman out to eat, and then she was supposed to put everything in her life at risk, even her health, possibly? For them, it was easy. They could go to bed with a woman, then stop, drop, and roll . . . just like her husband had done. Just like the countless stories she and her girlfriends had lamented about. And in the end, who was left cleaning up after the elephants once the circus pulled out of town? Women.

Nicole turned over on her side and stared at the streetlight filtering in around her miniblinds. *That's right. Stay focused.* A moment's pleasure was not worth the carnage that dealing with a man could create. She'd be hurt, then would be depressed, which would affect her interaction with her child. Or worse, her child could grow attached, and then be hurt again. Nope. There was just too much at stake. That was why she never argued with Gail's decision to stay a nun until her daughter was old enough not to be affected by any man drama. In fact, she respected Gail—even though she didn't know how she was able to do it.

Ten years . . . Nicole flopped onto her other side. Ten years of not feeling special, or pretty, or sexy . . . Well, she was more than halfway there. After she'd gotten pregnant, her husband hadn't touched her for almost whole year, and was always out or on the road. When the baby came, it was intermittent contact, and it sure wasn't with wine and roses, or much foreplay for that matter. And when the fights got serious, he packed his bags and went to live in his old apartment; that was two years before the divorce could be filed, she noted. Then, when the papers came, she did go on a couple of abominable dates that were never consummated . . . and that was two years ago. *So, yeah, five years,* she reminded herself. All she had to do was remember.

So what the heck? She could do ten more until Lydia was a teenager whom she could talk to in the kitchen. Ten more until her daughter was old enough to have her own social circle, or to tell her if someone put his hands on her.

The thought made Nicole shiver. What if she'd been so desperate that she chose a guy who was a pedophile, or was violent or dealt drugs, or had some other crazy secret like she saw on *Montel?* Nicole flopped onto her back and shut her eyes tight. Her mind focused on the face that had sent the roses.

He didn't seem like any of those things; in fact, he was in law enforcement. *Okay.* But what did that mean? She heard stories every day about cops who beat their wives, or molested kids, or did some underworld type of business.

She allowed her memory to rove over every inch of the handsome face, settling on his mouth, and the way it curved up on one side to accommodate the stick and a smile. He was obviously into good health and fitness. That was a plus. Didn't seem like the type to drink or do drugs. *No, not with that body.* Okay, so he wasn't a drug addict. He did have a steady gaze and a cool countenance . . . not the type of jittery behavior that one could detect from users. Also, he didn't seem to have the hard edge associated with people who dealt contraband, at least not on the street level. Being around Delores had taught her something.

Feeling a bit calmer after having gone through a diagnostic battery of thoughts, she allowed herself to lazily drift in and out of possible scenarios. What if this guy wasn't any of those horrible things, and he really did want to see her again? She was working three nights a week, and she supposed that he, too, had commitments to his profession—assuming that he wasn't married, wasn't living with someone, and wasn't in a relationship. Then, if all that wasn't in the way, when could they get together to get to know each other better . . . in a noncompromising, neutral place without her little girl present?

Then, suppose she did go out on a date with this new man, just like Gail and Delores and Victoria had done . . . what would she wear? Well, that would depend on where he took her . . . but what would they talk about? How much was one to divulge on the first date? You had to give the person enough information to let him know your boundaries and parental parameters, but you didn't want to get into the sordid details of why you were no longer married. At the same time, you didn't want to be so closed and cryptic that the person might be left to wonder whether or not the marriage broke up because you were just an unreasonable type of person, or had been the one to flagrantly violate your vows—because then that would set the tenor for how they might decide to treat you in the future.

Nicole found herself flopping onto her belly. This was way too hard, and probably the reason why all the women she knew didn't date until their kids got out of the way, or why they just got a quick sexual fix, but kept the person at a distance from their homes and hearts. The quick sexual fix wasn't her style, but she could understand it. She had to admit that as she felt herself swell and moisten. It had been such a long time.

But all of it was too complicated to figure out. Yeah, this was why you were supposed to do all this dating stuff, hook up with someone on a permanent basis, and then have kids.

Doing this with children's lives and hearts to consider was just way too hard, and it was way too easy to make a mistake that could hurt the one person in the world you loved more than life itself.

Taking in shallow sips of air, she tried to banish the glowing ember that was between her thighs. Her nipples had turned into tiny, hard pebbles, and the gentle friction of them against the sheet that her breathing caused made the ember feel like it had cracked and split, flowing like molten liquid between her thighs.

She would not give in to the desire to slip her hand below her belly. That was too dangerous. She knew that if she did, she'd put a face with the touches once and for all. She'd gone months without having to give in to doing that for herself. All she had to do was think about all of the realities associated with that face. Yes, it would take months before she could trust him enough, if he hung in there that long. Most didn't. After the first couple of dates, if not the first date, the brothers would start pushing up on a sister.

The ember had spread and turned into a full ache that had hollowed out a torturous, burning ring. She could feel involuntary contractions riddle it as she pressed her hips down hard against the mattress to stop the ache, but as she lifted them, she found that she needed to quickly grind that swollen center down again hard against the soft resistance of the bed. The slow thrusts forced a gasp up from her diaphragm, and the sound of it sent a shiver down her spine that made her nipples sting so much that her palms immediately cupped them in reflex. With her eyes shut tight, she reached for a pillow and wedged it between her thighs. Anything to mute the sensations that were driving her hips in what had become a frenzied rhythm.

Pulling at the distended skin between her fingers and her thumbs she soothed the angry pebbles beneath her flannel nightgown, rolling them back and forth in time to the movements of her rising and falling buttocks. But the ember between her legs just seemed to burn hotter.

Frustration formed tears in her eyes, and as she rolled over onto her back winded, yet not sated, she cast the pillow aside and pulled up her gown, reaching beneath it to make skin-to-skin contact with her breasts. Clamping her thighs together hard, and pulsing them to put out the flame between them, she kept her eyes shut tight, allowing the tears to fall from the corners and run down the sides of her face. It had been so long.

Just one touch, one insertion of a finger could make this agony go away. . . . She took her hands from her breasts and almost convulsed as the cool night air replaced her palms. It was as though the sudden temperature change and addition of the draft in the room had stoked the fire between her legs to become a blaze out of control.

When she allowed her thighs to fall open, the air rushed between them, licking and teasing the tender, overexcited surfaces that had swollen to greet it. Her hips responded by lapping against it, as her hands clutched the sheets and she could feel the blood drain away from them. No, she would not do this with this man in her head, this person whom she could not afford to feel this way about.

But without consulting her brain, one hand abandoned her side and found an angry pebble to pay homage to . . . while the other plunged into the fertile, wet valley that was burning with wildfire.

Chapter 12

"Like those NASA boys say, Houston, we have a problem!" Jo Jo allowed his gaze to scan the salon, offering it a scowl of disgust before he went toward the telephones that were ringing off the hook. "By my guesstimate," he yelled over his shoulder, "there's over a hundred people coming tonight and nowhere to comfortably seat them all—or even to stand them all. Miss Vic, this place is just not big enough."

"What!" Gail and Delores said in unison while Nicole and Victoria just shook their heads.

"I'm calling Shawn now to get his hips over here to help with the designer collection, and to see if we can get a red carpet, and velvet aisle ropes to go outside."

This time Victoria was the one who yelled, "What?"

"Jo Jo, tell me you are not going to roll a red carpet down the sidewalk," Gail screeched, aghast. "That's just over the top. Delores, talk to the man!"

"Well, if people are falling through here like it's the Academy Awards, then we're going to make some of them wait outside, checking invitations, and make it feel real exclusive for those who get on the inside first. We must preserve the buzz-buzz, honey."

"Jo Jo's right," Delores affirmed, smoothing down the front of her winter-white tuxedo halter jacket and glimpsing with dubious appreciation the total plunge effect Shawn had said she could pull off. "The way you keep people from tripping about a place being overbooked is to simply make that a part of the entire process. I'm going to pour wine and butler it to people on the outside with Jo Jo's cream mink thrown over my shoulders like a cape. It's all presentation, right? So Gail, if you can hook up a fruit-and-hors d'oeuvre tray, I'll give them in-line silver service. Jo Jo can check invites in the line, and that will slow down the inflow a little until Nicole can counsel 'em and make room."

"Yeah. Good plan. Send them to the front desk to get their consultations with Shawn; that way we keep Jo Jo on the door until it slows down," Victoria commanded.

"Oh, y'all are putting a serious strain on this caterer," Gail snapped. "This is double the amount of people we expected, and how am I going to keep from slopping up a winter-white crepe silk suit dress, huh?"

"Chile, just get to it," Jo Jo shot back.

"But there's not enough food!"

"Well, stop feeding them like you'd feed your family. Break those portions down into a quarter of the size, and add some more garnishes on the trays to make them look pretty. I cannot argue with you at a time like this, Miss Gail, when Benzes and Beamers are pulling up, and women are falling out of cars with men and furs like it's Hollywood! Oh, if I could get a searchlight out there and have them step in cement, I would, but this caught me by surprise, too. So move it!''

All hands made ready as Jo Jo furiously barked orders into the multiple-lit phone lines and raised a crew of brothers who already had tuxedos in their wardrobes.

Everybody did a little of everything, and while the place slowly filled with patrons, Nicole did her best to stay out of sight, helping Gail with the food in the background.

''You've barely said two words all afternoon,'' Gail noted. ''You okay?''

''Yeah, I'm fine,'' Nicole evaded. ''Just have the pre-event jitters.''

''I can dig it,'' Gail replied, sounding relieved. ''The entire place looks like a winter-white wonderland, and is so pretty. Well, I used that as my theme. Everything is white chocolate and lemony colors on the table. But what he did to you,'' Gail murmured with appreciation, turning Nicole around, ''you look like a bride.''

''A bride . . . Oh, Gail, puhleeze . . .''

''No, for real. That winter-white silk crepe sheath gown that Shawn pulled out for you with the slit up the front, and covered with a hand-painted, cream organza one-button floor-length coat with a pearl-crusted button . . . and your hair up all high and pretty, with the pearl teardrop earrings, that four-strand pearl choker with the old gold settings, and pearls scattered in your hair . . . Oh, sweetie. To me, you look as pretty as a bride . . . and you look as nervous as one. You sure you okay?''

Again Nicole only nodded. What had she gotten herself into?

''We figured out why the place is so jam-packed,'' Jo Jo said in a low whisper as he slipped into the all-winter-white velvet and chiffon room he'd created for Nicole to use for the private sessions. "Three quarters of the people want to be seen as couples."

"Are you kidding me?" Nicole gasped. "No . . ."

"Yes, doll. They want to go in by twos this time—just like on Noah's ark. They are out there *thick,* and everybody is talking about how the elixirs of love actually work."

"Does Gail know this?"

"Yeah. She has some guy out there who wants to distribute the stuff through his bottling company and who's trying to pin her down on a number, with that attorney who is on Miss Vic arguing and negotiating on her behalf. Then the construction guy is about to square off with the deacon, and Delores is swatting men away from her like they're flies. Girl, Shawn and I are doing our best to speed up the image consultations. . . . Miss Victoria doesn't have enough days in the week to take all of the appointments, and I can't manage the number of appointments she's trying to book. Oh! It is pure *chaos* out there, honey. So please tell me that you are ready to go on."

"Okay. Okay," Nicole said, taking a deep, cleansing breath. "I'm as ready as I'm ever going to be."

"My husband and I can't thank you enough," the older woman before her said with a giggle. "We tried that potion, didn't we, honey?"

"Yeah, we did," the older gentleman said with a wide grin. "We tried a lot of stuff."

"Oh, Burt," she said with another giggle, slapping his arm and looking away.

"Well, we did," he repeated, giving her a little peck that made her blush even more. "We're friends again, too," he added with a broad smile as he looked over at his wife with adoration. "We told all of our friends about you, and just

wanted to come back in here to tell you all about it ourselves.''

When Delores slipped through the door alone, Nicole let
out a long sigh.

"Girl, I am so glad it's just you!"

"Here's your water. Couple number fifteen is getting
antsy.''

"I have never been so embarrassed in all my born days,"
Nicole whispered. "I'm going to have to leave Philly just
so I can go into the supermarket. People are telling me stuff
that nobody should hear except the two people doing it.
Older people, too . . . people my mom and dad's age.''

The fact that Delores was holding her mouth and giggling
hard didn't help matters in the least.

"I'm serious, Dee!"

"I know, I know," Delores wheezed. "But people are
even getting eyes for each other in the line, and that crazy
Jo Jo started passing out free aphrodisiac when Gail couldn't
get the food trays down and outside fast enough. Some folks
just handed Jo Jo a twenty for the bottle, picked a partner,
and rolled. Girl, this is out of control!''

"Twenty dollars a bottle?"

"Yeah, girl! Twenty a bottle and—''

"Have you all lost your minds!"

"Tell that to Byron Redfield.''

"Who?"

"Miss Vic's new man.''

"Oh, Lord!''

"The attorney set the price when we realized that we
wouldn't have enough for everyone in the room. We're sold
out, and Gail can't whip up another batch that fast. Would
take hours.''

"How many people have the placebo?"

"I don't know what she puts in it, but I would stop calling it a placebo. People are sweatin' us for it like it's crack. You should see the brothers. They've been asking if she put Spanish fly in it, yohimbine, or if she's been grinding down Viagra in it."

"Tell me she didn't put anything like that in it!" Nicole's gaze searched Delores's face with panic.

"No, chile. You know Gail is a nurse and isn't that crazy. But the women have been telling me about how after one bottle, their man can keep it up for—"

"Don't tell me!" Nicole said covering her eyes.

"Girl, the brothers have been saying they feel like they're eighteen again, and can hang for hours. They're out there bidding on the last bottle now. The wives and girlfriends are out there smiling and laughing, and whispering about how long their man can eat—"

"I said *don't tell me.*"

"But you just asked me—"

"I know," Nicole said, losing her breath as she spoke. "Just tell me how many people I'm supposed to see tonight think that we are bottling a real elixir of love?"

"Everybody, practically. Gail's upstairs now trying to strain and season some frozen green beans to get the runoff juice to pass it out to folks who are waiting. Her aunt is up there with her, praying out loud and walking the floors with a Bible in her hand. She said the reason it's working is because Gail ain't had none in ten years and is a good woman, so when she puts her energy into making the batches with prayer, and dropping all her love into the pot, the Lord, who hears what's really in your heart, knows how much she wants to—"

"Just stop," Nicole shrieked, covering her ears. "I don't want to hear any more!"

"Well, last count," Delores said with a mischievous grin, "Miss Vic said the door had dropped five grand, and the number was climbing with the bullet. That ain't no placebo."

"You are lying. . . ."

"Nope. Since we didn't set a price, and Jo Jo put out those velvet ropes and red carpet, people got concerned that they might not get in, or might not be allowed to come back. So folks been dropping like seventy-five to a hundred dollars a pop, and that ain't counting the potion purchases. Even those not on the appointment list paid to get in—just to be seen, chile."

"Why in the world would anybody—"

"Because this is the hottest new club in town."

"New club? New club? Oh, my God! We don't have a license for a club!"

"I know. But we aren't calling it a club. It's a client-appreciation gathering. We don't charge for food, we don't charge for liquor . . . . But there's music and food and entertainment. People donate whatever they feel is appropriate. Besides, we've got attorneys in the house to keep us straight. So it's all good."

"It's all good? It's all good!"

"You're repeating yourself, doll, as Jo Jo would say. You ready for your next appointment?"

"Hide me," Victoria said in a rush as she burst into the room.

"What's going on?" Delores paced to the door and threw the bolt.

"Oh, my God, the police came, didn't they?" Nicole stood and began pacing around in a tight circle.

"No," Victoria said, clearly flustered, fanning her face and straightening the front of her strapless, rhinestone-rimmed taffeta gown. "I gotta get away from Byron. He just made me an offer I can't refuse."

"What are you talking about, Vic? Is he an attorney for the mob—they're the silent backers?"

"No, no, no!" Victoria whispered harshly. "But I have to get away from him."

"What happened?" Delores grabbed Victoria by her arms and held her fast.

"He was cool, doing his normal negotiating rhetoric thing to impress me; then Jo Jo gave him a vial, and he was teasing me about selling marked-up vegetable water. He took a swig; then he put it down real slow, and his eyes sorta closed, and he pushed up on me so hard by the buffet table that I thought I was gonna pass out. Right in front of all those people! Chile!"

"Stop lying . . . ." Delores dropped her hands from Victoria's arms.

"Made me wet my panties. Ain't had that happen to me in almost a decade."

The threesome stared at each other for a moment and exchanged nervous glances.

"He said he wants to sink a million dollars into a Center City re-creation of this entire scene, with real agreements drawn up for a limited-liability partnership . . . then he ran his hand down my back, pulled me close, bit me on my neck, and told me that tonight, after the event, was not negotiable, and it was his final offer. Y'all, I don't know if I can make it until the end of the party with him breathing on me like that."

Her voice held a plea in it that they'd never heard coming from Victoria Jones since they'd known her. It left both Nicole and Delores momentarily speechless. As if both of their wrists were connected to the same cosmic string, Delores and Nicole's hands slowly went up to cover their mouths.

Victoria turned around and grabbed the back of her gown to inspect it. "Taffeta stains so bad," she wailed in a low, trembling voice. "Please tell me I don't have a wet spot on my gown ... I can't sit down in it ... I have to go back out there and greet guests ... but I need to freshen up. I don't have a spot, do I?"

"No, you're good," Delores assured her. "I'll cover the front desk while you slip out the back, and I'll shot-block the attorney. You can't make a sound business decision all jacked up like this. You need some space."

"Thank you, girl," Victoria said, then giggled. " 'Cause if he follows me out the back door, I can't say if I'll return unmolested."

"Okay, get a grip," Nicole urged. "Deep breaths. Deep, cleansing breaths. Steady."

"Right. Nikki is making sense. I just needed some air."

"Okay. Now on three, we go out together, we split—you go one way, I'll go the other, and you get your tail upstairs and don't come back down until Gail is flanking you. Got that?"

"Yeah ..." Victoria said in an unsteady voice. "But, see, the problem is, I took some too."

"Oh, no ..." Delores and Nicole groaned in unison.

"Does it really work?" Delores whispered.

Victoria nodded, and tears had risen in her eyes. "I've got five grand in a drawer at the door and all I want to do is go upstairs and—"

"Don't tell me," Nicole whispered hard. "No, don't tell me!"

"She's been doing that all night," Delores said with a hearty laugh. "If it really works, then tell Gail to save a batch for the house—before she messes around and gets laid, and her energy gets diffused."

"You don't want to take this," Victoria warned. "It's dangerous."

"All of this is crazy," Nicole said, becoming peevish.

"Look, I've got some right here," she added in a flat, clinical tone. "Jo Jo gave me a vial when he brought me a glass of wine and something to eat. This is vegetable pot liquor, okay? The man turned up your volume because you're already interested in him." She took a swig from the bottle, downed half of it, and recapped it while her friends held hands and stared at her. "See, no Jekyll-and-Hyde effect . . . no fangs . . . no transformation, just a lot of vitamins and nutrients my body hasn't had in a while. Now will you guys stop fooling around and please get these people in and out of here so we can go *home?*"

"You don't feel a thing?" Victoria asked in an awed whisper.

"Not a thing," Nicole assured her.

"For real, for real?" Delores asked, folding her arms over her bosom in disbelief.

"No, but it sure is getting warm in here."

Victoria and Delores exchanged a smug glance as Nicole began fanning herself and sat down.

"Really, y'all. I don't feel a thing."

"Mr. Adam, can I talk to you?" Jo Jo asked in a discreet voice, pulling Adam Bastille out of line.

"Sure, brother. What's up?"

"Now, I know you made a generous donation last time, and I know you put down a significant placeholder to get back in here, but last time you upset Miss Nikki, and we can't have that. So here's a free bottle of elixir on the house," Jo Jo said as he pulled a vial out of his breast pocket, handed it to Adam as if it were a cigar, and waited until he accepted it. "On the house. If you want your money back, step inside and we'll return it to you at the front desk."

Adam stared at the tall, lean brother in front of him who

was dressed to the nines in a winter-white fur draped over his shoulders like a cape, with matching-color tuxedo with tails. He briefly thought about his own club-casual outfit and suddenly felt out of place as he slipped the vial into his coat pocket. Maybe he should have worn a tie with his suit instead of a collarless silk shirt. Adam let his breath out slowly and tried to remain calm. All he wanted to do tonight was to get a chance to tell Nicole himself how sorry he was for upsetting her.

"Look," Adam finally said in a cautious tone. "I know that she may have seen a few things during our session that could have upset her, but that was truly not my intention."

"Well, Miss Nikki is like a sister to me," Jo Jo pressed on. "While she didn't go into any details, I know when my baby girl is upset. And you upset her royally. So I'ma say this one time to be sure we are clear. If you upset her, it's me and you—and while we may have different proclivities, I will wax your ass up and down this sidewalk the old-fashioned way, man to man, if you make me go there. Now, I might be a nonviolent Christian, normally, but that child has a little girl to take care of, her husband left her, and she's all by herself, so she doesn't need to have anyone lurking around and making her feel afraid. She's a gem, and has been through a lot. And just because all her blood family is in Florida doesn't mean her Philly family won't represent. I do know some people who know some people, and we can do this smooth, or we can go for broke. Your choice—but don't be going back there upsetting my baby. Hear?"

If the outburst weren't so genuine, Adam might have laughed. But it made him more determined to get in to see the woman who now haunted his thoughts. She had that effect on people, to bring out the chivalry in them.

"She is a wonderful, sweet, honest sister," Adam said in a gentle voice to let Jo Jo know that there would be no testosterone contest. "I can understand why you wouldn't want anyone to hurt her. I do not intend to be that person."

A male exchange without words transpired between the two, and Adam took the posture of speaking to a woman's family . . . as he'd have to if he were trying to get past a father or an older brother. Jo Jo seemed to begrudgingly accept the olive branch, and he no longer appeared to bristle as much, but that by no means meant that Adam was in the clear. All it meant was that he'd possibly be granted an audience on this round; however, Jo Jo would be keeping his eye on him to be sure that his intentions were honorable. Adam could dig it. He'd been raised that way. It was a rite of passage.

"Look, we just got off on the wrong foot," Adam said, extending his hand to Jo Jo, who slowly accepted it. "I'd like to go in there and have a chance to apologize in person. If she doesn't want to have a session, that's fine, but at least let me fall on my sword face-to-face. I think the roses might have spooked her, since she never did give me her address formally. I assume she said something about that by the way the salon crew has been giving me the fish-eye."

"That's right," Jo Jo said with a frown. "You just ought to go right in there and fall on your sword, and tell her how you came by her address. That scared the bull crap out of her, and she called Gail up all in a tizzy about being stalked by some fool who carried a gun and whatnot. We don't have that kind of drama in our salon—you take that mess up to the bars. So you can apologize; then get your hat. And know that when it comes to Miss Nikki and her baby girl, I can pack heat, too. Momma ain't raised no fool—I used to work the clubs as a bartender, honey, and can bounce if I have to."

Adam only nodded, but was pleased. In all of Jo Jo's defensive posturing, he'd told him all he needed to know.

She was an old-fashioned girl—the flowers didn't mean a thing because of the way they were delivered, without a proper introduction. *Deep.* That was definitely old-school. There was no suitor or husband on the horizon, either. She'd received the flowers. She had people who rallied around her and chaperoned her like family .... That meant she had roots. He already knew she prayed, and had a little girl, and that that child was one cherished by many. But most important, he was going to get to see Nicole Gordon again, one-on-one.

Chapter 13

The wait to get in to see Nicole Gordon felt interminable. Despite all of his polite conversation as he moved through the crowd engaging in meaningless dialogue with people he really didn't want to talk to, none of it had provided a diversion to thinking about her. Plus, it was clear that there was nothing here at the salon for him to track. He'd been wrong and had gone down a blind alley in search of clues . . . but what a wonderful surprise that calculated error had been.

He supposed he owed his family a debt of gratitude for sending him on a wild-goose chase—since they had actually been the ones to lead him here, by whatever means necessary. Their superstitions and antics had created the strange confluence of events that now had him milling through a posh throng of people to see a woman whom he couldn't wash out of his system.

"Adam Bastille, right?"

He looked up from the wineglass that he'd been studying as a sexy female voice accosted him. The voluptuous woman whom he recognized from the bar was standing beside him, and the way she'd silently sidled up to him disturbed him. It was something in her eyes that told him she wanted to say more than hello.

"Yeah," he murmured, taking a casual sip from his glass.

"Delores Thompson. Can I talk to you for a moment?" she asked, peering around nervously and extending her hand for him to shake.

"No harm in that; shoot."

She hesitated as he released her palm, then peered around, and gave a few people false smiles as she moved in closer.

"See that brother standing over there?" Her voice had lost all of its sexy resonance, and sounded a bit nervous by his judgment as she motioned to a tall, distinguished, conservative-looking guy in a blue pin-striped suit.

"Yeah. Some sort of attorney, right?"

"That's the one," she said, her breath coming out upon a sigh of relief. "Well, word is that you're a detective. And we may need some help."

"Such as?" He waited and looked at her hard. The last thing he needed was to have to take on another domestic case at the moment.

"Well, I want to know if he's on the up-and-up."

"I'm not working here tonight; I'm just a client like everybody else. Besides, I'd have to have more than that to go on," Adam replied with a casual chuckle, immensely disliking the fact that his profession was probably well known by half of the people in the room.

"I know, I know," she said quickly. "I hate to ask you, but I figured you might have some instincts about men, just like I can usually pick up a vibe . . . no heavy investigation, but just vibes."

makeup was even different. Classy. Smooth. You couldn't judge a book by its cover.

He repeated that to himself as he unobtrusively made his way over to where the attorney had been left standing. Yeah, she was smooth. Only another woman could have pried Victoria Jones away from the guy breathing down her neck. Would have been tough for a man to do it, as it is an unspoken guy thing—Don't interrupt a brother while he's panting hard. That would have definitely made polite probing difficult.

Looking for a way to open the conversation, Adam stared at an empty silver decanter on the buffet table, motioning with his head toward it. "Don't know what's in that stuff, but it seems like a brother is late. They ought to bottle and sell this."

The distinguished gentleman he'd addressed smiled and shook his head, then wiped his hand over his jaw. "I'm going to give you this one," he said with a low chuckle as he reached into his jacket pocket and handed Adam a vial. "This other vial is going to a lab."

"A lab?" Adam replied, his hackles going up.

"Brother, let me tell you. This stuff is dangerous. It opened more than my nose to a woman I just met in here behind this potion. Now, I'm a man of logic, and been divorced . . . no woman in the world is that good for me to mix business with pleasure."

The pained expression that the guy standing beside him openly displayed made Adam chuckle.

"Get out of here," Adam retorted, joking with the attorney as he studied him for fraud. "This ain't nothing but some vegetable juice, probably."

"I'm testing it for drugs, dude. All I know is that I have half my clients in here and they're all saying the same thing. I was a skeptic, too, until I downed a bottle. The shit kicked in within five minutes, now I can't take off my suit jacket, if you know what I mean."

Adam stared at the man for a moment, then burst out laughing. "Get out of town!"

"Try it," the attorney urged. "You'll see."

Adam held the vial up to the dim twinkle-lights and squinted. He'd seen Jo Jo hand it off, and there wasn't any time for the bottle to be tampered with, unless it was spiked prior to the attorney's accepting it. He didn't like it, but there was only one way to find out if there was something fishy going on.

"Looks like and tastes like the greens or string beans your momma used to make, dude, but for real, for real, it's got something else in it."

"Okay." Adam sighed. "If you say so." Thoroughly unconvinced, he sniffed the concoction, then took a swig and let it roll around on his palate, then downed the rest of the vial. It was a necessary thing to keep the conversation going. But he noticed that a couple of men standing nearby just shook their heads, and he could hear the ladies that had seen him do it titter before they went into a huddle. "I'd say string beans."

"Yeah, all right," the attorney said with a friendly laugh. "The name's Byron Redfield," he added, extending his hand. "If you need representation for having been drugged senseless and giving up all your worldly assets to a woman, my partner does litigation; I do tax law. We got you covered."

Adam laughed with the seemingly friendly fellow, but he was still on guard. *You cannot judge a book by its cover,* he reminded himself as he loosened the top button of his shirt. It was getting warm in there.

The attorney looked at his watch, then over to a few brothers who were standing nearby. "Five, four, three—"

"What are you doing?" Adam said, growing agitated, and suddenly losing his humor for no reason.

"Counting down to impact."

"Give me a break," Adam scoffed as he took in a deep inhale.

"Hope you brought your wife or your girlfriend here," the attorney pressed on with a chuckle. "The caterer who makes this stuff said her aunt who does the batches said that the one you're supposed to be with is the one you'll send a heat-seeking missile for, more or less. Said it doesn't work unless you're already into somebody . . . whatever."

"What the hell are you talking about, man?"

"Dude, look, they tell me that you're gonna feel this way until you connect with Ms. Right—if she's around, you won't be able to stay away from her. If she's not, you're gonna be one miserable SOB until you find her, because no one else will be able to get this monkey off your back."

"I've heard a lot of bull in my day, but this beats all. Sounds like the stuff my grandmom and old aunts used to kick around down South." What he didn't tell the man beside him was that he was having trouble keeping his line of vision on him as a target, as it kept straying to the back-room door. Concentration on this conversation was becoming next to impossible.

"I said that, too. My people are from North Carolina. Where you hail from?"

"New Orleans," Adam replied, not wanting to. This crap was like truth serum, too!

"Oh, you're from real Doctor Buzzard country." Byron Redfield laughed. "Got any connections down there who can give us an antidote?"

Breathing through his nose was indeed becoming difficult, and Adam reached into his trouser pocket, produced a business card, and flipped it to the attorney with two fingers. "When you get lab results, a brother would be interested."

"Here's my card, too, man. PI . . . that's excellent," Byron said, his gaze scanning the room. "How come women go to the bathroom together all the time?"

Adam had noticed that all the mirth had left Redfield's demeanor—but it wasn't a sinister transition; it was the kind of waiting that was reminiscent of adolescence. He tried to keep his mind on his target as he watched a full-grown man almost pace as he waited for Victoria Jones to come out of the bathroom with her friend Delores. *Pitiful.* This did not seem like a mobster. But why was he finding it difficult to keep still himself?

"Is it warm in here, or what?" Adam finally admitted to the guy who was looking past him toward the back of the salon.

"Kaboom," Byron said in a flat tone, still looking toward the door and not at Adam. "Now you are going to feel the hydraulic effect, which will make you start talking stupid . . . If they ask you anything, you are going to tell them the truth, even though your mind has been trained not to give up the tapes. And you are going to want that woman so bad, brother, that you'd take a bullet for her." Byron cocked his head and offered Adam a weak smile. "Now, I ask you, doesn't that sound like drugs?"

"Yeah," Adam admitted, rubbing his chin and focusing as hard as he could on his objective to obtain information. "But, if you don't mind my asking, what did she make you give up? I'm only asking because I don't want to get jacked, too."

"I'm a tax attorney," Byron admitted again, "and the one thing I know is, you have to keep investing and rolling the money over, or Uncle Sam will suck you dry. The stock market has been real touch and go, strong one minute, then the bottom drops out the next. Was already looking around for a vehicle to salt away a bit of earnings . . . had a very good couple of years. Then, on a lark, I came in here because my sister told me about it—actually I came in here to make sure she wasn't getting rooked. Then I saw what they had going on, and thought, with the right location, and solid investment to provide working capital, this could be a dynamite establishment. That was as far as I was going to go— the thinking-about-it stage, a fleeting thought that crossed my mind. But then I met the woman who owns it, and . . . well. You know, you know.''

"You're the sole backer?'' The effects of what he'd just drunk were obviously pulling at his focus, and his responses were less obtuse than normal. That had to be it, because he could have kicked himself for what he'd just asked, and he could only guess that the effects this stuff had on Redfield were wearing off—since the attorney had obviously taken some of it a lot earlier in the evening than he had.

"Yeah,'' Byron finally murmured, his voice distant as he watched Victoria Jones slowly approach him. "I don't want her to get it from anybody but me.''

The comment made Adam look at the brother hard, but Redfield's line of vision was focused on the approaching female. *Deep.* "The money to expand this joint, you mean, right?''

"Yeah. That's what I said, didn't I?''

"What you said could be taken two ways.''

"Maybe I meant it both ways. Aw, man . . . see why I'm having a lab go over this? I don't do attached. Been there, seen it, done it . . . and I definitely don't get my money snagged up in a love triangle between me, a woman, and it.''

"You ain't said a mumblin' word,'' Adam agreed on a strong exhale. "This is crazy, and there is definitely something in this elixir, as they call it. Maybe it ain't drugs, but we've been rooted, man. I've heard about this sorta thing, even though I don't go by superstition, generally.''

"Me either . . . generally.'' Byron chuckled. "I like you, man. Maybe we can do business together one day. I always need an investigator, as does my partner. He's a good brother. I'll introduce you to him later—we can have a drink, or do lunch . . . but, er, listen, uh . . .''

"Cool,'' Adam said, giving Byron's shoulder a hard cuff of support. "Go get her, man. I'll catch you later.''

"Well?'' Delores murmured as she moved next to Adam to fill Byron's vacancy. "Did I keep her in the ladies' room long enough for you to find out anything?''

"Seems like a straight shooter, at first sight,'' Adam admitted. "But you can never judge a book by its cover,'' he added as his gaze went toward the back door. "I'll do some more digging in the next couple of days, and will let you know if I turn up anything shaky. I can go down to the courthouse and find out whom he's represented in cases of public record. That'll give us a baseline. But who he deals with privately is going to take a little more legwork. Do what you can to get your girlfriend to take it slow, at least on the business side of things, until I can get back to you. Okay?''

"We'll do our best. Thank you so much,'' she crooned, and swept his cheek with a kiss. "I feel so much better just knowing somebody will at least be trying to watch our backs.''

"I don't mean to be rude, but how much longer do you think it'll be?''

"Might be about an hour,'' she said sadly.

"Damn . . .'' he murmured, then caught himself. "I'm sorry . . . I'm just tired . . . edgy from the wait.''

Delores looked at him hard and moved in front of his line

of vision, and it was all he could do not to peer around her to get better sight of the back-room door.

"You took some of the elixir, didn't you?"

"Yeah. Byron gave me a bottle, said you guys were drugging people."

"You didn't . . . oh, no . . ." She had whispered the words as she covered her mouth and laughed.

"Why, are you ladies drugging people?"

"No," she replied with a deeper chuckle. "We don't know why it works. Old Miz Inez, Gail's aunt, adds some down-home spices to it with some git-down prayer, and then they bottle it. Said it's supposed to heighten whatever is the truest desire of your heart, and make you pursue it with honesty and passion."

"This mess is making men act stupid in here," he said in all seriousness. "I don't know whether that brother, our attorney in question, is under a spell, or if he's a front for the mob, but something is messin' with the dude."

"How're you faring?" the woman standing in front of him with her arms folded over her bosom said with a broader smile than he would have liked, obviously teasing him.

"Truth?" he found himself asking. "I'm dying, sis."

"Well, I suppose a down payment on that favor might get you bumped up on the list."

All his cool was blown as his breath exited his body hard and fast. "For real? You can do that?"

"Oooooweeee," she whispered, "Miss Gail has definitely gotta bottle this."

He'd watched Delores like a hawk as she left his side and quietly consulted with Victoria Jones, and his shoulders dropped two inches with relief when she issued him a discreet thumbs-up and led him to the back room.

"Now, as soon as the people before you come out, it'll be your turn. But Jo Jo told me to remind you that when you go in there you are to be on your best behavior,'' Delores cautioned him with a giggle. "So go sit down somewhere— you're making me nervous—and try not to upset her when you talk to her this time.''

He couldn't sit as his gaze locked on the doorknob. Every few moments he glanced at his watch and tried to ignore the broad smiles offered by the others who were also waiting. When an elderly couple came out of the room, he literally had to count to ten to keep himself from bolting past them toward it. Glancing back once at Delores for affirmation, all he could do was nod as he crossed the room and slipped through the door.

He squinted for a moment as his eyes adjusted to the soft dim light inside the room, and he stood stock-still as though frozen while he absorbed the vision in front of him. She looked like a bride, if not an angel . . . the room framed her like creamy clouds lit by tiny white starlights. The candles cast everything, especially her, in a luminous gold, and she was there, with those large, smoky-brown eyes, in the center of what he could only imagine heaven to look like.

They should have prepared her. Nicole swallowed hard as she stared at the man who had entered the room wearing the unstructured black suit with a deep turquoise shirt that was unbuttoned at the neck. Her gaze slowly traveled from his eyes down the bridge of his nose to his mouth and lingered there for a moment before returning to his eyes.

"I wanted to apologize in person,'' he murmured. "May I sit down and explain?''

All she could do was nod as something in her belly ignited and caught fire.

"I had no right whatsoever to find out where you lived without asking you for that information directly. I'm a detective, and sometimes old habits die hard.''

"I understand," she said in a gentle tone. "But it frightened me, and I didn't like that at all."

"Well, that's why I'm here." He found himself almost pleading. "I want to make it up to you and start again on the right foot."

"That's not neces—"

"Yeah, it is," he said quickly, ashamed that he'd cut her off, but not wanting to give her the opportunity to make up her mind about him without first hearing him out.

"Look, when I came in here, I was working on a case that I was preoccupied with, and I didn't consider that it could affect you." He waited for a moment and watched her countenance, which did not seem to tense as he spoke; in fact, unless he was deluding himself, it appeared that the more he talked, the sultrier her expression had become. But, then again, he'd taken that crazy elixir and it was probably just wishful thinking.

"What I'm trying to say is," he pressed on, "I was a skeptic at first. So it never dawned upon me that what was going on with me could affect someone who might have this sort of gift. And I researched it a little bit . . . you know, the police departments in a lot of counties work with gifted people to locate . . . Aw, I'm not trying to get into that, but you know what I mean. I believe you have something that other people don't have, and—"

"Is that why you came back in here?" she asked, seeming hurt.

"No, for real, wait. Reset. Let me start again." He was babbling like a madman! "Okay," he said, letting his breath out slowly. "I came in here as a skeptic, and now I believe in something that I cannot describe at present. The fact that I came here caused you some duress, because of the thoughts going on in my head, maybe. Anyway, I wanted to apologize, but went about even that the wrong way . . . but the apology was genuine. And the fact that I want to make it up to you is real.'' Then he sat back and searched her eyes for some glimmer of hope that he'd gotten through to her.

She could barely breathe in the room sitting so close to the handsome face and lush mouth that had spilled forth words in a fluid, baritone rush. Every syllable was still reverberating through her bones, and she could feel her arms being pebbled by gooseflesh.

"Apology accepted," she breathed. "But I can't engage you in a session while you're working on this case, or whatever. It's too disturbing.''

"Yeah, that's cool, no problem, fine,'' he blurted, then held his breath for a moment before he spoke. "But, uh, could I still see you? I mean, not here—like to go out, maybe, or—''

"I don't think that would be a good idea," she said quickly. "No.''

Her words crushed the air out of his lungs. He wanted a cigarette, and briefly thought about reaching for a licorice stick, then changed his mind. He didn't need anything else encumbering his clumsy tongue right now.

"I know I made a first bad impression, probably a second one . . . what's this, the third contact? First we met and I upset you, then I botched it with the flowers thing, now I'm tripping all over my own tongue and putting my foot in my mouth because . . . I've *never* had a woman make me act like this—honest. I'll pray with you about it; if you take my hands, I'll swear it on the Bible if you've got one back here, but I really want to see you, and not as a client.''

There, he'd said it, and he could feel his heart racing inside his chest so hard that it was making his ears ring.

Oh, my Lord, he'd said it. She could feel her heart trying to crash its way out of her rib cage. She was definitely not trying to get to know this man any better. Not when he was sitting across the table, looking at her so intensely that all she could think of was leaning over and . . . She had to stop it.

"Okay," she murmured nervously. "One should always pray for guidance in any situation."

"Yeah, let's do that," he replied in a low tone, sliding his hands across the soft, cream-colored, velvet-laden table and taking her hands. His eyes closed in reflex when the sensation of touching her satin palms shot through him. It was so intense that he needed to suck in air through his mouth, but didn't dare. But he found himself taking short breaths through his mouth as the heat of her hands traveled through him and boiled in his groin. He hoped he'd been right the first time and this woman couldn't pick up on thoughts.

She sat there, staring at a man across from her who had fused his hands to hers, and whose face had the most riveting expression of desire on it. The way his nostrils flared and his lips parted slightly as he took in long drinks of air . . . and his eyes had rolled back beneath the lids. How could she pray like this? His Adam's apple moved up and down in his throat as he swallowed hard . . . and the voltage that ran through his hands into hers felt like lightning.

"I can't do this," she whispered quickly, releasing his palms, which made him open his eyes. "I can't."

She was breathing hard, and all he could do was hope that she hadn't seen something ugly in him again. But the damp sheen on her brow and the bridge of her nose, and the way her petite breasts rose and fell breath the filmy fabric . . . Dear God, he wanted this woman.

"I promised Jo Jo I would be a gentleman and on my best behavior," he urged. "I got the green light as an okay guy from Delores, too. And I'll talk to anyone else you want, but please don't say you won't give a brother at least one more chance.'' His own words felt like they were slapping him in the back of the head. He hadn't begged a woman for her time since he was sixteen years old. Oh, this was definitely some sort of drug.

''I just don't trust myself; it's not you,'' she found herself saying to her own horror. What was in that stuff that Gail had cooked up?

Her admission seemed to cause him to again swallow hard, and his breathing seemed to be labored now. What had she just said to a complete stranger?

''Oh, no, I mean . . . what I meant to say was that my life is complicated, and I don't trust that I'd be good company, is all.'' Her rebuttal of her own previous statement even sounded contrived to her own ears. She was babbling, for chrissake!

Help him! The way her eyes had taken on that heavy, lazy look when she'd said what was really on her mind, and the way her voice had dropped a decidedly sexy octave, then she'd practically breathed out her statement. No way in the world was he getting up from this table without a collar.

''I'd like to take that chance,'' he murmured, not caring that his voice had gone to a low rumble within his chest. ''You're somewhat of a local celebrity now, and rather than have to fight for your attention at a restaurant, why don't you let me fix you something special at my place?''

Was he nuts? The woman was already spooked, and without diplomacy, patience, or decorum, he'd invited her to his spot. He never brought women to his house—that was the Batcave, his bachelor's sanctuary. He'd lost his mind! Jumping in to rebound his own foul shot, he pressed on with urgency, and tried to rationalize his ill-timed request. *A restaurant, take her to a restaurant, man. She'll think you're cheap, or think you think she's cheap*. But his course had been set, and it was too hard to turn the trajectory of his battleship on a dime.

"Listen, I found out a lot about you without your permission, and I think it only fair that I come clean with you so we can start on the right foot. I'll show you where I live, you can give your friends my address, my home telephone number, my beeper number, my cell phone, my license plate—"

"I don't think that will be—"

"No, I'm serious." God, he needed this woman. "I can pick you up—"

"I don't think I could—"

"You can call Jo Jo when you get there." *Please let her say yes.* "I'm in Medford Lakes and—"

"I'd feel better if I drove . . . I don't like the idea of being stranded with a guy I don't know and—"

"Sure, sure, I can meet you in front of your building, and you can tail me over, and I'll give your big brother all the info he'd need to hunt me down, if I don't hold to my word and be a gentleman. Okay? Is that a date?"

"I guess it's—"

"Tomorrow night? Saturday, six o'clock?" *Please, girl, say yes.*

"I'd have to get a baby-sitter, and—"

"Seven?"

"Seven is better, but I'm still not sure that—"

Thank you, God!

"I fix a mean Cajun shrimp and sausage jambalaya and grits, with okra—you aren't allergic to shellfish, because if so I can make—"

"No, I love seafood, and I'm from down home; I eat pork upon occasion."

Thank you, Jesus.

"Good, good." He breathed out fast when she giggled

and shook her head. It was the first time since he'd walked in the room that he was able to relax a little.

"Wow," she said with a warm chuckle. "I didn't expect this."

"Wow," he replied, chuckling with her. "Me either. Let me say it slower this time . . . . I'd like to take you to dinner, talk with you and learn more about you without half of Philly staring down our throats, and then bring you home, and I'll be a perfect gentleman. May I do that with your permission, tomorrow night at seven o'clock?"

"Yes," she whispered, looking away shyly.

"Even though I delivered them the wrong way," he asked in a quiet tone, "did you like the roses?"

"Yes," she whispered again. "Very much. Thank you."

It was all he could do not to wipe his brow in front of her. This was a deep way of beginning to talk to God again. "No, thank you for accepting them."

A tense silence had enveloped him, but her shy whisper still resonated in his ears. Staring at the halo of light around her soft, brown hair made him want to reach out and touch it, but he knew better. Instead he stood while he could still get out of there without offending her. "I'll leave my info with Jo Jo, and I'll see you tomorrow night around seven."

She nodded as he turned back, smiled, then slipped through the door. How was she going to talk to anyone else after that? Delores should have sent him in last!

Nicole looked up quickly when the door opened again, and she watched Delores and Gail pile into the room like bandits.

"Wow . . ." Nicole murmured to her friends as they glanced at her with excited grins. "Wow with a capital W."

Giggles rang through the room, and again the door opened to make them all fall silent when Jo Jo came in and leaned against it.

"Chile, the man dumped his pockets out on the front desk, wrote down every electronic means to track him from here to Alaska, and asked my *permission* to take you out. It started another deep buzz-buzz among the brothers, and folks are adding to the basket as we speak. Now, if there ain't something miraculous going on, then you tell me!"

"Where's Victoria?" Delores asked Jo Jo, as all eyes in the room watched him for a response.

"The girl done left about a half hour ago . . . trembling with that attorney on her heels. I couldn't stop her. If the screens weren't covering the sinks, I'da hosed them both down."

All three women looked at each other and spoke in unison: *"Wow . . ."*

Chapter 14

When the doorbell sounded, Nicole felt as though she was going to literally pass out, and she accidentally dropped her makeup case in the sink with a clumsy clatter of spilled lipsticks, pencils, and powders. "Oh, no," she groaned as she paced to the living room past her daughter, who was sitting on the sofa sucking her thumb and watching a video, to reach the intercom. "Who is it?" she asked as pleasantly as she could manage while her nerves crackled like the static coming through the black device on the wall.

"It's just me and Michelle," Gail said with a loud laugh, "not Prince Charming yet!"

Without answering, Nicole pressed the buzzer, then dashed past her daughter back to the bathroom.

"Are you going out with a real prince, Mommy? Wow," a little voice yelled over the Rugrats movie.

"No! Your aunt Gail was just teasing Mommy," Nicole

hollered from the bathroom. "Open the door when she and Michelle come up and say it's them through the door."

"Okay!"

Nicole glanced at the bathroom clock and new panic settled in her bones. What was she doing? Six-thirty. All her friends were in her business, Gail had insisted on sleeping on the sofa while Michelle baby-sat and slept in Lydia's bed, and everyone was waiting on the scoop from this date she was now going on for the first time in too long to calculate. It felt like getting ready for a prom!

The knock on the inside apartment door made her drop her eyeliner in the sink.

Soon Gail's gregarious boom echoed through the small dwelling, and she could hear Michelle's incessant teenage banter following it—and she couldn't even put her makeup on without freaking out.

"Guuurrrrl . . . You ready?"

"Yeah. I'm cool," Nicole said as casually as she could when she spied Gail's reflection in the mirror leaning against the bathroom door frame and watching her apply her mascara.

"Whatchu wearing?"

"Jo Jo and I had a big fuss about that," Nicole admitted with a tight chuckle. "He wanted me to go in some gold lamé ball gown. I chose that simple, violet scoop-neck dress with the long sleeves over there on the closet. Then I picked out some simple amethyst drop earrings with antique filigree settings, and one silver bracelet. Simple. I'm trying to keep everything simple, basic, and not over the top. I thought he'd have a coronary."

"I think it's pretty," Gail said with a wide grin. "Not too fancy . . ."

"You think it's too plain, don't you?"

"Well . . . no, you want the man to see who you really are, and you want to find out if he can deal with that, right?"

Gail's rationalization was making Nicole's stomach tie itself in knots.

"Yeah, I suppose so. Yes. I do."

"Well, then, go with what you think is right. You're a basic, no-frills, very practical kinda girl, and—"

"Oh, it is too plain . . . ."

"He'll love it. He's taking you out, not the dress."

"Jo Jo was right . . . I thought he'd practically slap me he was so indignant about the choice I came back to the shop with from Shawn's."

They both laughed.

"No," Gail soothed. "You know Jo Jo is just in a snit because Miss Vic went AWOL on him on the most hectic day in the salon, Saturday."

"She did not . . . is she all right?"

"Yeah, girl," Gail said with an even wider grin, and her voice became singsong in the process. "She called in *after* the shop was open, and Jo Jo had been wringing his hands for an hour. Sounded all breathless and giggly, and said she just needed a day to herself. Jo Jo went O-F-F—off, do you hear me?"

"Noooo . . . I don't think she's missed a Saturday in the salon since I've known her!"

"Yeah, chile. It was so live in there that he had Dee Dee and me doing manicures, pedicures, washing out perms, and whatnot, without a license."

"Whaaaat?"

"Half the girls called in with fake colds; clients were backing up over the runway to the chairs like a bad day at the airport. Him and Shawn temporarily fell out because he asked Shawn to do something, and Shawn was in a snit because his studio was crazy too, and he didn't have time. So you know it's chaos, girl.''

Nicole just stared at Gail for a minute with her hand over her mouth. ''This is not good.''

''It's too good, is what appears to be the problem,'' Gail said with another deep chuckle. ''Just promise me that you'll be back tomorrow in time for us to switch off so I can go on my brunch date.''

''Tomorrow?'' Nicole blinked twice. ''No. I'll be home tonight. A few hours, then I drive home. Got that?''

''Okay, if you say so,'' Gail replied coolly, moving from the bathroom into Nicole's bedroom with Nicole in fast pursuit. ''I think a dark color and heavy fabric was a wise choice,'' she quipped in an amused tone, holding out the dress from its hanger on the outside of the closet door. ''Hides the wet spot better.''

''Shut up, chile. You are so crazy and your mind is in the gutter. I'll be back before midnight,'' she added, dropping her lipstick twice on the bed before she could manage to open her beaded clutch and put the tube in it. Ignoring Gail's smirk, she discarded her robe, yanked down the dress and put it on, then slipped on her black pumps that had been waiting.

''You are not wearing those.''

''What's wrong with these shoes?'' Nicole folded her arms over her bosom, which was now heaving with exertion for no reason.

''The dress is so plain; it's pretty and all, but don't you have some nice straps, something a little sexier that tie at the ankles?''

''Gail Jackson, I am convinced that you did not come here to baby-sit—you came here to torture me and to get on my last nerve!'' Nicole continued to fuss as she rooted through her closet and Gail continued to laugh.

"You are going to mess up your hair, chile. Let me dig in the bottomless pit for you."

Exasperated, Nicole plopped down on the bed and waited.

"Now, see, these go much better with the little straps, your pretty toes out, and crusted with the dark beads that sorta match your purse."

"It's *February*," Nicole said in a flat tone as Gail produced a pair of shoes that would hurt her feet. "Having your toes turn black from frostbite is not sexy."

"The man drives a Lexus. He got heat in his car, girl!"

"I'm driving my car and the heat doesn't—"

"Wait. Let me get this right. You are making the man cook for you, then leave his stove on warm, drive almost an hour to Philly to come to your door, so you can drive your raggedy struggle-buggy over to Jersey, after he dropped a king's ransom in the shop, bought you two dozen roses, and—"

The doorbell stopped Gail's roll and they both looked at each other.

"Want me to get that, Aunt Nikki?"

Nicole could hear the teenager pop up from the sofa, and before Gail could move, Nicole had practically hurdled the bed, clopping in her strap shoes that were yet unfastened as she slid into the kitchen. "No! Let me get it, please, Michelle."

"Okay, okay," the astonished teen fussed. "You and my mom are acting too weird."

"Hello," Nicole practically shouted into the black box on the wall.

"Uh, Nicole?"

"Oh, hi, yeah, it's me . . . . I'll be down in a minute."

"Tell me you are not leaving that man standing outside, in the cold, in February," Gail snapped in disbelief.

"He can't come up here," Nicole said as she spun around

twice, then headed for the bedroom, almost falling over the straps of her shoes as she plopped down to fasten them, then sprang up to run to her dresser and slap on her jewelry.

"Why in heaven's name not?" Gail stood in the bedroom doorway like her mother would have—arms folded, a look of serious disdain in her expression, and shaking her head.

"Because. Because . . . I'm not ready for him to see my place, or my daughter, or for my daughter to see him, much less Michelle. And . . . and . . . because the bathroom is a mess and I have dishes in the sink . . . and—"

"Okay. Okay. Calm down, deep breath, put your coat on," Gail said as though talking to a psychiatric patient. "Walk down the hall slowly, be cool. Smile pretty and remember to breathe and push the elevator button."

Nicole bobbed her head, becoming dizzy as she did so. "You'll be here when I get back, right?"

"Yup," Gail answered, obviously trying not to laugh.

"Okay. I can do this," Nicole said in an unsteady voice as she steeled herself to go out and kiss Lydia and Michelle good-bye.

"Now you girls mind, and have fun. I'll be back in a few hours," she said, kissing them both and donning her black church coat.

"You look pretty, Mommy, and you smell good, too. I think da prince will like you."

"You are all that, Aunt Nikki."

Nicole felt her mouth go dry. "Thank you, ladies," she squeaked as she gave them another kiss.

"Uh, your keys, sweetie," Gail reminded her as she opened the door.

"Yeah, right, keys, where are my keys?"

"In the door, perhaps," Gail calmly remarked.

"Yeah, right . . . in the door."

* * *

Adam walked back and forth on the top landing, occasionally boxing his arms and cupping his hands over his ears as he watched his breath come out of his mouth in white, steamy puffs. If he stood there in the cold for another ten minutes, he was sure that the cops who were cruising by might eventually check him for drug possession. Why else would a brother be shivering his behind off at the doorway of an apartment building in February? Even the crackheads had enough sense to go find an abandoned shack somewhere, but did he? *Nooooo*.

"I'm sorry I took so long, but I had to get my daughter and the baby-sitter all squared away before I could leave."

It wasn't that cold outside, after all. Just a little nippy.

"No problem. Is everything all right up there? You need a little more time?"

"No, I'm ready . . . . I'm parked over there," she said, motioning to her car, which he had already spotted.

"I'm down the street a bit."

"Okay, I'll follow you," she said quickly, not waiting for him to escort her to her vehicle.

He took two long strides and caught up with her, taking her elbow before she slipped and broke her neck. It never ceased to amaze him how women could be so impervious to the elements, and would attempt to ice-skate in spike heels regardless of the ground condition. When she looked at him and smiled, he immediately understood. She was as nervous as he was—she just moved faster than he did to show it, like a wound-up top.

"The roads are icy in patches," he warned as they made their way to her car. "I don't mind driving, and I promise to get you there and return you safely," he added. Bending down, he looked at her tires. "I'm not trying to be funny, or to comment out of line, but I'd be less than a gentleman if I didn't tell you that the tread on these ain't gonna get you to Jersey in one piece."

"Really?" Her expression was crestfallen, and she stooped to look at where he was pointing.

"How long have you had these on here?"

Nicole let her breath out in an exasperated rush. "This is my dad's car, and I haven't changed them since ... I don't think I've changed them. Well, they got me up here from Florida just fine."

Adam shook his head. "Tread on these isn't as deep as my thumbnail, honey. Now I suggest—"

"Maybe we should stay local?"

"Well, we can do that, if you like, but there's shrimp and—"

"Oh, yes, that's right. You're cooking. Where are my manners? I'm sorry, it's just, well ..."

"What time would you like me to bring you back?"

"Huh?"

He felt himself smile.

"What time did you promise the baby-sitter that you'd be home?"

"Uh ... uh ... midnight."

"Okay," he said in a slow drawl designed to put her at ease as he handed her his cell phone. "Why don't you call upstairs and tell the sitter that you decided to let me drive, so that she doesn't think you were abducted from the front door, and that I'll have you home by midnight?"

She could only stare at the man for a moment as she accepted his phone and he showed her what buttons to push to get a signal. Her toes were freezing and she walked in a tight circle to get the blood to go back into them as she dialed.

"Gail, it's me," she said when the line picked up. "I'm

going to let him drive me because the tread on my tires is bad, okay?''

To her chagrin, instead of talking into the receiver, Gail opened and leaned out the third-floor window.

''Gurl, now you know that makes sense,'' she shouted down for the whole neighborhood to hear.

''Gail, go back in the house right now,'' Nicole hissed into the cell phone, totally undone that her girlfriend was holding the telephone receiver away from her ear.

''What? What's that? You're breaking up,'' Gail said in a sonic boom that echoed against the cold bricks. ''Y'all just go ahead and have a good time. Don't rush back. I'll be here all night.''

Nicole waved, shut off Adam's cell phone, and handed it to him. There were no words. Simply no words in the English language for this. She could not look at him, much less speak. Her cover for getting home, along with her transportation, had been blown . . . it couldn't get any worse than this.

''Uh, I take it it's all right for us to get into my car now?''

She only nodded.

He had to wait a few moments as they were walking before he could speak. He didn't trust himself not to laugh, and right now, keeping his eyes in front of him and on his car was the only way to ward off a true laughing fit. God, he enjoyed being in this woman's company. It was her, plus the company she kept, and the way the unexpected always seemed to follow her. Kept him on his toes.

When he opened the door for her and she slid into the seat, then looked away, he had to bite the inside of his cheek. But when she looked away again as he got in the driver's side, he thought everything could give way at the slightest provocation. He wanted so badly to just put his head on the steering wheel and roar. But instead he turned on the motor and hit the CD player while she fastened her seat belt.

He could only hope that the tranquil jazz would smooth her ruffled feathers. Now was the hard part . . . coaxing pleasant conversation from a woman who had balled her hands up in her lap, and who was craning her neck to look at the buildings as they passed by.

"You know," he murmured, unable to keep himself from teasing her any longer, "I've driven felons to the station with more conversation than this."

When she opened her mouth, then closed it and looked down at her hands, he pressed on.

"And you don't have to sit there like I've cuffed you. It's okay to stretch out a little for the forty-five-minute ride that's ahead of us."

This time when she looked up a sly smile graced her face, and her eyes seemed to sparkle with merriment. Then, without warning, she leaned forward, straining against the seat belt, covered her mouth, and laughed hard. The sight of her being so tickled made the restraint in him snap. Wiping his eyes as he drove, he clutched the steering wheel hard to hang on to it.

"See, the people in my life are crazy," she began. "You should know this, since you wanted to get to know me better. It's a wild package deal."

"You forget, honey, I've already met them. Good people . . . colorful, but good people." Deep, resounding laughter pulled its way up from his core, and as it filled the cab he suddenly realized how long it had been since he'd laughed like that.

"I was not trying to ride with you—you know that, right?" she fussed through her giggles.

"I know, because y'all think I'm the bogeyman, but I'm not."

"Well, you sure have a strange way of gettin' to know a girl."

"I know, I know, I apologize. My approach was unorthodox, but you have to admit, so was yours."

"Mine?" She gasped, pointing at her chest. "What did I do to meet you that was so unorthodox?"

"Gotta admit that it's not every day that you meet a girl wearing a blue turban and a veil, selling love potions out the back of a hair salon, who knocks you off your feet."

"See, now," she wheezed, doubling over again, "just stop it . . . why'd you have to go there? I told Gail and them this was some conjanglement . . ." Her words trailed off as she hiccuped with laughter and dabbed at the corners of her eyes. "Oh, Lordy Miss Claudy, you have no idea how crazy all of this has been."

"Try me." He chuckled, loving the sound of her voice.

"See, I don't normally roll like this," she said between gasps.

"Yeah, that's what they all say . . . . Stop, girl, before you make me have an accident." Tears of laughter threatened the corners of his eyes and he waved at her with one hand to try to get her to cease and desist the story until they'd parked.

"No, no, see, brother, it's on now. You wanted to get all in my business, so blam, here it is."

"Woman, please . . . I'm driving; I can't take it."

"Well, Jo Jo came up with a way to thematically present an event, hon," she said, waving her arms and snapping her fingers.

"My vision is blurring," he pleaded. "Stop, girl!"

"Naw . . . no way. Here's the dealio. See, I was a telemarketer, and they fired me last week 'cause I was giving more advice than selling toasters, so, since Gail was at the hospital, she was getting test tubes, but security busted her, so she was unemployed . . . then the tax man jumped on Miss Vic, and Dee, well, I won't tell all of her business, but suffice it to say that she needed to leave the bar . . . and—''

"No, no, please, baby, please, not till we stop driving. Plead the Fifth. Don't tell me!" he begged her, totally undone as wave after wave of riotous laughter shook his body, making his car occasionally weave in its lane. "Not while we're going over the bridge."

"No, no, but you're a man who likes to live on the edge," she taunted. "You're Five-O, you can take it. You wanna get to the bottom of this. . . . So we started praying, right, and the people started coming, both literally and metaphorically—''

"Y'all was praying for people to get some . . . ? Girl, stop!" he howled as they passed the toll plaza. "No, you did not take that kinda information to God!"

"Why not? Don't people—for real, for real, when it's been a looong time since you had anybody special—get that nervous twitch that makes 'em say, 'Oh, Jesus, just if—' ''

"Stop, please, you're killing me. I can't breathe."

"Well, they do," she continued. "Be honest. Tell me you've never once in your mind thought that. And when you do, what's the first name you call . . . ? Oh . . . God!"

Even though he was still laughing, her question and statement were a bit sobering.

"Truth," he said feeling good from the endorphine rush. "There have been days like that."

"Try years," she said with a little calmer giggle.

"I have tried years," he admitted, now only smiling.

"Oh." What else could she say?

Chapter 15

Had she lost her mind, playing around with some man she just met like that, and broaching such a serious subject? As the giggles abated and they settled into a more innocuous conversation about jazz, Mardi Gras, and playful arguments about New Orleans versus New York City being the actual jazz capital of the country, it dawned on her that she hadn't truly just let her hair down and enjoyed a date's company this much in years. A definite *wow*.

She was also unprepared to pull up to the immense cabin-style house that was framed by serene forest and a still, black-ice covered lake that looked like glass. It took everything in her to keep her composure as he hit the garage-door opener, and slowly brought the vehicle inside a spotless three-car garage.

"Okay, last stop on the Metroliner," he said pleasantly, coming to her side of the sedan to let her out. "Everything is right through here,'' he added, pointing toward the inner door.

Without making any comment, she followed him through it, but did allow a gasp to cross her lips as she stepped into the kitchen. The stained pine in deep honey brown took her breath away as she entered the room and ran her hand over the center butcher block counter that hosted a range hood and built-in stove. Gleaming black state-of-the-art appliances made her pulse race, as did the beautiful tiled surfaces that greeted her as he turned up the lights.

''Oh, brother . . . can I just say it plain . . . this is fabulous.''

He smiled, and her words sank into his bones in a way that he hadn't expected them to. But it was also the way her eyes drank in the environment. Not in a gasping, hungry look, but holding a certain appreciation in their expression. Then she closed them and took in a long filter of air through her nose that made him need to hold on to the edge of the kitchen table.

''Something smells *so good.*''

The resonance with which she said it made him ponder whether or not the jambalaya was the best thing on the menu, or her.

''Let me take your coat,'' he said quickly, needing to move. But when she turned, smiled, and slipped it off to reveal her body sheathed in lush velvet, he was sure she might see his hands tremble. ''You look fabulous,'' he murmured. He also wanted to tell her how much better she smelled than his cooking, but thought that might not be the thing to say so soon.

''Come on into the living room,'' he urged her. ''I'll light a fire, you can warm up your pretty toes, and then I can finish preparing the meal. Can't leave grits on the stove simmering like the other stuff, so I haven't done them yet.

Would you like some wine?'' She had him babbling again. Why did this particular woman make him babble? It wasn't funny now, but yeah, she was the one who had made him try to cut a deal with God.

Wow . . . Her mind was fixated on the word as she spied the living room through the black-hooded fireplace that separated the kitchen from it. She'd seen a lot of places, but never one like this owned by a bachelor. He had to be a bachelor; he'd given her every conceivable way to contact a person, even his fax number and e-mail address. Her attention was drawn to the expansive black leather sofa and matching armchair, and she glimpsed the wall of male-oriented electronic equipment, track lighting, and black arc lamps. She cast her gaze up to the twenty-two-foot ceiling that held huge, exposed wood beams amid eggshell-colored walls. Yeah, definitely a bachelor lived here. No window treatments save vertical blinds, no feminine touches, no colors—basic black, and no art. Everything was massive, and dark, and digital, and male . . . but too clean.

"This is so lovely," she murmured as her heels sank into the sand-colored deep-pile carpet when they left the tiled kitchen floor. "But how on Earth do you keep it so immaculate?"

"Don't be fooled. I live in three rooms. The bedroom, the study, the bathroom . . . and occasionally I go down to the laundry room and to the family room to lift weights—but not as much as I probably need to."

She laughed. He was a good sport.

"But your kitchen was spotless . . . all those black-finished appliances in there . . ."

"Secret," he whispered, bringing his finger to his lips as he slipped off his coat and hung it up. "Promise you won't tell anybody?"

"I promise," she said with a chuckle as he winked at

her. But it was difficult to keep her humorous perspective when he shed his coat, and she watched him turn and lean into the closet for a hanger. His back expanded beneath the dark fabric, and she could get just a hint of the rise and fall of his behind. She dropped her gaze quickly as her face burned. When he turned around, she smiled, allowing her eyes to drink in the way the dark cranberry silk shirt swept across his chest and back into place under his conservative black suit.

"Normally I don't have time to cook, and this place stays like a museum—dusty, and without a lot of change. I order out way too much, and this is the first meal I've had in here with anybody since I built it several years ago."

"Get out." She put her hands on her hips, looked around at the sumptuous environment, and shook her head.

"I swear."

"You did not build this lovely home to sit in here all by yourself. You did not."

"No," he corrected. "My hope was to share it with somebody someday, but somebody never came ... so ... I got a head start on someday. You want some wine?"

"Yeah," she said slowly.

"You want to look around first?"

"Yeah."

"You still don't believe I live in here by myself, do you?"

"Not entirely."

He laughed. She was a good sport.

"Come on. Grand tour. Fifty cents a ticket."

He walked her through to the dining room, which had another black metal fireplace and a huge oval walnut table and high, ladder-back chairs with black leather cushions. It was already set with black china and tall crystal wine flutes with black stems, and in the center of it was a crystal vase with two dozen white roses flanked by tall white tapers in onyx candleholders.

"This is truly beautiful," she murmured.

"You like the roses better this way?"

His voice held a mixture of anticipation and gratitude when it dropped an octave as he asked the question. The charm of his being that concerned about what she liked would be her undoing. This man was definitely making her forget her promise to push him away and to be home by midnight.

"Yeah . . . I do. Thank you."

She watched him light the dinner candles, then hit a remote control that she hadn't noticed when they entered the room. Immediately mellow music filtered into the space, making it feel cozy, despite the giant-size sprawl of all she'd encountered. He dimmed the top lights and pressed a switch on the side of the fireplace to ignite it. She could understand how the cold metal unit felt . . . he was pushing all her right buttons and she was definitely igniting.

"That's all on this level, save the powder room down the hall. Up these two steps, and those four, are the master bedroom and bathroom, and three smaller guest bedrooms— one of which I have decimated as I turned it into my office. There's a full hallway bathroom on the second floor, and a powder room in the basement by the family room."

She cocked her head to the side and smiled. He chuckled. Of course she wanted to see those rooms—if there was another woman afoot, no man was good enough to keep every shred of evidence out of sight.

He didn't say a word as she followed him from room to room, she noted. But again, the two unused bedrooms had that utilitarian male feel to them. No sentimental items on the dressers, beautiful though they were. No pictures on the walls—although he had enough perfect gallery space to make a curator envious. White sheets and plain blue comforters—like he'd just seen two of the same color that matched the size of the beds and figured, What the heck, it covers the beds. Jo Jo would have run screaming into the night if he'd seen this environment going to waste. She chuckled inwardly at her own crazy thoughts. What did any of that matter? She was just inspecting to be sure that no banshee would roll up on her and accuse her of something she had unwittingly walked into.

The bathroom in the middle of the hall was just like the powder room. Deep cranberry porcelains, awesome hand-crafted tile, gorgeous modern gold fixtures, and as clean as a hotel—and even less appointed. One white hand towel and some antibacterial soap. Deep. He really didn't live in these rooms.

"All right, brace yourself," he finally said. "The study looks like a bomb hit it, and I don't even let the cleaning lady go in here when she comes twice a month."

He had a cleaning lady? *Okaaaay.*

Her eyes scanned a room that she could not comprehend. Files were stacked up on the floor, banker boxes were overflowing, he had two computers in there, plus a desk that she could not see the top of, and all sorts of electronic gadgetry that she had no name for. But she did note the locked gun case on the wall, and the maps of the area, and how he'd pushpinned stuff up against it, totally destroying the eggshell paint job and natural exposed-wood panels. *Criminal,* she thought as she let her fingers cover a thumbtack hole in the wood as though that would repair it.

"I do not have a dark side," he said quietly with concern. "I'm a PI, so I have equipment for the job, and the guns are part of the job—for protection. If you want to run a rap sheet on me, you'll find that I've been honorably discharged from the service, and left the police department with a clean record. I have a license for everything on that wall . . . . I'm not a weekend warrior or Internet gun collector. And I don't leave that equipment around the house for little kids to pick up and hurt themselves with, either. Used to be a cop, and my partner . . . well, he had small kids, and I was their godfather. We both made a habit of putting that stuff up, locked and safe—since we had to have it for the job.''

"It's not my business, and I had no right to—"

"No," he said in a patient, good-natured tone. "Yes, you do. People, I think, have a right to know what and who they're dealing with—up front. Not after the fact."

She nodded, but her mind was fixed on his comment. What he'd said was true, but after the fact . . . *After what fact? After you got to know them better, after you slept with them, what?*

"Okay, this room isn't as fixed up as I'd like it to be," he said, apologizing as they entered it and he cut on the light, "but this is my room. All I do is sleep here, watch the news in here, and bolt."

His comment was not lost on her. Not much action going on in his bedroom either? *Hmmm* . . . From the looks of that man, with this house, that was too hard to believe.

Her gaze immediately swept the expansive room that hosted only an armoire with a television on top of it, a big leather chair that didn't go with the armoire and looked as though it belonged in the living room—but that matched the black television—and the biggest four-poster bed she'd ever seen.

Hunter greens and burgundy reflected off the mirrored closet as he turned up then muted the canister track lights. A fireplace in the bedroom and no sumptuous rug in front of it? She wasn't bold enough to check the man's closet space—too tacky. She could imagine that it was a walk-in, but bet that he hadn't appointed it with things that would make his life easier. She just hoped there were no woman's clothes in there. Why were her fears all deciding to come out of hiding on her tonight?

She glanced at the wood ceiling fan and he offered her a timid smile as she entered farther into the room. He was definitely a bachelor. No plants . . . no pictures . . . a criminal combination of putting a digital television on top of an antique. Leather in the bedroom—unheard of. Soft, gentle touches went there.

"Can I say something—and promise not to get mad at me, or throw me in the lake?"

She enjoyed the way he smiled at her.

"A few plants and some warmer colors in here would bring this beautiful room out more . . . I'm just saying."

She was nesting . . . . God was good. He was on time, all the time, just like the elders in his family always said. The woman had come into his house and was nesting. She was redecorating it in her mind, claiming space, deciding color schemes . . . his boys had told him about this phenomenon, but he was still a virgin when it came to this. The woman was walking through the Batcave and laying claim to it . . . . *Wait.* Was that a good thing? He wasn't sure.

"You put a nice, goose-down comforter on this big, beautiful bed . . . add a few throw pillows, add some wrought-iron candle stands," she murmured as she allowed her line of sight to travel to the fireplace. "Oh . . ." she moaned, "look at this. You need some art to show this high mantel off right; this has to be your sanctuary—after you work as hard as you do, honey."

It was suddenly difficult to breathe in the room. He needed to sit down, but couldn't. No. That wouldn't look right— she'd read it as an improper invitation. His legs felt like jelly. Maybe it was the way she said that long "oh . . ." Or was it the way she called him *honey,* when referring to how hard he worked? Or was that the generic *honey,* like *honey-chile?* Whatever. He liked it. A lot.

"What about in the bathroom? You think I should do something in there? It's just all white and gold tile, nothing fancy." He knew he was baiting her to stay in his lair a little longer, but he was loving the effect she had on him.

The man had asked her a decorating question for his bedroom and bathroom? *Nooooo way . . . Wow. Oh, wow.* This one was for-real interested, and there was no predatory female in sight. What to do, what to do? Follow the man into the—

"Oh, my God, Adam . . ."

"You like it?"

She put her hand over her heart to make sure it was still beating. "Yes," she said. "Absolutely."

Her gaze swept the double sink, built-in hair dryer, sink-to-ceiling mirror, and the way there was a smoky glass divider between the toilet and bidet and washbowls. The opposite side of the room hosted a hot tub and a separate double shower with little marble seats inside, and a stained-glass skylight let the stars wink in. Plush white towels were beside every water-bearing fixture in the room, and there was even a linen closet.

"I was wrong," she whispered as she closed her eyes. "Oh, Adam, you should turn *this* room into your sanctuary. . . . Can you imagine coming home from a hard day of work, slipping into the Jacuzzi with a glass of wine, putting on the jazz, lighting the candles, turning off the lights, and letting the water just beat all that tension out of you . . . then going into the bedroom and relaxing by the fire. . . ."

Yeah. He could imagine it. Actually, right at the moment, he could feel it with every pore of his body. "Baby," he said with a smile, making her open her eyes and smile back. "Standing in the middle of my bathroom, going through said graphic description of the pleasures of relaxing, is working on the wrong side of my brain—the nongentlemanly side. So, since I promised Jo Jo, how about if we end the tour here, go back downstairs, and you take off your shoes while I pour you some wine, salvage my jambalaya, and make some grits?''

Honest was all he could be at the moment, because the woman had blown him away in his own home . . . and she was worried about his locked gun cabinet. He just hoped that he hadn't offended her with the truth. But she looked so much more appetizing than dinner, standing there with what seemed to be a shocked but pleased expression on her face.

As he moved aside so that she could retrace their steps ahead of him, the thought of her slim, nude form in the water holding on to his shoulders as the hot tub jets beat against his back . . . *Oh, yeah.* She could transform his sanctuary into paradise without a trip to Home Depot. The thought almost made him bump into the wall as he came down the steps and made the turn at the landing.

''Sit yourself down, kick off your shoes, and I'll be back with the wine,'' he said in a rush, hitting the fireplace button to turn on the one between the kitchen and where she stood in the living room. *That's right, create a diversion in your mind so you can take off your jacket after dinner. Put a wall of fire between you and something that's burning hotter than that blaze that torched your bedroom. Basic training: seal one fire off with another if you have to.* This one was definitely sucking the oxygen out of the air, he noted as he struggled with the bottle of wine to get the cork out. How was he going to sit all through dinner, and watch her eat?

He paced into the dining room, got the two stem glasses, poured the wine, recorked it, and put it back in the refrigerator. What was he thinking of when he had brought her

chocolate-covered strawberries for dessert from Reading
Terminal? Huh? Was he insane? And he gave his word as
his bond to her play big brother to keep his hands off her.
He couldn't watch her eat those in front of him.

When he reentered the living room, she was sitting on
the floor, close up to the fire in the dim, recessed-lit room
with her eyes closed. The colors thrown from the flame
dappled her flawless complexion with deep golds and reds.
She'd taken off her shoes and was leaning back on her
elbows and twinkling her toes with a lazy, sexy smile on
her face. The front of her dress scooped down in a low U
shape that gave him a hint of the breasts that swelled beneath
the velvet's edge. Tiny pebbles disrupted the smooth texture
of the violet fabric that draped her, and his palms stung with
the urge to run his hands down the front of it. This was no
angel; this was a goddess . . . a love goddess . . . someone
destined to make him lose his mind. Heaven help him.

"Your wine," he murmured with a husky voice, bending
to give it to her.

"I took liberties," she nearly purred. "We've all been
under so much stress at the salon, and have been so crazed,
and the fire felt so good, but the sofa was too far away from
it to—"

"I can move it closer if you want me to."

He'd move heaven and Earth for her at the moment; all
she had to do was ask.

Her eyes opened from sexy half-mast and she looked over
her shoulder at the furniture, then shook her head. "Don't
be silly; that stuff weighs a ton. I'm fine."

No lie . . . the woman is fine.

"What can I help you with?"

Controlling the urge to pounce on you right on the floor.
"Uh, nothing. I'm good."

Yes, he is good . . . good enough to eat instead of dinner. "Are you sure I can't help you?"

Hell, no. But it was the right thing to say.

"I can stir the grits for you."

She's already stirred my grits. "No, no, you're a guest tonight. Like you said, it's been a long week."

It's been a long two years . . . five years . . . a damned lifetime since I've felt like this. "Don't you want some company back there?"

I want some company in my bedroom. "Sure, sure . . . you can sit on a stool and watch me work. I have to drop some cornbread, too."

Oh, God, would I love to watch that man work . . . on me in those mirrors.

"Come on, let's eat. We're both probably starved."

Chapter 16

It had been so long since he'd seen a radiant woman, a woman filled with earnest laughter and true joy in her heart, a passion for others in her soul. It had been even longer since he'd been able to share mutual stories with someone about how he grew up, or swap family history and the names of relatives, detailing each of their idiosyncrasies. And he had no frame of reference for the way he was telling this woman about his various career fortunes and misfortunes as though she were one of the boys, until it slowly came to him just how lonely he'd been.

He watched Nicole, whom he'd been granted the privilege of being allowed to call Nikki, wrinkle the bridge of her nose when she giggled and told him countless stories of her recent job-to-job antics.

What others might have considered depressing, she ultimately found funny about her necessary career changes, laughing at herself and chastising herself for being too naive.

But did she know what that did to his jaded worldview, to be in the presence of a spirit so dearly, rapturously, gloriously unspoiled by the bumps and bruises of life?

The only thing he would not let her laugh away was the passion for writing that she summarily dismissed. There was something in her eyes that flickered so sadly, then burned away when he'd asked her if she still put pen to paper. She'd given him a flippant response, and had told him that was passe—real writers used a mouse and keyboard—then she moved on to something else.

"You haven't answered my question, though," he pressed, enjoying her comical escapades and hoping that his instincts to dig deeper wouldn't spoil her mood. He couldn't explain it, but he wanted to know everything about her, not so much to satisfy his bent for investigation, but to savor and soak up all of the light her spirit shined upon him.

"You've asked me about a hundred questions by now. Be more specific."

"Do you still write?"

She paused. Then she took a sip of wine. "Nah."

She was smiling, but her demeanor had changed—just ever so slightly.

"Why not? You have more stories and funny stuff happen to you than anyone I know does. Your family alone, like mine, is like a book all by itself."

She stared at the man sitting across the table from her and was glad that he'd finally relaxed enough to remove his jacket before they ate. The deep berry color of his shirt made his skin seem all the more like delicious chocolate. Had he any idea how what he'd just said made her feel?

No man had ever wanted to know so much about *her* on a date. During the few encounters she'd experienced, the men only talked about themselves. Not one of them, not even her husband, had cared about whether she wrote or

not. None of them considered that writing was her true
heart's desire, and none of them ever took on the concerned
expression his eyes now contained when she'd been honest
about stowing away her dreams.

"I went through my poetry *noir* phase, and I'm over it,"
she said with a sad chuckle.

She'd laughed, but he noted that it was a hollow laugh.
It had the echo of innocence lost. Ridiculous, if not perilous,
thoughts entered his brain. If this were his woman . . . if
this were his wife, he'd make a way for her to have a room
facing the lake, or if she preferred, facing the woods . . .
and that would be her lush sanctuary that he'd work like a
slave to maintain. Anything to take away the flicker of
sadness in her eyes. Anything to let a woman like her be
able to tell her stories and share her gift of laughter with
the world.

"Poetry *noir?* You'll have to inform me of this genre.
I'm not up on all the literary specifics. I plead ignorance on
the subject, but I'd like to read some of what you've written
sometime."

Read her work? No man had ever wanted to read her
work. They always assumed that because what she wrote
was written by a woman, then it had to be about only things
that would concern women . . . but didn't they know that
she had sown pearls of wisdom about her species in every
line? Her husband hadn't known this, much less respected
this, and the man before her now was connecting to the
innermost core of who she was. The effect was disorienting
as her synapses grasped at the fragile concept, then backed
away. It was as though her insides craved this brand of
nourishment, but it had been so long since she had been fed.
And the awareness began to release a dangerous chemical
aphrodisiac throughout her system: hope.

"You know," she said, smiling, "poetry *noir* is that mess

where you go to the dark coffeehouses filled with smoke
... or to the tea salons, and you stand up on a rickety stage
with a mike that produces feedback until you hold it far
enough away from your face, and everybody in the audience
is dressed in combat fatigues or retro seventies gear, and
you stand there and rattle off a run-on sentence about life
just not being fair; then you sit down while the people clap
and talk about how deep your rhetoric was. Did it. It's group
therapy onstage. I'm done."

Her words did make him chuckle in earnest, because he'd
been in so many of those places, and in so many dark holes
that he'd come to accept sunlight as a natural disaster. And
he respected that those places also stole one's inner light.
They had practically snuffed out his own.

"I hear you. Sometimes we have to go certain places until
we're done being there."

A man who understood?

She peered at him sheepishly as she pushed away her
dinner plate. "This was fabulous, Adam. I'm going to get
that dish in a minute, but at the moment I have so many
spices running through my mouth that, as they say where I
come from, 'Boy, you got me puffin' and blowin' at your
table.' "

He laughed with her from deep down in his bones. "Don't
you worry about these plates. You just puff and blow some
more. Would you like some coffee to top that off?"

"No, thank you. I cannot squeeze another bite of food
into my mouth. See, I know you're from down South, the
way you feed people—just like Gail. She's from Georgia.
If a person says no, y'all say, 'Oh, chile, just have a little
bit.' Then when the person finally relents, y'all heap a huge
spoonful on their plate. That's what you did with those grits
and shrimp, and then you put that soul-shakin' okra on my

plate, with that spicy cornbread. Brother, the way you cook will make a person slap her momma.''

"Compliment duly accepted. I am so glad you came here and filled this old empty house up with your sweet voice.''

She looked down shyly, and he didn't care that he'd made her blush. He'd meant what he'd said. It was so nice to hear the sound of her bounce off the walls.

"This was so much nicer than going to a restaurant, and I'm sorry that I gave you such a hard time about coming here. It's just that—''

"A woman can't be too careful, in this day and age,'' he said, finishing her sentence.

She looked at him with a quizzical grin.

"What? It's the truth.''

"Yeah, but, you're not supposed to say that.''

"Why not?''

"Because if I'm sitting here with you, and you tell me that it's not safe . . .''

"I wasn't talking about me. I was talking about all my years of collaring bad guys. Trust me, love, if I had a daughter . . . humph.''

"What's that supposed to mean?'' Nicole chuckled and shook her head as he stood to take away the plates, and she followed him bringing the small ones into the kitchen.

"I wouldn't let her go on a date until she was thirty. I'm old-fashioned. I'm not evolved. I know what brothers think and do.''

"You are not endorsing the species, huh?''

He looked at her; she had a tiny plate in each hand, her neck bobbing slightly as she talked, one hip jutting forward, in her stocking feet.

"No. You look beautiful like that.''

"Like what?'' she said, becoming a little more shy and looking down at her dress.

"Standing in the kitchen arguing with me about nothing."

"What, boy!"

"I love it. You want some chocolate-covered strawberries?"

"Noooo . . . you did not get some of those?"

"Yeah, I did," he murmured as he set down the two large plates he held, and removed the smaller ones from her hands to put them on the counter. "I had to."

"Did you investigate me and find out that—"

"I witnessed it with my own eyes, that first time we had a session, and I couldn't breathe while I watched you eat one. Couldn't shake the thought," he said, giving her his back to consider while he turned to root in the refrigerator for the dessert. "Like I said, I'm not letting my daughter date until she's thirty."

"Well," Nicole said, clapping her hands once and backing away from him with a giggle. "Can't argue with the facts."

"Aw, c'mon, girl . . . I didn't scare you, did I? I told you I'd be a gentleman, and I was just playin'—sort of—so why don't we take these with the wine into the living room and sit on the sofa? I'll get the dishes later."

He loved the way her mouth turned into a peevish smile and her eyes sparkled with mischief. It was so weird, but for the life of him he couldn't remember being out with a woman who made him so nervous, yet so relaxed at the same time. It was as though one minute she was as close to him as family, and he could just tell her anything; then the next minute, he was on pins and needles with his blood boiling for her. Then she'd say something to crack him up, and they'd be back to being friends. He liked both extremes and all the places she took him in between.

Once she'd settled herself on the sofa, he handed her the small cold plate, and went to fetch the remainder of the wine and their glasses. When he returned, she was studying the plate hard, turning it slowly as she decided upon which chocolate-swathed berry she wanted. He set down the glasses on an end table.

"Tell me something," she said brightly. "You don't want to eat these in the dining room, just in case some chocolate gets on this light-colored rug, or falls and hits this expensive leather couch?"

"Nope. Things can be replaced. Good times and good people can't. I try not to buy anything that I'd be upset about losing, breaking, or messing up. I figure, if I can't enjoy it, why have it? Guess that's why I don't spend that much on clothes, 'cause I always rip something, dirty something, mess them up, ultimately. I prefer jeans and a T-shirt, or sweats, most times, to be honest."

"Me too, to be real honest. And once I'm inside, the shoes are the first thing to come off."

He smiled as he looked at her pretty feet. Yeah, he could get used to coming home and seeing her without her shoes on, comfortable and relaxed like this.

"So, if someone spilled wine ... or red juice on this carpet, you wouldn't care?"

"That's why they make carpet cleaner."

"Even in your car with the plush interior? What if the expensive paint job on it got scratched?"

"That's why they have insurance, honey."

"Oh."

"What?"

"Just oh."

He smiled. He could tell that she was looking around and trying to visualize a child in his space. It was in the way her brow wrinkled when she'd first spied the fireplace switches, and how she really had a problem with his gun cabinet, although it was locked. Or maybe it was the way she stared out of the cathedral windows at the woods and the black ice on the lake, then sighed and looked down at the berries, trying to decide whether to taste one.

"This place doesn't pass inspection, does it?" He caught the edge of her plate before a berry tumbled off it.

"Whatever would make you say that? This place is lovely . . . gorgeous, and who am I to talk? You saw where I live."

"No. First of all, I do a dangerous job for a living and they pay me well to do it—so let's not go there. I'm into you, not your digs, and I can tell you are not the kind of person who cares about what somebody has, even if you might appreciate it. But you have something that is more precious than any of this," he said with a sweep of his arm. "One wrong step down that floating staircase, one wrong push of a button that turns on the fireplace instead of the TV, chasing one butterfly too far . . . this place is not child-proofed. I'd have to work on that. You gonna eat one of these berries?"

She picked up a piece of fruit and bit into the tip of it quickly to keep her mouth from hanging open. The man had said what had been on her mind. And the crazy thing was that he was discussing it all as though they'd known each other for years, and this was all perfectly logical. He was talking to her as if they were husband and wife, just sitting on the sofa after work, discussing plans to remodel!

"Can I ask you a series of deep questions?" She licked her fingers and sucked the juice out of her berry, and held it by the edges where no chocolate resided, using it to make a point as she spoke.

Why did she have to do that while she was about to launch into a series of deep questions? It wasn't fair. These were torture tactics designed to make a man give up his name, rank, and serial number.

"Yeah. Shoot," he replied. *And please, God,* his mind

begged, *let her torture be short, sweet, and simple, right between the eyes.*

"Why aren't you married?"

Point-blank range like a professional hit. A neat kill.

"Haven't found the right one, I suppose. I told you that."

"No, that's the cocktail-party answer. You tell me why you aren't married, and I'll tell you why I don't write."

She must be an undercover cop—no, special division, narcotics unit.

"Fair. I was on my way to being engaged, and the person I was going there with decided that she loved pretty things more than she loved me. She set my partner and me up . . . my partner lost his family and therefore took his own life. We went through this before."

"Not the part about you—you talked about what happened to him, not about what happened to you. Thank you for being honest about that, though."

"It's cool." He shrugged. "Happened a long time ago."

"Then why aren't you married?"

"Why do you keep asking me that?"

"Because I'm trying to decide if I want to date a brother who has all this going on—nice home, nice car, decent profession—but no woman anywhere around. It doesn't add up for me; I'm sorry," she said, biting into the strawberry and licking the part that had melted on her fingers. "I like you, though. A lot. But I like to know what I'm dealing with. I've got a daughter. I have to know such things."

Another point-blank shot. He liked her style. But he was packing heat, too, and needed to back her up.

"You can't judge a book by its cover. I could look at you and see this gorgeous woman having a ball with her friends, and ask myself, Why haven't fifty brothers scooped her up by now?"

She sighed and smiled. "I went through a bad divorce.

Got burned. Not as badly as you, but bad enough for me. My husband was a pilot. Liked to travel the country and make a conquest in every city he touched down in. He also liked money more than me and my daughter; in fact, he moved out of the country so he wouldn't have to pay child support and left me with a five-digit bill. So, hitting the streets with that kind of baggage, I was very skeptical about dating again. Plus, early on, I didn't want to leave my kid to go out gallivanting, and I had to work so much to make ends meet, there wasn't really time—that's also why I haven't been writing . . . you come home tired, you get up tired, have lots of stuff on your mind . . . blocks the creative process, unless you do wail poetry.''

He sat back and watched her eat around the edges of the strawberry and leave the pithy center. The process of witnessing her do that while she talked so casually about her reality was working him down to the core as well.

"We both have been residing in the same place," he ventured, offering her the plate so that she could select another berry.

"How so?"

"Have another berry."

"Aren't you going to have one?"

"I like watching you eat them more than eating them myself."

"You are missing out, brother," she said, this time putting the whole tip of a new berry in her mouth and pulling it out slowly. Then she turned the fruit on its side and licked away the chocolate in broad strokes. Once she had removed all evidence of the chocolate, she put the whole berry in her mouth and sucked on it, letting it push out one cheek, then the other, before flattening it with the bridge of her mouth, chewing it, then swallowing it.

"Okay, you win." He did not object when she giggled.

"That was a simplistic demonstration of the two ways one can decide to go through life. The first way is to pick apart everything, leaving the core, and not fully enjoying the layers and textures and coatings while getting to it. The other way is to luxuriate in all the thickness of it, with the little divets and bumps, the sweetness and tartness, the smooth and the rough together . . . Do you understand what I mean?"

"Yes," he said hoarsely. "I stand corrected for getting into your business, and trying to match wits with a writer." The agony of watching her had sent phantom sensations to his groin that matched what she was doing to the berry.

"So why aren't you married?"

"I'm not married because I haven't been in the right places, or taken the time to stop and savor anyone who made me feel anything close to this."

"Oh," she whispered.

He set the plate on the side table.

"You want to know something about men . . . a really big secret?" he asked without smiling, all the mirth having left him now.

"Yeah," she replied, looking down at her sticky fingers.

"It doesn't take us years to decide on a woman we want to be with permanently—like a husband. We make that decision in a matter of moments, usually, within a meeting or two. We lock onto target, and we know that's the one. We don't intellectualize about it. If it doesn't hit gut level, then we ain't going there. If you see a guy hanging around for a long time, dillydallying about it, he's either not there because his finances are jacked up and isn't comfortable about that—and no, y'all can't help. Or he hasn't locked on target, and she's just not the one."

"You're saying all that to say . . . ?"

He noticed her tone was becoming defensive, and it made

him smile. Boy, talking to women was like traveling through a mine field.

"I'm saying all this to say that guys nest when they're ready."

"What?"

"We want a person to be there, to depend on, to trust. If the right woman asks us to do something, we will move heaven and Earth for her—if we were raised right, but that's a whole 'nother conversation."

"You're saying all this to say what, then?"

She had become so indignant that he feared she might pop up off the sofa. The sight of her feathers being ruffled made him want to chuckle for some odd reason. He was getting to her, and he enjoyed every minute of that sensation.

"I'm saying all this to say that a man doesn't drive to Philly, after going to the farmer's market to find crawfish and shrimp, drive back to Jersey, then drive back to Philly, stand in the cold trying to convince a woman whom he doesn't care that much about to not kill herself on the slick roads, only to drive her to Jersey and offer her dinner, but not before he gets down on his knees in his mind to thank his Jesus for letting her come to his house."

"Well . . . since you put it that way . . ."

"Naw, girl, I'ma read you, since you are about to read me. Yes, you were," he affirmed with a chuckle. "I read body language for a livin', don't forget."

"I wasn't—"

"A man just on the prowl doesn't let a woman he doesn't care about inspect him for spoilage like he is a USDA cut of meat, and check it out his Batcave, redecorate it in her mind however she wants, and be thinking of how he can address every specification to childproof it . . . while he's eating, he's trying to think of what day off he's going to do this handiwork himself, or pay somebody to get it done . . .

while this fine, and I do mean *fine,* woman sits on his sofa asking him about all the past people who couldn't hold a candle to her. And if sex were his sole focus, he wouldn't spend the time to get to know her when she was turning him on like this . . . and he wouldn't be trying so hard to keep his hands to himself as a demonstration of respect, either. That's what I'm saying all this to say.''

"Oh.''

"Yeah. Oh.''

"I'm sorry.''

"Apology accepted, but you cannot have any more strawberries in my house tonight!'' He laughed as the bridge of her nose wrinkled with a giggle.

"Why not?''

"Because I told Jo Jo I'd act like a gentleman, and so far I have. Correct? Ain't that what your play–big brother made me promise? I want your family to like me too. I'm saying all this to say, when you hook up with someone, it's a package deal, right?''

He wanted her family to like him too? He respected Jo Jo as someone important to her? Did he know what that meant, not to have to defend the people she loved?

"But you're single, and you don't have to accept any package deals.''

Was she crazy? To not accept the package meant leaving half of the gift on the table! How could he not accept her, or her friends, or that beautiful little girl?

"My family is alive and elaborate, too. I told you that. Cecilia is a trip, and my dad . . . hell, the man got in my face about sending money home and trying to buy him and Mom a house. Said my mother was *his* wife, and until he died, he was the man of the house. Told me to go get my own. So I could only send my parents on little vacations and stuff. Package deal. Take it or leave it.''

The man was nesting . . . he'd set up a castle and was looking for someone to . . . *Oh, dear Lord!* Half-complete, half-decorated, the house was in stasis. But she'd just met him!

"Things are moving awfully fast."

"True," he admitted with a chuckle. "But no more strawberries until you're ready to go farther than a cursory investigation. I may be a gentleman, but I am still a man."

"I won't eat them like I did before, okay? That was wrong and, like my mom would say, fresh. But I am not trying to be funny . . . they are good."

She smiled and leaned across him, peeking at the plate he'd set on the end table beside him. Although her comical expression made him laugh, when she brushed against his knee again, it wasn't funny any longer.

"Let me ask you something," he said, retrieving and handing her the plate.

"Like you say, shoot."

He watched her pick out a fat strawberry and put the china in her lap.

"How long has it been since you've been with anybody?"

"What!" She threw her head back and laughed. "That is too out of line and not a cursory investigation!"

"I'll tell you the truth; it's been over a year, and I can't watch you eat that strawberry like that."

"Over a year . . ." she murmured, carefully placing the bitten strawberry down on the china, beginning to lick the chocolate off her fingers, then reconsidering. "I'm sorry, I shouldn't have been playing around. Let me wash my hands."

She handed him the plate and he set it aside again.

"You got so serious all of a sudden," he said, gently taking her wrist and turning over her chocolate-stained fingers. "Why?"

"Because I know what it feels like to want to be with someone special, when there's nobody like that around . . . awful."

He said a silent prayer of thanks. She'd been in waiting, like him.

"Yeah," he murmured. "But like you said, we have to savor the chocolate. . . ." He placed her forefinger into his mouth and allowed his tongue to clean the sweet confection from it. "I've been hankering to do that since the first time I saw you do it," he said softly into her palm, then kissed the center of it. Then he repeated the act slowly with her thumb.

She said a silent prayer of thanks as the wet heat of his mouth burned her fingers and scorched the center of her palm, then traveled up her arm. He'd been in waiting for a special somebody, just as she had.

"It's been a really, really, really long time for me, too. I can't play like this anymore, Adam."

She'd said his name—more breathed it than said it—and whispered the words so softly that he'd had to strain to hear her. It had been a *really* long time, she'd almost moaned . . . did she understand what it was doing to him to know that? And those smoky eyes had gone to mere slits when he'd placed her fingers in his mouth. He was teetering very dangerously on the edge of no longer being a gentleman. And he didn't want to scare her, but . . .

"When you walked into my bedroom, and started telling me how to fix up the bathroom," he murmured, moving close enough to smell the spicy fragrance of the dinner mixed with the sweetness of the berries on her breath, "and started describing how I could relax . . . I haven't been able to concentrate since then."

"Oh," she murmured, her mouth looking as ripe and full as the berries she'd suckled.

"And I know it's too soon to even think about it, but a man can't be blamed for keeping hope alive . . . you smelled so good when I came up close to you to take off your coat . . . and you had on this soft velvet that reminded me of sliding my hands against it as I held yours the first time we met, and girl, you are sitting two inches away, and I'm not trying to blow it, or make you angry, or disrespect you. But if I taste your mouth, I'm going to want to taste more than that, and for real, for real, I can't play like this with you right now. I'm already messed up behind just licking your fingers."

He watched her eyes close even more to mere slits, and her breathing seemed to quicken as the swell of her breasts rose and fell. Her lips were slightly parted and his heart was slamming against his breastbone as he watched her silent desire. His finger traced her jawline, and found its way to her collarbone, then along the edge of the scoop of her dress to her shoulder and to the delicate lobe of her ear. Although his palm ached to cup the small orbs that had tiny pebbles at the tips of them, he didn't dare. As a compromise he coaxed his trembling fingers to settle for the silky wisps of hair that they found at the nape of her neck.

The way his hands trembled as they touched the edges of her dress, then stroked her skin, made a shiver run down her spine. She could barely catch her breath, and in reflex she tightened the muscles in her thighs as the point between them burst with liquid want, and shame burned her cheeks.

"I can't. Not yet, not this first time we've been out. I mean, I really want to, but . . ."

"I know," he whispered. "That's why I'm not kissing you. A man has a limit. Your mouth is my personal limit."

He watched her squeeze her thighs together tightly, and that slight movement almost fractured his composure.

"I want to lean you back on this sofa so bad, you just

don't know, girl. Either I've gotta take you home, or you
have to call your baby-sitter and stay.''

He watched her bring in air in short pants through barely
parted lips, and the sight of her poorly camouflaged arousal
did something to the rational side of his brain. He was back
to bargaining with the Almighty—then he laughed to banish
hope from his mind. Hope was poisoning his judgment.

''What?'' she whispered.

''We're both sitting here, two inches from each other,
and two seconds from me throwing you down on this sofa,
and I'm doing what you were laughing about in the car.''

''What?''

She looked so breathless and disoriented—and he hadn't
even touched her—that he had to do something to break the
tension and the mood or it would be over. Laughing at
himself and his predicament was his only option.

''I was bargaining with God; I was asking him to change
your mind.'' He chuckled. ''I was saying, Please, Lord, let
this woman call her girlfriend and stay here tonight. You
know what's in my heart.'' He moved farther away from
her. ''Get thee back,'' he playfully warned, slapping at her
hand when she edged closer toward him, giggling. ''Seriously now, woman, I'm a man on the edge.''

''You did not say that . . . you couldn't have been thinking
that at the same time I was fixin' to call Gail.''

''You were gonna call Gail? For real?'' All mirth evapo-
rated. ''Don't tease me.'' His groin felt as though she'd
loaded cinder blocks into it. ''You were considering it?''

''Yeah, I couldn't take it. I don't ever do this, but there's
something about you that I just really, really like . . . it's
like one minute we're as close as best friends, but the next
it's all hot and thick between us . . . then, the next, we're
kidding around, and—''

His mouth captured and stopped the flow of her words,

and the deep taste of chocolate fused with Cajun spices and wine. The soft feel of the inside of her mouth jealously competed with the softness of the velvet at her back, and he felt her falling with him as her legs tangled themselves around his, and his movements echoed the way he'd needed to move against her all along. Dear God, she smelled so good, and her hair smelled so good, and her mouth, and her neck, and her shoulder tasted so sweet. Lord help him if this woman wanted to go home.

She could not pull him against her hard enough or fast enough, and the barrier of the fabric between them was definitely stronger than her will. It was the only thing keeping her from having him inside her, and the agony that distance caused made a moan work its way up from her belly. Dear God, he felt so good, and the cranberry silk shirt that she clutched in her hands felt good, just as the steel body beneath it felt way too good . . . and he smelled so good, and his earlobe, and his neck, tasted better than the chocolate.

When her hands found the deep sway in his back and treasured the feel of the tight, sculpted-granite muscles in his behind, she brought them up the gorge of his spine to allow her legs to untangle themselves from his and freely wrap around his waist; then she arched. The force with which he returned her thrust made her cry out. And the alignment of their bodies was so perfect, as though his had been formed just for her, and every downstroke landed on its mark. And then he stopped, pushed himself up, and looked down at her, taking in huge gulps of air.

"I have to get up. Now. This is how babies get made."

"You're right. You're right. I wasn't thinking . . . I couldn't think."

"Neither could I. No more playing with strawberries."

"We shouldn't be playing this close to the edge at all . . . not yet."

"I know," he said in a ragged breath. "I shouldn't have kissed you, then gone for broke."

She watched him hover over her as if he were doing a push-up, and the sight of his ability to suspend his weight that long with his arms trembling, breathing hard, made her want to pull him down to her again.

"I gotta get up. Now," he said in a stern voice, not moving away from her. "We could torture ourselves like this all night until one of us breaks, or I can take you home. Your last chance. You want me to drive you home?"

"My body wants to do this all night," she murmured, "but my mind says you have to take me home."

"What does your heart say?" It was hard to talk. She had him hovering there, inches above paradise, panting. He closed his eyes tightly. *Please, baby . . . I have honorable intentions. But I'm only human.*

"My heart says I like the concept of a package deal . . . and I don't want to spoil it by unwrapping it too soon."

He kept his eyes closed as he tried to catch his breath. He could feel the heat from hers rising in invisible waves to his and pulling him down as his arms struggled to hold his weight away from that temptation.

"Just give me a second to pull myself together, baby."

Was she crazy? No one had ever made her feel like this so fast and so furiously. She looked up at his pained expression and it ignited another charge in her. Contractions rippled from the valley between her thighs and shook her womb as she peered at him. When he emitted a low groan in his throat and lowered himself an inch, then pulled back, her thighs opened wider in response to his voice. She was so close to the edge of momentary oblivion . . . but so close to something lasting.

"We can't . . . I'm sorry, Adam. Not yet."

"It's all right. I shouldn't have gone there," he said, panting. "I knew better than that."

Was he crazy? She'd said her body wanted to do this all night. Just one more contact . . . all he had to do was to drop his weight against her and feel her long legs wrap around his waist, and sink into the luscious sweet center that was driving him mad. If he could just undo his belt and get out of his pants, he could feel how wet and ready he knew she had to be. But she wanted to go home, as much as she wanted him, and why in the hell were women so complicated?

"I know, I know," he said, grazing her mouth with a kiss as she closed her legs beneath him. When he pulled back to a sitting position he ran his palms over his face.

"Please don't do that to me yet," he said in a pained voice when she reached out to touch his face. Then he turned her palm against his mouth, planted a kiss on it, and stood. "I'm still not in my right mind."

She couldn't help herself as she allowed her gaze to make a slow descent from his face down the length of his body. Her hand still burned where he'd kissed it hard.

"You've gotta take me home right now, Adam Bastille, because my mind is going places that it cannot come back from right yet, either."

"Maybe . . . I don't know, baby; the cold air will do us some good, huh? But you sure you want to go home?"

"No, I don't want to go home, but I have to go home." She stood and smoothed her dress, and adjusted her earrings and hair.

He'd blown it. She was leveling off. He could feel the air leave his lungs with the hope that had been extinguished.

"Why don't you stay . . . call Gail . . ." His pride was shot. She'd driven him to begging.

"I can't. First date, and look at us."

How did women do it? How did they master mind over matter?

"You're gonna make me go back and pull out some old dusty Motown line for you, suga—back when brothers had to rap, and they weren't too proud to beg."

"Baby . . ." she crooned. "Please . . ."

"Don't talk to me like that . . . oh, girl . . ."

She laughed. "I'm sorry, I'm sorry, I'm so very sorry." She walked in a little circle with her arms wrapped around herself; then she fanned her face with her hands. "We gotta shake this off. Oooh, boy."

He laughed and pulled her into his arms, kissed her hard, then let her go fast.

"C'mon, baby, lemme take you home," he urged as he brought back her coat and handed her her shoes.

"I loved tonight," she whispered. "All of it."

"C'mon, baby, lemme take you . . . home. Stop whispering, too; it's sending shivers down my spine."

"I have to put on my shoes."

"You're stallin', and messin' with me, and I'm gonna carry you to the car," he said with a laugh when she giggled. "Them ain't no shoes no way," he teased. "They just pieces of material with beads glued on 'em tryin' to act like shoes in the wintertime."

She doubled over and laughed. "You know you sound too country. Did you notice as the night went on we started sounding more and more like from home?"

"That's because, girl, we ate like we was back home," he said, scooping her up and carrying her toward the kitchen.

She let out a tiny squeal and laughed harder.

"All the blood was rushin' from my brain to parts indecent, and *they* wanted to go home. But the woman in my arms says it ain't proper yet, so I gotta take her home. Now what's wrong with this picture?"

They both chuckled as he plopped her on the hood of his car, and opened the passenger's-side door while she clutched her shoes in her hands. They both laughed even harder when he looked up with a wry grin and winked at her.

"I'm just an ol' country boy at heart, ya know, and you are doing something to me sitting on the hood of my vehicle. You giving me ideas."

Nicole hopped down and got into the passenger's seat and pulled the door shut when he moved out of the way.

He was a good sport about this . . . too good a sport. She should have stayed, and now it was too late. But she wouldn't have regrets in the morning—or would she?

"Better call ahead to Gail, and tell her to make sure the baby is asleep . . . 'cause I sorta got you all disheveled back there. I'm sorry. You need to use the cell phone?"

"Don't apologize. I enjoyed every moment of it, but yeah," she said, looking in the visor mirror, "I'd better warn Gail that I'm coming in with one engine and no landing gear."

She sat still for a moment. That was weird. Why on Earth would she use an airport phrase, something to flash her back to her ex-husband—after a wondrous evening like this? *Yeah.* It was too soon. She had some serious baggage to unload, first, lest she spoil this good man's intentions.

Keep it light, she told herself. *Talk about funny stuff, crazy stuff, but nothing serious.*

"Who are the guys around you in the uniforms?"

The thought popped into her head from nowhere.

"I told you I used to be a cop and in the military, but I don't work with guys in uniform anymore," he said in a concerned voice as they drove. "Why?"

"I don't know . . . but I just thought of uniforms. Security guards. Wild, huh?"

"Yeah, maybe you were just thinking you needed armed guards to keep me off you," he said with a strained chuckle.

"Yeah, maybe," she added with a laugh, then shook the eerie feeling.

Chapter 17

She practically floated in the door as she opened it, and Gail's wide-eyed expression didn't even bother her.

"Oh, my God . . ." Gail said on a long breath, adjusting her scarf over her big pink rollers as Nicole sauntered in.

Nicole dropped her bag and her keys on the coffee table and plopped down on the sofa next to her.

"Yeah . . . Oh, *my* God . . ." Nicole repeated, then threw her head back and laughed.

She and Gail exchanged a glance and both laughed hard.

"The full scoop, and nothing but the scoop. Chile, what happened?"

"I think he's the one, gurl."

"No!"

"Yes!"

"No!"

"Oh, yes."

"Noooo . . ."

"Oh . . . help me, Father . . . yes . . ."

"Oh, yes?" Gail sat back and covered her mouth as Nicole stood and removed her coat.

"No," Nicole replied, shaking her head and making a sad pout. "Oh, no."

"Why on Earth not?" The tone of Gail's voice was thoroughly indignant as she looked at Nicole's disheveled condition.

"I have no idea."

"But look at you . . . he tried, right?"

"Yes," Nicole mewed, her voice sounding pathetic to her our ears. "He tried hard . . . but then . . ."

"Are you crazy?" Gail shot off of the sofa and paced behind Nicole as she fussed. "Have you lost your mind! He's fine, eligible—"

"I know, I know, I know, and he's *nesting*."

"Whaaaaat! And you're home by midnight!"

"Shush! You're going to wake up Lydia and Michelle," Nicole warned with a giggle as she went into her bedroom. "I have to get out of this dress."

Gail leaned on the door frame and shook her head. "The man made you wet your panties, didn't he?"

"I can't talk about it," Nicole said with a shiver. "I can't discuss it."

"Oh, my God . . . that good?"

"Oh . . . girl . . ."

"No."

"Yes."

"No! Stop it," Gail pleaded. "Tell me."

"That's all I'm going to say. I have to get out of this dress and take it to the cleaners Monday."

"No."

"Yes."

"Mommy . . . you came home by twelve."

Both Gail and Nicole looked at each other.

"Suga, what are you doing out of bed so late? I put you down about a half hour ago. Only let you stay up that late 'cause you and Michelle were watching a movie."

"Mom," a sleepy teenager intoned as she entered Nicole's bedroom. "I thought Aunt Nikki was coming in tomorrow?"

"Gail, are you crazy? Why would you tell the child something like that!"

"I only thought that—"

"I told you Mommy would be home by twelve. The prince always has to get Cinderella home by twelve."

Nicole stared at her daughter, then at Michelle, who wrinkled her nose, then at Gail, who shrugged.

"Mommy was not with a prince—"

"Were too!" the five-year-old challenged.

"Okay, Lydia, tell Mommy why you think she was with a prince, and who standing here ever told you something like that?" Nicole put her hands on her hips and gave Gail and Lydia her most serious warning glare not to say a word.

"Nobody haf to tell me. I could tell."

"Why, honey-bird?" Nicole forced her voice to be gentle, and she stooped to be at eye level with her child.

" 'Cause I never see you so pretty and smile so much. Aunt Gail is my godmudder, right? And she came over and helped you get pretty; then you lef' and came back by twelve. And jus' like Cinderella, your shoes ain't all tied, and your clothes are wrinkly and messed up. Did his car turn into a pumpkin . . . is that how you got messed up?"

Unable to hold it in, Gail and Michelle turned their backs to Nicole and the little one and howled with laughter. Nicole hung her head to keep the child from seeing her wide grin.

"Go to bed, sweet pea. It's late and I'm really, really tired, too."

She escorted her daughter to bed with a kiss, tucked her

and Michelle in, and went back to take off her clothes. Gail was lounging across the comforter, swinging her feet and whistling a merry tune, when Nicole entered her bedroom.

"Do *not* say a mumbling word, Gail Jackson," she warned in good humor, taking off the dress and snatching up her robe.

"Told you to wear a minipad, didn't I?"

"Shut up, Gail Jackson."

"When you seeing him again?"

Nicole stopped her jerky motions of removing her jewelry, stockings, and underwear and turned to face her girlfriend. "I don't know." She sighed. "You think he'll call?"

It had required getting her safely to her apartment door, then half the drive back to Jersey before the cold air began to take effect and numb the burning she'd left in his groin. Never in his adult life had a woman opened his nose like this! It didn't make sense. But as he continued to struggle with the options of how to get her to visit again, he could feel the tension begin to ignite the ember that he was desperately trying to snuff out.

"Think about work, fool!" he yelled into the empty car. The exertion of hollering felt good and helped kill the pain. "Damn!" He slammed his fist against his steering wheel. He'd definitely be working this off tonight in the basement. Maybe that was why all bachelors needed an in-home gym. The gloomy thought made him chuckle to himself as he switched off the CD player and hit a button to turn on the radio. *Yeah*. Mind-numbing rap. Very loud music. Erection-killing lyrics. Maybe that was why the young boys loved it.

But his resistant brain scavenged every word that she'd said, and some of the glimpses of sadness that she'd revealed.

He felt connected to it all as he drove down the highway, bopping to an insane beat, and trying to yell portions of the lyrics at the top of his lungs. Anything to clear his head. But what did she mean about men in uniforms?

Adam turned off the radio and drove in silence. This was not why he was supposed to be in Philly. Now the woman was messing with his work. He hadn't been able to think of a thing since he'd spotted her. Not a good sign.

Okay. What did he and his cousin Cecilia have in common? A last name. What did the insurance companies he'd investigated all have in common? Clients. Dead end. Okay. What did the clients of large insurance companies, ones large enough to mean anything, have in common? His mind tore at the puzzle. What did every major company have? Security guards. Guys in uniforms like his gifted baby mentioned.

Dread filled his gut, and this time he couldn't shake it. Yeah, he'd be awake all night. It was time to rouse a few sleepy people and get a printout of all the security firms on retainer by his client's clients—and that would take all night.

The sound of his telephone ringing brought him around from the stack of papers on his desk that had been his pillow. Without lifting his head, he peered at the digital clock face and groaned. Who in the hell was calling his office telephone at ten on a Sunday morning? The last thing he remembered was that same clock telling him it was around five. Didn't they know Sunday was a day of rest?

"Bastille here," he said in a flat tone. He didn't care who it was. The lack of sleep and a lack of Nicole had turned his mood foul. "Talk to me."

"Redfield here. Byron. We need to have a conversation, man to man."

"Look, dude, it's Sunday morning and—"

"Have you spoken to your cousin?"

"Which cousin? I'm from down South, and have lots of cousins."

"Cecilia. Cecilia Sampson—maiden name Bastille."

Adam paused. Sampson was her old married name. What freakin' games was she up to now? He hated games.

"Who told you she was my cousin?"

"She did."

"When?"

"When she called me today and I told her I couldn't help her until tomorrow. She said that she'd have to just call her cousin who was a private detective, then. I put two and two together, found your business card, and decided to call you."

"Why?" The attorney's short statements of fact made Adam sit up straight and removed the haze from his mind.

"She called my house and it caused some tension with my guest."

Adam let his breath out hard. "I don't deal with domestic squabbles, brother. That's the province of divorce—"

"Listen to me," Byron Redfield insisted. "She was crying hysterically and said she needed an attorney and didn't know who else to call."

"Okay, and?"

"She said her new boss at some security company she's working for was trying to push up on her, and when she backed him down, he went ballistic and is now trying to fire her."

"Which company is that?"

"A.S.A., Inc. Allied Security Agency."

"I'm listening," Adam murmured, riffling through the papers on his desk and looking through the A.S.A., Inc. employee list. That was when he spotted it—C. Sampson, date of hire three weeks prior. Status—part-time, night shift, clerical. Right about the time he received that call from his aunt and mother. *Damn!* Cecilia never mentioned moonlighting there as a temp. Working under an alias. No wonder he'd missed it.

"So I told her that there was nothing I could do until Monday—when I could give her a referral to people who do EEOC types of suits," Redfield pressed on after a moment of hesitation, then fell quiet.

Adam let the silence form a few questions in his mind, and he roved over the mental list of Cecilia's paramours. None of the names she'd given him appeared on the security company lists, but what did that mean? Where was the link, and how did this Redfield character factor in?

"And she came to call you, in particular, at home, because?" Adam finally asked, growing more agitated as the fact that Cecilia had been running him in circles sank into his bones.

"Because I was foolish and gave her the digits when I met her at the salon the first night I visited there."

"Uh-huh. And this caused a problem how?"

"Because I wasn't alone here when the call came in, and when I explained who it was, the person who was here snapped a mental twig."

"And that person might be?"

"Is that important?"

"Possibly."

"You know the sister who runs the salon, Victoria Jones."

"I know her. Good people, from what I understand."

"Very good people," Redfield clarified. "VIP, for me. Okay?"

"And she didn't like my cousin calling you, I take it."

"No. Not in the least."

"Any particular reason why a very prominent Philadelphia attorney wouldn't have some clients call his home—as a professional courtesy? What's the problem?''

"I don't know how to put this delicately, but ... well, Cecilia is known. Let me rephrase that—"

"Yeah, dude. Please rephrase that. Although I'm aware of my cousin's rep in some circles, she is still that—blood.''

"Well, Victoria took exception to her calling me and jumped to conclusions."

"Were those conclusions accurate?"

"Not in the least."

"Then why was she calling you?"

"She was in a tizzy, and wanted somebody with an 'Esquire' behind his name to send this guy a letter of intent to sue, just to show him that she meant business, without having to actually go all the way.''

"With the attorney in question or with the suit?"

"The suit, man! The suit! I never put my hands on the woman. Sure she's gorgeous, sexy, and all of that, but that's not what I was looking for, so I never pursued it.''

"Chill. Okay. But I'll ask you again. How did she get your private number?"

He could hear Byron Redfield let out his breath in a hard rush.

"I knew this was a bad idea," Redfield said evenly. "No matter what I tell Victoria now—"

"Look. You're the attorney. You're used to grilling people, right? Then bear with me as my PI brain takes down just the facts and cross-references them. Before I take on anybody's case or cause, I have to know in my gut that they're dealing with me on the level. Cool?"

"Cool."

"Okay. Now let me ask you again, so I can establish motive; why did she have your particular number, if indeed, she's not your type of woman, as you say?"

A long pause hung between them, and as he waited for
Redfield to answer him, or hang up, he looked through the
list of companies to see if any other names he knew from
his past came up. Dead end. But damn if Nicole hadn't
called the part about it being a man at the nexus of this. It
wasn't a bull's-eye mark, but she had hit an edge of the
target. There was also some mess with his cousin and a
security company—guys in uniforms—and if there was
some jerk pushing up on Cecilia, well, then, it was logical
that he might try to spook her or harm her.

"I'm tired, man," Adam said in a surly tone. "I ain't
got all day."

"All right," Redfield snapped in an exasperated voice.
"It's embarrassing."

Adam wiped his face with his palm. This crap was getting
on his nerves.

"She came into the salon after I had my session. I was
about to leave, and I saw this stunning thing walk through
the door. I had been thinking about going up to Victoria,
but hadn't worked up the nerve at that point. Cecilia was
hanging around—said she was on her way to handle some
business at the bar . . . I was hanging around . . . I'm not
proud to admit that I didn't feel like going home by myself
after I took some of that elixir, so . . ."

"So," Adam said in a weary voice, rolling his shoulders
to work out the tension as he tried to keep rage from clouding
the information he needed to obtain, "you didn't have the
nerve to make a play for Victoria Jones—the babe you really
wanted to get next to—so, being horny and all, you figured
you'd try the pretty sister who you heard was an easy mark.
Are we on the same page, or did I misunderstand you?"

"We're on the same page," Redfield murmured.

"Okay, just so I'm clear."

"Look, it's not something I'm proud of, but, man to man—"

"Do not go there, brother. A—that's my cousin. B—being a man does not give you the right to play Chinese checkers with these women—guys like you give us all a bad name. C—Victoria Jones is a good friend of a friend, and I'd hate to see her connected to a sorry sack of sh—"

"Hold it! I apologize for your cousin, man. I can't take that back. That was how I was rolling at the time, and what's done is done. But I didn't screw her, although the opportunity did present itself. We chatted a couple of times on the phone, and I was going to hook up with her, but changed my mind."

"Why? The elixir wore off?"

"Because of Victoria Jones."

"You had this overnight transformation, right? Give me a break."

"Unless you have ever gotten to know a woman like her, or ever clicked with somebody so perfectly, then you wouldn't believe me. But on this one you have to trust me. I met Cecilia before I had a chance to get to talk—just talk—to Victoria, and get into her as a person. After that, I tore up Cecilia's number. I'm not even thinking about going anywhere else to jeopardize what I have with Victoria."

While Redfield's argument seemed like a plausible alibi, parts of what he'd said disturbed him. Too much of it was familiar to the way he used to roll . . . too much of it reminded him of his own twenty-four-hour transformation.

Shaking it off, he pressed the knife of truth closer to the attorney's jugular. After all, the man had offended his cousin's honor, what little of it she had left; had pushed up on a friend of Nicole's; and another friend of Nicole's, Delores, had asked him to check out Redfield's intentions.

"I suppose none of this honorable passion you suddenly feel for Victoria Jones has anything to do with wanting to expand her salon, steal her staff, wrest her elixir from her, and bottle it yourself after the results of the ingredients come back from the lab, push up on her designer contact, and have the entire operation, including the love adviser, for yourself . . . chivalry not being dead, and whatnot."

"I suggest you call your cousin," Redfield shot back, "find out what she needs help with, and look in the yellow pages for an attorney that specializes in EEOC matters, then tell her to lose my home number."

"Yeah, I'll do that."

"And just for the record, since I assume we'll be bumping into each other in polite company—I'm not trying to steal anything from Victoria Jones. There's nothing to steal—her ex-husband already did that to her a long time ago. The salon has been financially hemorrhaging for years, she's been drowning in taxes because she didn't know how to shelter her income properly, and she was bent on conspicuous spending to prove to the world that what he did to her didn't break her heart. Look at the salon books, and you'll know I'm telling you the truth—the other set, not the set she shows the tax man. I'm trying to bail her out because I love her, man. Where I come from, that's what you do for the woman you love—you don't just let her drown in her own blood!"

Adam looked at the telephone receiver when a hard click shot through his eardrum. "Too true," he murmured. "Can't judge a book . . ."

Deep.

The disturbing call made him reach in his desk drawer for his pager. Sure enough, there were five calls from Cecilia's home number. Raw nerves had him on his feet as he returned her calls while pacing. The one night—the one single night that he'd tried to turn off the world, and all hell had broken loose! Where was she? When the answering machine came on, he left a brief but direct message: "It's me. Call me ASAP. I'll be in Philly within the hour."

Adam paced out of the study and down the hall. *If this don't beat all, first thing on a Sunday morning!*

Chapter 18

After five minutes of pounding on the knocker and ringing the bell incessantly, Adam pulled out his spare set of keys, opened Cecilia's town house door, and looked around.

"Yo, Ceil, what's up! It's me." Then he waited. The last thing he wanted to witness was his baby cousin in the act.

"Hold your horses, hold your horses," she hollered from her bedroom. "I thought I told you to call first before you put a key in my door!"

Adam counted to ten before he replied.

"I did. Several times. Then I rang and knocked and rang and knocked, and I was hoping that I didn't come in here and stumble over a body," he said evenly as she sashayed into the living room where he stood.

"I was getting my beauty rest. I was up late last night."

He was so angry that he could only stare at her for a moment, and he thrust his hands into the pockets of his leather bomber to keep them from finding their way around her neck.

"Want a drink?" she asked calmly as she turned on her heel and headed for the kitchen.

"It's eleven-thirty on a Sunday morning," he called after her as he followed her down the long hallway to her kitchen.

"And?" She'd spun to face him and put her hands on her hips, not appearing to mind that her red silk robe was giving him more of her to view than a cousin needed to see.

"I've got Bloody Mary mix and vodka, if you're a purist about morning," she said with a sly smile when he didn't answer her immediately.

"I'll pass."

"Coffee?"

"I'll pass."

"Then I take it since you're here looking madder than a wet hen, it's probably to fuss at me again about something?" She put a long red talon to her lips, made a little clicking sound, then ran her fingers through her tousled, sandy-brown hair. "Not in the talkative mood." She sighed as she shook her head. "Well, let me pour myself a drink and sit the hell down to be read at my own kitchen table."

From his position in the doorway, Adam watched her saunter over to the cabinets and pull out a bottle of bourbon, then reach for a tumbler. Taking her time to move to the table, she set down the glass and the bottle hard, poured liquor to the top of the glass, sat down with attitude and took a deep swig, then smiled. "Okay, shoot."

For a moment, all he could do was stare at the beautiful but hardened green eyes that met his. Sadness took the edge off his anger, as he looked at her café-au-lait complexion that was now becoming sallow, remembering when it used to glow bronze in the bayou sun. This was a woman who could have had any brother she wanted jumping through hoops of fire. What in God's name had happened to the little girl with pigtails whom he'd doted on?

"Sit down, sit down and be pleasant this morning, A.B.," she purred. "Now what did cousin Ceil do that was so bad this time?"

"Do you have company back there?"

"Oh, no, puhleeze, I know you are not going to try to get in a lady's business with a morning bed-check call? I'm not in the army and don't have to—"

"Cecilia, stop. Do you have company?"

"Sit down."

"I prefer to stand. I need to talk to you about business that nobody else needs to hear. I don't care if you have company or not, but I do care that your private business might be—"

"You hit the jackpot. I'm alone. Can't you tell?" She raised her glass and took another swig.

Adam removed his hands from his pockets and folded his arms over his chest.

"I got a disturbing phone call this morning."

"Do tell."

"Very disturbing, so stop being cute."

Cecilia put her hand on her exposed cleavage in mock dismay, and batted her eyes, then picked up her drink again. But it was in the way she glared at him over the rim of the glass that disturbed him the most.

"Think you ought to slow down so we can have a productive conversation?"

"Just tryin' to bite the snake that bit me last night. One little ol' drink won't keep me from—"

"Dammit, Cecilia, I'm not playin'."

"Oooo, my, my, my, my my, my, my! Somebody is testy. What's the matter, big cuzin," she drawled, "ain't been laid in a while?"

"You are testing my patience, Cecilia. Do not test me or—"

"Or what? You won't play on the swings with me?"

"Or I will drop this freakin' case like a hot potato, and from what I've gathered, you might need a little help keeping a guy with a baseball bat from trashing your car, or your face."

"Okay." She sighed, allowing her shoulders to drop, and she sat back in her chair, put down her drink, found a pack of cigarettes on the table, and lit one.

When she motioned for him to share one, he declined, but she'd awakened the nicotine jones, and he reached for a licorice stick in his jacket breast pocket instead.

"Can't shake the oral fixation, huh?"

He didn't answer her as the poor substitute for the smoke he craved sent the familiar flavor of his abstinence through his mouth. But the brief thought danced through his mind that he hadn't reached for a stick the entire evening he'd been with Nicole—then he banished it.

"Tough guy through and through. Cold turkey on smoking two packs a day, cold turkey on my best girlfriend in the world, Carole, cold turkey on women, cold turkey on Louisiana, cold turkey on all that cold cash you coulda been setting your family up with—but *nooooo*, you got principles."

"It's a way of life. You might try it sometime. And I told you not to mention Carole again to me, ever."

"Touché!"

"We're not here to talk about me. We are here to talk about why a prominent attorney called me about you—at ten o'clock this morning, and why said attorney would know you and I are cousins—or, better yet, why he had to be the one to tell me that you are moonlighting under your former married name. Let's start there."

"Well, now I have to arrange all of these questions in

logical order, since you're firing them at me so fast and blowing your load here in broad daylight, suga. How am I supposed—''

"Stop jacking with me, Ceil!"

"Okay, all right, for goodness' sake!" She let her head hang back and shook her shoulder-length tresses as she dragged her fingernails through them, cigarette still between her fingers as she did so. The action caused her robe to gap even more to expose her nudity under it.

"Sit up, fix your robe, and talk to me."

"I'm not shy," she murmured as she honored his request and closed the front of it. "Ain't nothin' you haven't seen before."

He would not be baited into a diversionary argument, nor embarrassed about the way they used to skinny-dip before she grew breasts.

"All right, fine. But you need to put all of these circumstantial coincidences into proper context, A.B."

"Talk to me, Cecilia—without another sip of bourbon."

She let out a long sigh and took a drag from the cigarette that he'd worried might torch her hair when she'd raked her fingers through it. She'd missed her calling. She should have been an actress.

"It's all very simple," she purred in a blasé tone.

"Talk to me, then. Make me understand how simple it is."

"I ran up a few credit cards a few weeks ago and needed to get the bill down before Mardi Gras . . . you do remember Mardi Gras, don't you? Some of us still go back home for various holidays."

"Skip the editorial commentary and stick to the facts. Okay, you had bills. What's new?"

"Well, since you declared a moratorium on helping damsels in distress—even family, blood—"

"Don't go there. What I told you was that I wasn't your sugar daddy, and that I would help you with things that made sense, or real emergencies, but I was not the one to be buying you diamonds and furs, so—"

"Okay, okay, that's old news. Sorry."

"Fast-forward to the part about this new job using an old name."

"So, with all the pressures of having to make ends meet, I did the only thing I could do, and that was get a clerical job at some stupid company at night. Big deal, nothing spectacular about it. And it had to be part-time, a coupla nights a week, so that it didn't interfere with my day job at the hotel. And I used an old name, that I still have ID for . . . because, frankly, I was embarrassed to have to stoop so low, and I do have a higher-profile *career* in sales and marketing at the hotel to keep up appearances for. Is that all right with you?"

He rubbed his chin and moved the stick to the other side of his mouth. "Why didn't you tell me about the gig, Ceil?"

"Because I knew we'd have this discussion about how Cecilia couldn't budget, Cecilia was a spendthrift, et cetera, et cetera, et cetera, and frankly, darlin', I didn't want to hear it."

"All right," he said, letting his breath out hard. "What next?"

"So I start this job, like I do everything else, with only the best of intentions. And my manager is a cute guy, but not my type—broke—so I'm nice to him, but he can't do nothin' for Ms. C. I'm cordial, and professional, and amicable, but the guy just won't take no for an answer. So I tell him, after enough is enough, that, well, enough is enough— buzz off, sweetie. He takes offense and gets in a bit of a snit, but since we do have to work together, he just gives me the shitty tasks and the evil eye, nothing spectacular, like I said.''

''And you didn't think any of this information might be helpful to me in finding out who might have thrown chicken guts on your steps, or who might have bashed in your car windows?''

Cecilia laughed and took a sip of bourbon. ''Pardon me, but I'm parched.''

''Ceil . . .''

''Oh, A.B., I didn't think anything of it at the time; he's such a wimp, and I never slept with the man, much less gave him a whiff. So, honey, I don't think he's the one behind all of this, honestly. And believe me when I say I would not stick around at a pitiful-paying little job like that if I thought I was being stalked by a lunatic. Now, a few wives might even shoot me if they ever found out what their husbands could *really* do in bed . . . that's why I went to the psychic. But she was no help. All she would tell me was some moralistic hoo-ha—''

''Look,'' he said, cutting her off as he grew agitated about any negative reference to Nicole, ''when I'm working on a case, and I ask a client about all the possible suspects, you let me be the judge as to who might or might not be important for me to check out. Got it? Are we clear from this point forward?''

''Aye-aye, Captain,'' she replied with a smirk.

''All right, granted,'' he shot back, trying to recapture his cool. ''I can understand why you took the job and didn't feel it important to tell me, twisted as your logic may be. I can understand why you wouldn't put this guy at the top of the suspect list. But if he was so harmless, then why did you call Byron Redfield all hysterical and crying?''

It was just a flicker of astonishment before her smile tried to mask it, but he'd seen it and imprinted it on his brain.

They'd known each other way too long for him to have missed it.

"Byron called you and told you I was hysterical?"

"Yeah, he did."

She laughed a hollow laugh and took another swig of her drink, then a heavy drag from her cigarette, allowing the smoke to slowly filter out of her lungs through her nose.

"That bastard has some nerve."

Adam just stared at his cousin. He'd heard a lot worse coming out of a woman's mouth, but the tone was too visceral to stomach on a Sunday morning. For a moment it flashed him back to his almost-fiancée, Carole. Sitting in that chair, Cecilia reminded him too much of his ex. They had the same tall, voluptuous body, same complexion . . . only Carole had auburn hair and steely gray eyes.

"I take it that's not how it went?" He waited. Something was not right.

"Let me tell you about your new friend, Byron Redfield, A.B. He is a flat-out liar and a cheater, too. He's running with that tired old broad who runs a tacky, wanna-be posh beauty salon . . . what's her name, Victoria something-or-other common . . . Jones. They can't make their money on doing hair and nails, obviously, so she's running psychic readings through there with some phony love elixirs to boost sales. I know all about it. All of 'em are scam artists, through and through."

Garnering patience, Adam took his time to choose his words. "You called Byron to help you—who by the way is not my friend, I know him on professional terms—and what, in your words, happened?"

"Am I on trial because I called a man I used to date for a little ol' favor, and he had another woman in his bed who freaked out and gave him what-for? Now, that was *not* my fault. *I am the victim.* Let's be clear on that, since we are setting the record on the straight and narrow.''

He didn't like the sound of it, but given Cecilia's track record, it made sense. It almost made too much sense. Something about it was too clean.

''How did he know we were related? Better yet, why did he know, and what made him think calling me would help the situation?''

''All of you men are so transparent, and blind at the same time. You can't see something when it's as plain as the nose on your face.''

''Call me stupid. Help me understand.''

''Don't you get it?'' Cecilia let out a dramatic sigh and looked at him with pity in her eyes. ''During pillow talk— I know it's been a long time since you've done that, but try to visualize the concept—Byron and I discussed a lot of things. I might have mentioned that my cousin was a PI, braggin' on you, since I really do love you, A.B., as much as I break your balls and tease you all the time, but I do love my big cousin. All the family has always been proud of you. And here I am in bed with this hotshot attorney. So sure, I might have put a little yeast in my description of my family tree to get him to like me more. Now, if that's a crime, plenty of women will go to jail. However, let's think this out logically.''

Now *she* was going to talk to *him* about logic? Adam sighed, but relaxed and leaned against the door frame. What in the world had his mother and his aunt gotten him into? ''Shoot.''

''I'm having a minor problem on the job, nothing earth-shattering, but annoying, right?''

''Right.'' He hated the way she ticked off her point using her fingers with a cigarette butt dangling between them. Carole used to do that.

"Now, who would you tell about your workday? Your big cousin who is high-strung, sees the bogeyman everywhere, and carries a firearm, or a cool attorney who has very powerful letterhead that can back up even the most hard-edged CEOs with a simple little missive?"

"You'd call the attorney," Adam admitted with a sigh.

"Right, honey. So that's what I did . . . but wasn't I the one so surprised when that banshee answered my man's telephone. She started screamin' and yellin', and callin' me all sorts of names, and wouldn't even put Byron on the phone. So, sure, I called back, he picked up, and I admit I was hurt, so a few tears fell, and I called you because I was pissed-off royal and needed a man's opinion on all of this . . . but do I look hysterical to you—or more wrung-out?"

She raised her glass to him in a lonely toast, and took a swallow. "I am not an alcoholic, but after a morning like this, who wouldn't turn off the ringers, climb back in bed, and have a bourbon, and be in a bit of a funk when someone bursts in her door with a list of accusations—based on the man who'd just broken her heart?"

Confusion tore at his mind as two big tears welled up in Cecilia's striking green eyes and glittered a moment before they streaked her face.

"Baby . . . don't cry. I'm sorry."

"Oh, A.B.," she wailed. "I was so humiliated by both of them. Then he has the absolute gall and audacity to bring my family into this and to try to turn you against me? Of course he called you! After I had spoken so highly of you, and told him all about your moral fiber, he *knew* you were the only one who'd be able to talk some sense into me and keep me from going over there to kick his pompous ass, and keep me from dragging that heifer out of his house by her half-bald, nappy head! Oh! The nerve of him. Adam

Bastille, trust me, Byron Redfield is no gentleman, and is no friend. But thank God that blood is thicker than mud!''

"Okay," Adam said in a gentler tone. "Makes sense. I apologize and fall on my sword. But that still leaves somebody out there who vandalized your property, and I don't like it."

"Nor do I." She sighed, wiping her eyes.

"I think I still might pay this guy on your job a visit."

"No, no, no," she cautioned. "Please don't do that. There has already been enough drama, and I've been humiliated enough. I just want this part of my life to go away forever. Just let it rest. It's not that big a deal, and it's not worth it."

"What's his name?"

"It's not important. A.B. Haven't I been through enough turmoil for one day without having to also lose a second job I need? Just let that silly man alone, and I'll deal with him the old-fashioned, dignified way. I'll tell him I'll sue him if he doesn't stop harassing me. He's married, he'll get over it, and he *will* leave me be. If necessary, I will tell him I'll call his wife. That always puts a man who won't take no for an answer in check. I've got this one covered."

"All right, Ceil. I'll let it rest. You go back to bed, put the phone on the hook, and try to lie low for a little while, okay? Can you do that for me?"

"Yeah." She sniffed. "Thanks for coming to check on me."

"No problem," he murmured; then he went to her, gave her a peck on her forehead, then paced through her sumptuously appointed town house toward the door. The high-maintenance requirements of his cousin, and her lifestyle, shadowed him as he passed each high-definition art-clad room. Reminders of Carole shadowed him—haunted him.

He needed air. Fresh air. *Let it rest. Like hell.* None of this felt right, all because it made too much sense.

He let himself out of what felt like a gilded tomb and descended the front steps two at a time. This was why he hated the business. Always finding out that everybody lied. Everybody had a scam. Innocence was such a rare and precious commodity. Adam wiped the imaginary film of emotional grime from his face, grabbed his cell phone, and began dialing as he drove.

"Hello, Pep Boys. Yeah. I wanna order four radials—and have them installed when the lady gets there."

Chapter 19

When the doorbell sounded, Nicole raced for it and hit the intercom so hard she almost knocked it from the wall. What was wrong with her? Adam Bastille wouldn't necessarily be coming over again, and unannounced like that, so soon. But it was too late. Hope had shot her across the room like a rocket.

Michelle smirked as Nicole glanced back at her and Lydia to see who was listening as she depressed the talk button. In that moment she vowed to remind Gail never to fuss about a teenager rushing for the telephone or any other communication device to the outside world again. "Hello," she said as pleasantly as possible.

"Nikki, buzz me up," Gail shouted. "Hurry up."

Nicole pressed the buzzer and stared back at the children, who were now ignoring the television.

"I thought Mom was going home to change right after

eight-o'clock service, then would be going on her brunch date?''

"She is, Michelle," Nicole responded coolly. "She probably just wanted to pop by because she needed a certain color makeup or something. Mind your beeswax. Both of you are too young to be in the Kool-Aid when you don't know the flava.''

The girls giggled as Nicole rushed to the door and opened it before Gail could begin pounding.

"In the bedroom," Gail commanded to Nicole, then spun on the kids before they could get up from the sofa. "I need some lipstick—stay on the sofa and do not move until we come out of the bedroom!''

This had to be deep. This was conference-level urgent. Nicole paced behind her girlfriend into the bedroom. She didn't say a word as Gail slung her by her arm farther into it, slammed the door, and hooked the latch.

"What's going on?" Nicole whispered harshly as she followed Gail's pacing. "You're supposed to be going home to clean the house, change your clothes after eight-o'clock service, then go to brunch and ring twice if you want me to keep Michelle here overnight.''

"I know, I know, I know," Gail whispered through her teeth. "But I *cannot* do it.''

"Do what?" Nicole grabbed her friend by the arm to keep her from wringing her hands. "Stop, girl, you are making me dizzy!''

"I can't do it, I can't do it. Oh, Lord, what are we going to do?''

"Can't do what?''

"Go on this date, or make the batches anymore.''

"Okay. We're out of the love elixir business, then, but the date—''

"You don't understand. It's what's keeping the business going, no offense to your advice sessions."

"No offense taken, Gail, but slow down. You are now a professional caterer with a good client base. You don't need potions—"

"There was something in it that I can't get my hands on anymore."

Nicole just stared at her friend. "Tell me, Gail," she said with a quiet but serious tone. "Tell me what's in what we've given to half of Philadelphia's judges and attorneys and doctors." She could feel her voice climb its way up her throat as her girlfriend's eyes filled with tears. "Tell me on a Sunday morning that you haven't done something completely—"

"It's not drugs, but it is a drug, sorta," Gail whispered through her teeth. "Calm down."

"What!" Nicole felt her body sway as her ears rang from the sonic blast of her own voice.

"Shush!" Gail hissed. "You'll frighten the kids."

"I have to sit down," Nicole muttered as she crept to the side of the bed, clutched her stomach, and pulled the wastepaper basket in front of her. "I'm going to be ill. We're going to jail; I am dating a detective . . . ." She dry-heaved twice and held her hand over her mouth. When the telephone sounded, tears formed in her eyes and fell.

"Mother of God, what have you done? It's the police!"

"Want me to get the phone, Aunt Nikki?" Michelle was yelling from the next room, but Nicole could only wave her hand to try to stop her as she tried to squeak no, then failed.

"Chile, pick up the telephone and tell whoever it is that Aunt Nikki doesn't feel good, or has cramps, or whatever, and can't talk to them right now. Pick it up, before it stops ringing!"

"Gail," Nicole repeated as the telephone ceased, sending

an ice pick through her skull. She could feel her voice begin at the low end of the scale in a very calm, soft tone and build to a screaming crescendo of high-pitched screeches. "What is in the freakin' potion?"

"I don't know, exactly," Gail said in a very calm voice as she sat beside Nicole.

"Tell me how you make this stuff and what you drop in your pots that me and my baby eat from."

"Okay," Gail whispered, "here's what happened. I make my greens and whatnot, like most everybody does. I make mine better, but why quibble. The recipe is fairly standard in our community."

"Gail Jackson, heaven help me—"

"All right. I'll get to the point. Well, for the last ten years, maybe fifteen . . . Well, I don't know when Auntie Joleen down South started consulting with Auntie Maybell up North, but . . . no wait, wait . . . it was after my mother died. That's right. Aunt May said she would look out for Bethann's baby, and I was indeed Bethann's baby."

"Gail Jackson, so help me . . ." Nicole allowed her head to find her hands as she rocked on the bed where she sat.

"Aunt Nikkaaaay," Michelle screeched through the door, "I told Mr. Adam that you had cramps like Ma tol' me to— he said he was sorry to hear you wasn't feeling well, but he left you some tires over at Pep Boys, when you feelin' better, and said the man over there will install 'em—he said to call him 'bout salon bizness when you up to it. Okaaay?"

"Thanks, chile, now git away from da door!" Gail smoothed the front of her lilac suede suit and took off her wide-brim white felt hat, then set it very carefully to the side of her on the bed. "Now, we was saying?"

"Oh, Lord have mercy . . ." Nicole groaned. "That child did not tell the man I had cramps, he did not buy me tires, and he does not want to know *anything* about the salon, does he, Gail Jackson?" Again the question had begun as a low hiss in Nicole's throat, only to rise and gain force like a hurricane by the time the last of it was said.

"It's not that bad," Gail soothed. "He's a full-grown man, and knows women get their monthly, so he won't pester you for a while, until all of this dies down. I think it was rather nice that he was concerned about your car, though; a lotta men—"

"Gail. The batches."

"Right. Well. Since I only had one baby, and the rest of my cousins have like anywhere between five to nine, my aunties thought I had female problems, see. Not physical female problems, but, you know, the other sort of problems." Gail looked down at her hands.

"They thought you were frigid?"

Gail only nodded.

"Oh, Lord . . ."

"I never thought it right to tell them that I wasn't giving my no-good husband none, or no other man for that matter, because he didn't treat me nice. My relatives were old-school, and woulda told me I was shunning my wifely duties. Then I only made matters worse by tellin' another lie to get out of the first one—well, not an outright lie, but sorta a lie by omission and implication. And they thought my no-good Luther Roy Jackson couldn't get his pole up to go fishin'— see, everybody wanted a boy so bad, although after Michelle, I was done making babies for L-Roy, but people thought that's what was wrong with him—he didn't get his boy.

"They also thought that some of it had to do with the move up here—the climate change musta done something to him. That is, till he made them three boys in the streets up here in Philly on me, but that's another whole tale. *However*, after they heard tell of what he done, they thought the roots worked, and sent me another bottle to get him to come back to me and tell the truth, then another to repair my broken heart when he didn't. I never used the stuff, just saved it away, not to hurt their feelings. I had all of these herbs in my closet, and—''

"Wait just one damned minute," Nicole whispered, hopping up from the bed as though she'd been burned. "You put an unknown herbal substance, an ingredient X, into the batches . . . stuff that you've had on your kitchen shelves for over a decade?"

"Yeah, kind of . . ."

"Either you did or you didn't, Gail. It's like being sorta pregnant."

"Okay," Gail whispered and looked down at her hands, "but I didn't know what else to do—we was desperate."

"You are a *registered nurse!*" Nicole was walking back and forth in front of the bed as she ticked off the charges. "One of those people in there could be taking nuclear medicine, chemotherapy, insulin . . . have pacemakers in their chests, especially these amorous men—girl!"

"Nobody died . . . and it works."

Nicole grabbed her hair with her hands and began walking in a circle. "Nobody died, she says, nobody died—yet!"

"That's why me and my aunt pray over it *real hard* that no harm comes to—''

"Gail, you have to call your aunts and find out exactly what's in it. Eye of newt, wing of country bat, toe of frog . . . toadstools, what the hell ever, we gotta know, and cannot, I repeat, *cannot,* distribute this stuff without going through the formal FDA approval—''

"Nobody knows what's in it . . . and there ain't no way to find out now."

Nicole stopped pacing and lowered her hands from her hair. "Why . . . not?" she asked in a very calm, quiet whisper. Perhaps too calm.

"Because old Miz Inez died about six years ago, and can't nobody make heads nor tails of the marking on her jugs. My aunt who's still in Macon is blind in one eye and can't see out the other, and my other aunt ain't doin' well enough to travel. But I did think of that when we first got started, more from the point of knowing we needed some more if this thing took off. So they called around to see if Miss Inez had some people, and spoke to another lady they said was in the know about all things mystical, Ms. Zelda in Louisiana—"

"What was her last name?" Nicole sat down slowly on the bed beside Gail.

"Wait, heard it around here recently—oh, Bastille. Zelda Bastille. She by any chance a relative of this new beau of yours? He's real sweet, but . . . Hope she ain't related to that Cecilia Bastille, 'cause, chile, now that one don't need to know how to root nobody!"

"I don't think so," Nicole said softly through the palm of her hand that was covering her mouth, as she shook her head no.

"You don't look good. You gettin' the flu? Maybe you should'nt have listened to me and wore those straps out in the cold."

"Uhmmm-uhmmm," Nicole mumbled from behind her hand, and she removed it slowly and took in a long, unsteady sip of air. "Tell me the rest of what you were saying, Gail."

"Well, nobody could figure out Miz Inez's recipes, and they didn't want to poison anybody. We couldn't find out exactly where she was from . . . the lady was older than dirt and had come to Macon by way of South Kakalacky, Geechie country, off them South Carolina islands . . . hear tell she mighta brought some mess over with her on a slave ship . . . but that can't be true; she was old, but ain't nobody that old. So that's why we used just a pinch, sparingly, and then we prayed real hard that whatever it was supposed to do would get done ... and boy, oh, boy ...

"But, like Jo Jo always says, Houston, we've got a problem."

"Do tell," Nicole said flatly, leaning forward on her crossed arms, which now rested on her thighs.

"Several, in fact. See, I'm down to my last batch, and Byron Redfield, that attorney who practically kidnapped our girlfriend, well, he took a vial to a lab for testing before he fully invests—"

"Why in God's name would Victoria allow him to do that?"

"She called me bright and early this morning, before I went to church. Was calling from the installed telephone in the man's bathroom—can you get to that?—said the house was off the hook, and she was talking to me while using the bidet, like rich people do, and—"

"Gail, the point!"

"She was happy ... the man was an animal, and she hadn't had none in years, and he was treatin' her nice, and he wanted to know what was in it—and hell, so did she at that point. Said it had her practically singing opera, the way the orgas—"

"Gail!"

"Well, she took some, too, and seems that since they left the party, the man hasn't let Victoria out of bed, not that she was complaining. And she signed some papers—"

"What papers?" Nicole had sprung up from the bed again and was hopping up and down.

"Papers that gave us all fifty-one percent ownership of this major club-restaurant-salon deal he and Victoria were negotiatin' in bed. He must have done it over the weekend, had the papers drawn up and the money wired .... She called to tell me that the man pledged a million dollars, I guess while he was coming, and—''

''Stop! She has to give it back. A million dollars—that has to mean federal.''

''Federal? Girl, what are you talking about?''

''Federal-level crime because the dollar value is so high. Fraud, extortion—''

''Oh.''

''Yeah, oh, Gail! Get rid of it.''

''I don't have any more; I'm down to a few vials.''

''Good. Then maybe we're okay, unless someone else saved one from before.'' Nicole's gaze shot around the room as though she expected federal agents to burst through the door at any moment.

''Well, that last batch *was* sorta strong, only 'cause I was rushin'. I told Jo Jo don't be rushin' me while I was cookin'—and so I just threw a little of everything in all the batches and didn't measure it out . . . everybody got a little of everything, so people was telling truths that maybe was best kept to themselves and left untold, and people was connecting . . . well. I can't duplicate the strength of what Byron Redfield took to the lab. From now on it will be real placebo. Gail Jackson's Curious Southern Cuisine is no more. Sort of a shame, too, in a way, since we've got a reputation to uphold, and I'm out of batch helper.''

Nicole found herself on the floor on her knees, tears streaming down her face. ''Help me, Father God, for I have sinned; please be merciful in your wrath against the wicked—''

''Girl, God is *not* mad. This is not a curse—this is a blessing. We didn't ask that man for anything, and we have plenty of witnesses to tell that we never asked for a nickel from him—he was the one sweatin' us . . . well, we did ask him for twenty-five dollars the first time around, but he was the one sayin' to sell the vials at twenty bucks a pop. And if givin' up a little to have a rich man invest in your business is extortion, then half the rich chicks, and a lotta the poor ones too, will have to do time. So nothin' we did will send us to jail, or bring down the wrath. It's just possibly the year of Jubilee. Me, you, Delores, and Jo Jo get ten percent, and Miss Vic gets a little somethin'-somethin' extra—since she did all the work and it was her salon.''

"I'm not hearing this," Nicole murmured as she shut her eyes and covered her ears while still on her knees.

"But we do have one or two other little problems."

"There's more?" Nicole opened her eyes but stayed on her knees, too weak to move.

"Seems that the way my eldest aunt says it ultimately works is, it's all tied to me, since it was, by design, for me."

"Go on," Nicole whispered, holding her head but keeping her line of vision trained on Gail.

"See, whatever this stuff is, it was made with a lot of love and a lot of prayer. My folks wanted me to be happy, to have a person be honest and tell the truth, and me to do the same, and they wanted me to be cherished and cared for—with a lot of babies to fill up our home with joy."

"What's the problem—besides the fact that you put an unknown substance, possibly a deadly, toxic root, into something people ingest, and an attorney has taken it to a lab, and signed over a substantial portion of his assets . . . while being worked down to a nub in his own home in his own bed? Sexual extortion, how about that for a new crime . . . so what little detail did I miss in all of this? Oh, we didn't have a license to distribute this stuff."

"It gets you horny, like a mug, but it also gets you pregnant."

"Dear God in heaven . . ."

"Now don't worry, don't panic. Miss Vic has her tubes tied. I don't think it can—"

"But do you know how many people took this?"

"Yeah. That's one little problem. It sorta brings on immediate ovulation, they say, no matter where you are in your cycle . . . puts you in heat, can't think of any nicer way to say it right now, 'cause I'm a little flustered. And it's supposed to triple a man's sperm count, so he ain't shooting no blanks, and it keeps folks who took it in the mood until it wears off."

"How long till it wears off?"

"Nobody but Miz Inez could tell you that, and she's long dead. And I never used any of it until recently, and mine ain't wore off yet, so . . ."

Nicole allowed her body to slowly ease back until she was sitting on her heels. If she had done what she was going to do last night . . . And Adam had correctly said, *This is how babies are made . . . . Dear Lord.*

"That's why we all come in here so hot and bothered, and can't shake it, Nikki."

"You said it was tied to you, though?" Nicole stared at her friend, who'd fallen silent.

"Seems as though once I find true happiness and connect with my true love, then . . . I would just hate to see all them happy people fall back to where they was before we started making the elixir. Didn't it feel good to make people happy the way we did for those three times we had the events in the salon, and didn't you really feel like Cinderella when that man looked at you the way he did?"

"Yeah," Nicole whispered, reaching for her friend's hands and clasping them with her own. "But you really like the deacon, don't you?"

"Yeah," Gail whispered, tears now staining her face.

"And you know that you won't be coming home tonight,

don't you?'' Nicole whispered the question softly and rose
to sit by Gail and put her arm over her friend's shoulder.
''Oh, honey. The herbs . . . well, like you said, nobody died,
right? We were lucky—no, blessed. But you're scared of
how strong these brand-new feelings are, aren't you?''

Gail only nodded and sniffed back the tears as she wiped
her face.

''Don't be afraid of that part of the miracle in all this
crazy mess. We might never feel like this for the rest of our
lives, all giggly and excited and treated so wonderfully,
awesomely good.'' Nicole wasn't sure if she was talking to
Gail or talking to herself. But a quiet calm came over her
as she said the words that felt so true in her heart.

''I know. . . .''

''And you know that there are some things in the back-
woods bush that modern medicine still can't define, not the
way them old dolls from home concoct it. If it's natural,
it'll pass the labs, and they won't be able to break the
code on the recipe for another hundred years—technology
notwithstanding.''

The comment made Gail chuckle and look up for the first
time since she'd sat down.

''And you can't break God's bonds of love once they've
been forged . . . those batches were prayed over real hard,
like you said. If people found each other, hooked up, told
each other the true desires of their hearts—because you and
your aunts were praying for a miracle from a good place in
your spirits—then, girl, get out of God's way. What do the
old ladies say?''

''Let go and let God.''

''Right.''

''So if this business partnership dissolves, and we're back
to doing hair, catering church affairs, and doing things the

old-fashioned way, we'll survive. Our friendship won't dissolve."

Gail gave her a big hug, and looked at her with a gentle expression. "I knew I wasn't going to make it past today ... not with the way this man makes me feel. And I didn't want to blow it for you, or Victoria, or Delores ... you all were so happy, all at the same time, for the first time since I've known y'all. You found Mr. Right, and Delores has been underground with a guy in the film industry and can't be found. Victoria is in seventh heaven. And Jo Jo was just beaming with pride, and felt like a part of something miraculous, a family, for the first time in his life. I didn't want one night to take that away from the people I love."

"You won't, sweetie," Nicole murmured, rocking her friend a bit as Gail's head found her shoulder. "You fix your face, clean your house, make yourself pretty. I'll watch the girls, and you down the last of the batch with your new man and have a spectacular night ... and call me in the morning. I love you, honey, with your old crazy self. Just the scoop, and all the scoop, so help you God."

Chapter 20

Nicole kissed her girlfriend Gail good-bye as she shut and locked the door. She glimpsed the telephone, picked it up, and carried it toward the bedroom, issuing a smile to Michelle, who returned an even broader smile of her own as Nicole slipped into the bedroom. Although it was her intention to call Adam to gracefully decline the expensive gift of tires for her car, suddenly the urge to call her mother first was stronger. All she could do was hope as she dialed Florida that her mom had gone to early service and would be home.

"Hi, sweet pea," her mother said as she picked up the telephone on the first ring and didn't wait for Nicole to announce herself. "I went to early service and rushed home, because I knew you was gonna call me today. Had me a feelin'."

Nicole laughed and cradled the telephone closer to her

ear. "How do you always know it's me before I even say anything?"

"Because you my chile. Of course I'd know," he mother said with a warm chuckle. "Sooo . . . how is life treating you in the big city, and how's my grandbaby?"

"Oh, just fine, nothin' special," Nicole hedged, simply enjoying the sound of her mother's voice. "Lydia's growing like a weed and getting just as fresh. How's Daddy, and everybody down there?"

"Same old same old," her mother replied pleasantly. "You know your father. Always fussin' and pesterin' me about this or that—but that means he's all right. Love that old buzzard, even though he does get on my nerves. But all in all, no aches, pains, no complaints. So how are you?"

Nicole hesitated, then sighed. "Fine . . . just wanted to hear your voice."

"Ah . . . that good, huh?"

"I lost my job, Mom—but I'm going out to get a Sunday paper later on and will find another one. I don't want to worry you, though. I'm fine."

"Well, I'm glad you lost it, truth be told. That job was too stressful on you, and it was just puttin' distance between you, my granchile, and your gift."

"I don't have a special gift, Mom. That's just it." Nicole chuckled sadly. "And I needed that job to—"

"First of all, I know you are not on this telephone on a Sunday afternoon telling me that there's nothing special about you, honey-bird. I am not hearing that nonsense from you today. And secondly, you *are* blessed. Been blessed and prayed over hard since the day you was born and became my gift."

Her mother's fussing was just what Nicole had called to hear. That special tone of indignation at her, but in defense of her. It was soul-strengthening somehow, and the conviction in her mother's voice summoned courage in her cellular memory that hailed back to generations of women who had gone before her.

"Mom, I have been drifting from pillar to post, and I'm not sure of what this special talent is. Maybe if I knew, I'd be able to—"

"But you do know," her mother cut in, her voice gentle but firm. "You have a gift to put pen to paper, and to tell wonderful stories that make people feel good. But you have to trust in the Lord to make a way."

"I haven't been able to support myself and Lydia with this gift, and because of that, I've had to take a lot of different jobs, none of which I particularly fit—"

"Stories," her mother cut her off again with a chuckle. "All good storytellers must take the road less traveled, or otherwise what they have to say would be kinda ordinary, wouldn't it? The disciples traveled all over and told the most wondrous true story ever told, didn't they?"

The comment and mother-logic made Nicole chuckle. "Mom, why is it that whatever I tell you, you have a rebuttal? You just won't give up, will you?"

"No, and that's because you're my child. Did you give up on Lydia when she was learning how to walk, and she stumbled and would plop down and cry . . . or did you help her up, kiss her boo-boos, and make that child learn how to stand and run on her own?"

The statement was so true, yet so profound, that Nicole was temporarily rendered speechless.

"You didn't want to try teaching?"

"No." Nicole sighed. "I didn't know if I could deal with the state of the schools up here, and really didn't know if I had anything in particular to teach a young person—plus, by the time I got my residency, things were bad . . . I was in the middle of the divorce."

"That's ancient history," her mother said with a sigh of her own. "Let go and let God. Well, maybe formal teaching isn't a particular path, but a student will turn up who's meant for you."

"Yeah, Mom, maybe you're right."

Again, silence hung between them like a comfortable blanket.

"Everything else okay, baby? You sound so blue . . . is it sunny up there, or all cloudy and rainy?"

Nicole smiled as she glanced toward the window. Why did her mother always inquire about the weather just before she was going to ask her about who she might be dating? "It's beautiful outside today. Cold, but sunny and just pretty."

"Now that's a good sign, and something to lift your spirits."

Nicole giggled. "Yes, Mom. That's why I'm going to walk to get a paper."

"Well?"

"Well what, Mom?"

"Anybody special to tell me about . . . maybe to bring home for the holidays? Easter is coming."

Nicole laughed hard and fell back on the pillows on the bed. "Mom!"

"Oh, don't 'Mom,' me. Tell me . . . ."

"Okay . . . but don't get your hopes up. I met a nice man recently, and he seems to be a good person. Nothing special has gone on, and we've only gone out once."

"Where did you go? I mean, where did this not-so-special nice man take you?"

"He cooked dinner for me—"

"That's serious!"

"Mom, we are in the new millennium and—"

"Child of mine, things ain't changed since Adam and

Eve, new millennium notwithstanding. I say he likes you more than you know.''

Again, loving silence passed between them as Nicole clutched the telephone and rolled over on her belly with a broad grin. "You think so?"

"You like him, don't you, sweet pea?"

"Yeah, I do, Mom . . . a lot."

"So where is Mr. Not-so-special from, and what's his name?"

"Adam Bastille, and he's from Louisiana."

"Oh, Lord, I knew you would hear my prayers, not in my time, but in yours!"

"Mom?"

"Me and Inez, God rest her soul in peace, been praying over you children since longer than I can remember."

Nicole sat up and blinked twice. "Mom, what are you talking about?"

"Now, I know you were disappointed by that no-good, Duane—and we all prayed and held out hope, but I told you before that I never liked him—and there may have been some that came along after him who were of that same ilk, but you can't lose faith, honey. Those others were just a test of faith, and to show you what you don't want, just so your eyes would be open to see what you do want."

"Mom, please, tell me what you're—"

"Inez Gibson—you remember Miz Inez, chile! Well, maybe you don't. She was an old woman when she left Florida and you was just a baby. Was from Barbados, I think—nobody can remember back that far . . . she was a hundred and two when she passed, God bless her. Good woman. Well, after her husband died, she set up housekeeping with her nephews in South Carolina, but eventually moved to Macon, Georgia, to live with her daughter . . .

poor girl, died young. Inez doted on everybody's children, even though.''

''Mom, get back to Miz Inez and Adam Bastille.'' Nicole could feel her heart trying to pound its way out of her chest.

''Well, he's her godson.''

''What!''

''Oh, baby—that boy has been under her protective prayer seal since he been born. She loved that boy, used to talk about him all the time. I've got baby pictures of him, pictures of him in uniform when he was in the service, in the police force, and—''

''Noooo . . .''

''Oh, yes. Miz Inez has godchildren all over. Has a god-daughter in Philly, I think she once told me. Poor thing had terrible trouble in her marriage, and me, Inez, and the child's mother, Miz Bethann, and her aunts, Joleen and Maybell . . . we lifted her up in prayer all the time. We put you on the prayer line too, along with that boy, especially during your troubles, and when that boy had all that trouble from them white folks down in Louisiana. Zelda was about to go out her nat'chel mind, she was.''

Nicole opened and closed her mouth like a fish. Her mother knew Adam's mother?

''Well, everything in God's own time. He's a nice young man, baby, and his people are good people. So when you goin' to cook for him?''

''Cook for him?'' Nicole was still trying to fathom what her mother had just told her, and answering a question was beyond her grasp at the moment.

''Cook for him, child. The way to a man's heart is through his stomach, they say. You just said he cooked for you, right?''

''Yeah, but—''

''Just be sure to use those good spices I always send you

from down home. Can't be fixin' a nice young man like that a bland meal. Make him some redfish, fried plantain, and rice and peas ... show off your skills, chile of mine; he's the marrying kind. That's the trouble with you young folk today: you eat in them restaurants all the time—they don't pray over their food, or cook it with love and—"

"Mom," Nicole rushed in, stopping her mother's words as a million questions and links too close to calculate formed in her brain, "what's in the spices you send me?"

"Oh, a little of this and that," her mother said with a warm chuckle. "I'll give you the recipe one day ... you'll need to have it, 'cause you have to teach Lydia how to simmer the pots right."

Nicole stood and slowly went to the window and peered down at her car, which was still parked down the block.

"He bought me snow tires, and I think it's too early to accept something like that from him. I don't want him to think I just like him for his money, because that's not the case."

"Just cook for him, baby. Return a kindness with a kindness. Be honest with him and nice to him. Don't let the past put a cloud over this sunshine moment. He's good people, and has a heart as big as can be. He knows you ain't that kind of girl."

Still stunned, Nicole returned to the side of the bed and sat slowly.

"Mom, how is it that you haven't left Florida in over thirty years, and you practically know, or know of, everybody I know?"

"I'm your mother, and the world ain't that big. Besides, I pray every day that God and His angels above will steer you only toward people who mean you well ... all you children is under the seal, baby. Gotta pray on your children, especially when they ain't under your roof no more."

ОKa

"I love you, too, Mom."

"I love you, sweet pea. Now let me talk to my granchile before I get off the telephone."

"Okay, Mom," Nicole whispered, too awestruck to argue with her mother's logic any longer. "You give Daddy and Grand a big kiss, and give the rest of the family my love."

"I will, suga. You have a nice day."

Dead end after dead end rubbed his nerves raw as he made one last pass by Nicole's house to see if her car had moved yet. It hadn't. He'd take up his complaint with Redfield on Monday, when he could catch him in his office and give him a piece of his mind, man to man, face-to-face, and eyeball-to-eyeball. He hated being played. But for now he'd have to go back to Jersey and work on the leads that he had on paper. Monday would also find him cruising by Cecilia's job—just to discreetly obtain the name of her boss. While Cecilia might be all right, and this might all be some lovers' triangle nonsense, someone had bashed in the girl's car windows, which was a much more serious message than chicken innards.

When his cell phone vibrated, Adam glimpsed the long-distance number as he pulled it off his belt and set it in the hands-free jack while he continued to drive. "Hi, Mom," he intoned pleasantly. "How's everything?"

"You don't even let a person say hello first, do you, boy?" she fussed, then laughed.

"Technology, Mom. We're in the age of technology."

"Technology, schmechology. How's my son?"

"Fine, Mom. Everything with you and Pop all right?"

"Your father and me are like two peas in a pod. Juney's doing well; so are Sissy and Beck."

"Good, good," he said by rote. "How was church?"

"Oh, minister outdid himself today," his mother replied, sounding happy. "When's the last time you been to church, by the way?"

"Aw, don't start, Mom." He chuckled good-naturedly, enjoying the sound of her voice as it filled the sedan while he drove.

"Well, that's not why I called, to get into how you need to repair your speakin' terms with the Lord, but you need to. He's been blessin' you."

"Yeah, he has," Adam said in a distant voice, suddenly becoming aware of the smile that would not leave his face. "That he has."

"I told you not to lose faith, didn't I, son? Even while you ain't been prayin', I been prayin' on your behalf."

"I 'ppreciate that, Mom; you know that."

"I love you, son."

"I love you, too, Momma."

"You comin' home for Easter? I know you hate Mardi Gras, with all them people actin' crazy and drinkin', but you comin' home after that for this Easter holiday?"

"I can't promise," he hedged. "I never know what my work is gonna entail, and I don't want to disappoint you if something comes up—"

"I dreamed of fish last night, and—"

"Mom, c'mon, now. You know I don't go in for dreams and—"

"That's 'cause you young and foolish, but you are a good man, Adam Bastille, despite your stubborn ways. So you comin' home for this holiday, and do I need to make up an extra room, is all I'm tryin' to ask?"

"An extra room?" Adam chuckled. She was at it again. Matchmaking. Didn't she know that after Carole, he wasn't rushing into anything? Well, maybe a little, but not headlong, like bringing somebody home to meet the family. Not just yet.

"What, you deaf, boy? An extra room ... the *guest room.*"

"No, Momma, there's nobody but me coming home, if I can make it."

"But I dreamed of fish, and Maisy Gordon told me you was sweet on her daughter—bought her some snow tires or somethin'. Now, Adam Bastille, that's a *nice* girl. You can't be—"

If he hadn't had both hands on the wheel, he would have driven off the road. "I'm the one who's the detective, Mom. How is it that you know more about my business living halfway across the country than I do?"

His mother's warm Southern laugh filled the cab of his sedan and poured over him like melted butter on hotcakes.

"Son, I'm your mother. It's my business to know. Been praying over you since you was born—you was my gift, not that I don't love all my children, but you're the one. My firstborn, chile. That's why I named you what I did— Adam, God's first man."

A loving silence fell between them, and Adam drove on feeling both confused and comforted by everything she'd said.

"Heard you cooked for her, too," his mother finally pressed with a chuckle.

"What else you hear?" His heart felt as though it were trying to crack a rib to get out of his chest.

"Oh, nothin' much, except that she was sighing on the phone and giggly when she called her momma about you this morning."

"How you know her Momma in Florida?"

"Oh, chile, we go way back. In fact, she met her husband in New Orleans, years ago. We was both helping out in the

USO, and she and I just clicked. When the servicemen all came in we was dolled up and they were so handsome. World War II . . . Met your daddy that same night—they moved to Florida before either of you was thought of. Oh, that Maisy is a peach. We stayed in touch over the years through letters, would pray for our kids together—nearly broke her heart when that girl married a man who hurt her. Anyway, I got Maisy's letters tucked in my Bible. I keep 'em there, and slip them into the pages of Psalms that will help whatever's worrying her.''

"But . . . but . . . I never heard you speak of her."

"Son, I have lots of friends in lots of places. You young folk are always moving so fast that when we mention a name or a person to you, it don't stick. The onlyest thing you remember are those people you see regular—like I know you remember your aunt Inez, your godmother, bless her soul in heaven."

"Yeah, yeah, I do . . . but . . ."

"Don't question every miracle, son. Now answer me this: when you cooked for her, did you use them good spices I sent you up?"

"Yeah, Momma, I always use your spices."

"Good."

"Why?"

"Jus' wanna make sure that you served her real Cajun cookin', not that old restaurant take-out mess you young people like to eat all the time."

He laughed and shook his head. "I cooked from scratch."

"Do tell . . . . She must be somethin' special."

"Yeah, kind of."

"See, that's your problem: you young folk don't commit. Either that nice girl is special or she's not."

"Okay, okay, Mom, she's special, sort of."

His mother's laughter connected to his own.

"When you seeing her again?"

"I don't know, Mom . . . Geez!"

"Oooooh, touchy subject. Well, I'll take that as a good sign. But son, throw away them licorice sticks I sent you . . . if you have to have 'em, go get them from the health-food store."

Adam laughed as he reached for one and put it in his mouth. "Why? I still have half a box of the ones you sent me. Besides, the last time I ran out, you had a hissy fit because I bought them from some street vendors up here—then you insisted that I get them from some friends of yours in South Carolina. She already knows I stopped smoking, and this is healthier and better for your teeth. So what's the big idea—"

"Young folk ask too many questions," his mother snapped. "The ones I sent you are the last of Inez's batch. She been gone for six years now, and everything of hers is runnin' out . . . have mercy. Glad you met that child before . . . well, before we ran out of sticks. But Inez must still have her hand on your shoulder from the other side, because when that nice girl of Maisy's is around, you don't need to be chewing on those sticks. You hear me, boy?"

Adam fell silent as he slowly removed the stick he'd been chewing on from his mouth and studied it. Curiosity and indignation became one as he turned the worn-down bark in his fingers.

"Momma, I'm going to ask you this in all seriousness," he said in a respectful but firm tone. "What did you and Aunt Inez doctor my licorice sticks with? Be honest on Sunday."

"Nothin' harmful," his mother assured him quickly, her voice strained and nervous-sounding all of a sudden.

"Momma, I'm asking you as your son to be honest with me about the hoodoo you and Aunt Inez—"

"It ain't hoodoo! We pray hard over all you children and ask God to give us guidance, wisdom, and clarity, and herbs from His good Earth for the medicinals to suit His purpose."

"Momma . . ."

"Oh, all right." She sighed. "A little salt peter, and nature killer . . . we didn't want you to get yourself tangled up with another Carole, and we'd been prayin—"

Adam dropped the stick and swerved to miss ramming into the back of the vehicle in front of him. "Momma, tell me how long you and Aunt—"

"See," she said in a demure tone, "we knew you'd act like that if you knew. Everything in its own time—"

"I cannot believe you would poison your own son! I cannot believe you and my godmother would collude against me like that and—"

"You're behind the wheel of a car, son. Slow down and calm yourself. Just throw away the sticks, now that you met a nice young lady, and let nature take its course."

"Momma . . . there are no words. . . ." He was popping, spitting, stuttering mad. His own mother?

"Next time you cook for her, use them spices I sent— and do bring her home for Easter. Well, I need to go now. I love you, honey. Gotta go put supper on for your dad."

Chapter 21

His palms were tingling as he reached for his cell phone and hit speed-dial. His own mother had inserted herself into his business and his most private affairs and even rooted him! Help him, Father, and now he was calling this woman whom his mother already knew? He hit the off button quickly and sat back. *No.* This was crazy. He was not going to be manipulated any longer. In fact, this ridiculous case had practically solved itself. He'd just pay Cecilia's boss a little visit on Monday, warn the guy never to go near or harass his cousin again, make him pay for her car, and then it would be over. His life would go back to normal.

When his phone immediately rang back he nearly jumped out of his skin. But when he looked at the number flashing on the panel of it, he took in a breath and picked it up so fast that he almost hit himself in the head with it.

"Hey, how you doin'?" Couldn't he have said something smoother than that to her? What was wrong with him?

"Hi, Adam," a soft voice murmured into his ear. "I just wanted to call to thank you for the tires . . . but it's such an expensive gift that I can't—"

"No, it's cool. I want you to have them," he replied so quickly that he cut off her words. "You and the baby can't be driving around like that in the wintertime; it ain't safe. You get them installed yet?"

"Well, no, see, I didn't think I—"

"You know our moms know each other?" he found himself saying to his chagrin. Anything to keep her on the line . . . "Yeah, fancy that. Coincidence, huh? Nice coincidence. Says your people are good folks, but I already knew that— not that I knew that our mothers had a connection, but that you were good people, were from good people." Again the woman had him babbling. He'd definitely been drugged. Yet he loved the euphoria of it.

"Isn't that weird?" she replied with an easy chuckle.

God, he loved the sound of this woman's voice.

"Yeah, in a good sort of way."

"Yeah." The feminine voice sighed.

There was that sigh again. . . .

"Hey, tell you what," he pressed, feeling a sense of panic that she might back away for some unfathomable reason, "wanna try out your new tires and come over? Just to hang out; it's a gorgeous day, and—"

"I can't. I'm baby-sitting for Gail, and I'll have the girls with me all night."

"Oh, yeah, yeah, I can dig it." Defeat claimed him as he spied a mall as he passed it. "Well, maybe some other time?"

"Definitely," she said in a warm tone.

"Monday night?" he said way too quickly, then admonished himself as he took the jug-handle turn to head back toward the mall. The silence that hung in the air created a static charge in his nervous system.

"I'd have to get a baby-sitter. . . ."

"Think you can?" He tried to control his breathing as he entered the mall parking lot.

"Probably, unless Gail and Delores have plans. I can't get in touch with Miss Vic."

"I'll cook for you."

Again, silence.

"What if I bring over some redfish, plantains, and rice and peas and cook for you this time?" she offered shyly.

"You've already done enough, and I don't want to wear out my welcome."

Wear out her welcome . . . she could wear out anything he had. "Uh, no . . . you don't have to go to all that trouble on my account, baby. I enjoy cooking for you."

Silence. His stomach was in knots.

"Why don't we both cook? I'll bring some stuff, and we can heat up that leftover okra and cornbread to go with the food I bring?"

Yes, there is a God!

"Cool," he said in a forced casual tone. "What time do you want me to swing by to lead you over?"

"Say, same time we did it before . . . but this time can I wear something more comfortable, like jeans and a sweater?"

Lord help him, this woman was on the same page.

"Yeah . . . that sounds real good to me. I'll see you tomorrow. Call me if there's any problem at the garage, okay?"

"Okay . . . 'bye. And thanks again," she murmured, then was gone.

He sat in the mall parking space and looked at the marquee choices. Pier 1. Candles, plants, new comforters . . . what did she say? *Oh, yeah, throw pillows.* Her sanctuary had to be perfect.

Nicole nearly petted the telephone as she hung it up and went into the living room. "Girls, get your coats and shoes on; we're going to Pep Boys, and to pick up a Sunday paper. Lydia, you go to the potty before we leave."

"Okay," Lydia said in a disgruntled tone as she tore herself from the program she was watching.

But Nicole noticed that Michelle's gaze was following her intently. "What?" She finally giggled as the teen continued to gawk at her.

"Aunt Nikki," she said in a conspiratorial voice, glancing down the hallway behind Lydia, and waiting for the bathroom door to shut before she looked back at Nicole. "My mom isn't coming home tonight, is she?"

The question caught Nicole totally off guard, and she found herself slowly approaching the sofa to sit beside Michelle.

"Uh, to be honest, I'm not sure," Nicole hedged. "Why?"

"This is the happiest I've ever seen my mother in all her life. She's running around, bumping into things, dropping things, humming in the kitchen . . . that other guy she went out with earlier in the week didn't make her act all crazy. What's up?"

Nicole stifled a wide grin and looked away as she spoke. "I think she likes this deacon a lot."

"I'm glad." The teen sighed hard, and let her body fall back against the cushions. "My mom deserves somebody to make her feel like that."

"Yeah, she does," Nicole murmured, returning her gaze to Michelle's and taking the child's hands.

"But I don't want her to give up her dreams, though . . . she is so much happier catering than she was working at the hospital. They treated her mean there, and worked my mom like a dog . . . that's why, when I grow up, I'm going to be a doctor, not a nurse."

Nicole blinked and stared at the young woman in front of her. "Have you ever told your mother how you felt, or what you wanted to be?"

"Nah," Michelle replied wistfully. "She'd only worry about how to pay for it, or it might make her feel bad that she never went that far."

"But your mom's dream wasn't to be a doctor. She always wanted to cook, but took up nursing because it was a good-paying job. She'd be proud to hear that."

"People think that just because you're young, you don't know things," Michelle murmured. "But we do. Like, I've seen my mother struggle by herself, and I know how much she loves me, and she's scared I'm going to go out there and get pregnant . . . or see her have a friend and think I'm grown, and mess up . . . but that's not true."

Nicole could only stare at the person who she suddenly realized had become a woman-child before her. All of Gail's deepest fears were being washed away on a Sunday afternoon as her daughter confessed maturity while holding Nicole's hand. The transformation that she witnessed put her own mother's words into perspective, and as the student taught her, Nicole developed a new respect for the power of a mother's prayers.

"See, Aunt Nikki," Michelle said with a long sigh, after taking a moment to gather her thoughts. "I have goals, and getting pregnant and having to raise a baby all by myself, or put that strain on my momma, ain't one of 'em. I don't think just because you're a woman, and want some company in your life, or want kids, that everything else you love has to get put on the back burner for someday that never comes. That's why me and Mom fight all the time. I already know that. I've already seen that happen to some of my best friends. I'm not them. But Momma keeps trying to act like I don't have good sense."

"Your mother's just scared . . . don't you know what it's like to be afraid of something bigger than you, and hope it won't hurt those you love?"

Michelle looked off in the distance and nodded. "Yeah, I do," she whispered. "My dad."

The child's honest comment, said without bitterness, just resignation, made Nicole taste tears. "Give your mom a chance to let go of her fear, so she can let go of you a little bit. Maybe finding her own happiness outside of just you and her will help her do that."

Nicole held her breath and waited for a response. She wanted so much for Gail to see this soon-to-be woman trying to fly, learning to fly—with the courage and eagerness to ascend up to her dearest friend's highest hopes . . . that the girl reach her full potential. It was like watching a young eagle flap its wings on her sofa, and she wanted to open the window and encourage Michelle to go for it . . . go for the top, till the clouds were beneath her. But it was not her place to open that window all the way yet. That was her mother's job. She could only stand on the sidewalk and cheer the girl on. Gail would have to let go first.

And God only knew that she wanted so much for this child to likewise accept her mother's need for independence without resentment. And Lord knew how much she wanted them both to be happy and safe in this evolutionary, revolutionary transformation of household change. One was learning to fly, as the older one with the battered wing was testing her flight patterns again. And God help them, there were so many rocks, and so many storms to consider if they did indeed fall.

"She trusts me, doesn't she? She just doesn't trust the world not to hurt me, right, Aunt Nikki? Is that what you're saying?"

Fly, baby, fly . . . Nicole's mind echoed. *God, lift this child up and protect her as she goes.*

"Yes, suga," Nicole murmured. "Your mother trusts *you* . . . she's just learning tonight to trust the world a little; give her time. But talk to her . . . she's a good friend to have— the best friend to have."

"My mom?" Michelle laughed gently. "She's so tough . . . and she don't play. And it's her way or the highway."

"She's just giving you a map until you learn the rules of the road."

"I guess so."

"My mom was the same way, and her mom was the same way, and her mom was the same way." Nicole chuckled.

"Really?"

"Really. And I thought I'd *never* get away from that woman . . . and now I miss her so much, and she's the first person I call to kiss all my boo-boos."

"That's who you were talking to all that time?"

"Yeah." Nicole chuckled. "Met a new fella, and had to call my mom."

"But you grown, Aunt Nikki!" Michelle giggled and blushed and looked away.

"Yup . . . but I'll always be her child."

The two exchanged a silent understanding and sealed it with their smiles.

"My mom doesn't have her mom to call anymore . . . Nana died." Michelle's expression immediately clouded over, and the sad acceptance in it seemed to be mixed with fledgling knowledge that her mother was also a daughter once.

"Yeah," Nicole whispered. "That's why your mom came to me. You gotta have good girlfriends—family. That's why she's always fussin' about who your girlfriends are, and what they're about."

"I hadn't thought of it like that. I mean, you never think of not having your mom around anymore, you know?"

"Yeah, and one day your mother will surprise you, honey," Nicole affirmed. "She trusts you and respects you and loves you, and I know for a fact that she prays for you in her heart every day."

"I just want her to be happy, Aunt Nikki—to keep that smile, ya know? In fact, I'm glad you have somebody nice to dress up for and to make you run for the phone, too. There's nobody special calling me yet," she said wistfully. "But I'll watch my play sister anytime. You all don't need to baby-sit me anymore."

"No, I guess we don't," Nicole murmured as she squeezed the young girl's hands. A dawning awareness captured her as she slipped an arm around Michelle's shoulders and pulled her to her breast and stroked her hair. "You're all grown-up now, huh? Where did the time go, baby girl of mine? One day you're gonna have somebody special call. Don't rush it, choose wisely, and be good to yourself in the process. Too many people love you, and don't want to see you get hurt."

"I love you too, Aunt Nikki. I won't disappoint you, my mom, and all those aunties who love me. Promise."

"Yeah, sweetie. You won't."

"All done!" Lydia yelled as she raced toward them. "Whatchu talkin' 'bout?"

"Just girl talk," Nicole answered, exchanging a knowing

smile with Michelle. "C'mon, ladies, let's go get some tires!"

He hadn't expected to get in to see Byron Redfield without an appointment; he was going to just leave word that he'd stopped by so they could meet on neutral ground. But when the secretary announced him, nodded, and stood up quickly, Adam followed her past the large walnut reception-area desk, down a long hallway, and entered the expansive wood-paneled space that Byron Redfield occupied.

Adam glanced around the room past the man standing before him. He'd expected Redfield to be smugly sitting at his behemoth leather-and-walnut show of power. But instead he was standing, looking agitated, and pacing in front of the huge picture window that framed Philadelphia's skyline.

"Let me get to the point," Adam said from deep within his chest. "I hate liars."

"Let me get to the point," Redfield boomed back. "I'm not one. And I need you to know that."

"What do you care? I only came here to look you in your face and to tell you that I didn't appreciate your using me to get my cousin to back off. Figured I needed to deliver that message face-to-face."

"Mr. Redfield, your nine-o'clock is here," a woman's voice chimed through the black multiline telephone on the attorney's desk.

"Tell them I need a few minutes, offer them some coffee or something, but I need a few, Jackie."

"Yes, sir." Then the voice was gone.

"You may be used to throwing your weight around, Redfield—"

"Cut the crap!" Redfield jumped in. "Your cousin was trying to set me up."

''What? You know, we can step outside and do this the old-fashioned way, brother.'' Sudden rage pumped adrenaline through Adam's veins as both men squared off, standing their ground.

''Not necessary,'' Redfield retorted. ''You know why she needed a letter from me on my stationery?''

Something about the indignant conviction in Redfield's tone gave Adam pause.

''I'm listening.''

''So she could scan it and make copies of an original, with my signature!''

''And may I ask how you came to this brilliant, twisted conclusion?''

''Because her girlfriend, one Carole Winston, used to work for one of my clients—terminated as of first thing this morning. She worked in the trucking company's New York central office data processing center, and just so happened to be in there on Sunday, electronically changing the manifest dockets on certain carriers to reflect lower inventory being shipped to the Philadelphia security warehouse than should have actually been on the trucks. You do know a Carole Winston—intimately, I take it.''

He could not speak. His ears were ringing.

''Right. I thought so. Seems you two have been around this particular bend in the road before. Only last time, she didn't get caught. It only singed her, but didn't burn her. We checked her background and found out about a little mix-up in the DA's office in New Orleans, and somehow she squeezed through the cracks with her charges dropped. Your late partner was the arresting officer. I like to know who I'm dealing with, too.''

''Seems you've done your homework on me. Why?''

''Because, according to one of the accomplices' confession, the trucks would get out of New York with a full load, they'd unload along the way as per usual, and sit in the company's secured lot in Philadelphia overnight—but would have too much inventory to account for.''

Acid singed Adam's esophagus as the old familiar scene unwound itself in his head.

''It was almost perfect, clean,'' Redfield raged on. ''When the drivers would prepare to park for the night in the security yard, they'd be confused because they'd have remaining boxes to unload—but nowhere to unload them. You following me?''

Adam nodded. Unfortunately, he did follow. *I was like an eerie déjà vu.*

''Yeah,'' Adam murmured. ''The drivers, naturally, would have questions, and would follow manifest discrepancy procedures to fax back the manifest to headquarters, right? No driver wants to get fired because he missed a drop location, and have to haul it back to its origination point. So he'd call and say that there was more on the truck than the paperwork indicated there should be. A fax would be sent back to the security company to instruct them to allow another trucking company to enter the yard and remove certain excess items—and someone would cite a mere paperwork error.''

''Right,'' Redfield confirmed, his voice still icy, yet calmer. ''This way, the bogus firm could drop-ship high-end electronics wherever my signature said to drop it. Since instructions would be faxed, no one would be looking for an original sign-off on the paper trail, until much later. The security company wouldn't be liable, because they had faxed authorization. The driver of the authentic truck would be none the wiser, because he was just following orders sent down from the top. The parent company wouldn't discover the inventory shrinkage until quarterly reconciliations were done—and when the auditors ultimately came through to investigate, the signature would be mine—the parent firm's attorney of record! And these manifests, when they arrived in Philly, would be checked and logged by none other than one Gonzalee Dieter, Cecilia's boss!''

A sickening feeling filled Adam's guts, and he unclenched his fist and wiped his face with his hands.

''Yeah, Bastille. I was the one marked at the salon, after they got to know my sister—who was talking about her hotshot lawyer brother in the damned beauty parlor! I was marked and picked out before I even knew what was happening to me. Thank God I didn't sleep with her!''

Adam could only stare at the man who was now walking in a circle around him.

''My client's internal security investigators nabbed that Carole person and pulled her telephone records, only to find dozens of calls going between Cecilia's house, her job, and her cell phone. What's more, did you know you had a wife?''

''What?'' Adam asked slowly.

''Oh, so you didn't know?''

''Talk to me, brother. I'm all ears.''

''It appears that your wife, Mrs. Adam Bastille, a.k.a. Cecilia Sampson before she married you, would be the one to receive payments from these shipments into her Internet firm's lockbox . . . for the sales of products which apparently they've taken orders for over the Net. Business-to-business sales only and deliveries to small stores in Philly that think they're buying legitimate goods through an Internet electronics wholesaler. Everything still in the box.''

''Sampson was her married name before she went back to Bastille! And I'm her cousin!''

''Right. Well, she flipped the script, just in case she got caught. Then it would be the poor Southern girl who just did what her estranged husband, whom she wanted to remain amicable with during the contrived divorce proceeding she claimed to be going through, told her to do for business reasons. She'd say she didn't know how to set up a Website all by her little ol' self. She didn't know where her husband got the goods. That it all seemed on the up-and-up because her husband showed her copies of papers with a big, well-known attorney's name on it—see why my signature is so valuable?'' Redfield glared at him with disgust. ''Do you *now* see why I don't just deal with anybody and everybody? My signature, brother, is a damned asset.''

''But that is so insane!'' Adam paced toward the window. ''First of all, she'd get caught in a lie about being married to me. They could pull marriage certificates to prove that, easy enough. The divorce decree would have some other brother's name, and—''

''But while all of this was under investigation, with cops going down blind alley after blind alley and eating up precious time, she and her girlfriend could cash checks and get out of the country beyond the reach of the law—Cecilia had identification as being both a Bastille and a Sampson.''

''We don't live together; there's no way she could make it look like—''

''You two have phone records between you . . . and you have a past that narrowly links you both to a similar scam in Louisiana. So once the cops got on the horn to each other, they'd drop her as the top suspect and pursue you, and by the time they woke up and smelled the coffee, she'd be history. That's why it was so important that you be played off as her husband, because your paths interwove so perfectly as a cover. Simple. You been had, my man, by blood.''

''I need an attorney, don't I?'' Adam faced Byron and silence sliced between them.

''No.''

''Why not?''

''Because you have one—who is very, very pissed off at

the moment, but who had the presence of mind to have that stupid son of a bitch, Gonzalee, picked up first. That's why she was hysterical, because I got the name first, then told her no. I've been around the block, and can tell when things are fishy.''

''Yeah,'' Adam conceded. ''I was gonna pay him a visit myself, after I stopped in on you. None of this sat right with me, despite what she told me. I needed firsthand information, just so I could sleep at night.''

''Well, now we're on the same page,'' Redfield replied, letting his breath out hard. ''Do you know that fool fell for it, and threw chicken guts on her steps after he slept with her the first time, hoping that they could run off together and get married? Then when she told him she was going to reconcile with her estranged husband—you—to get him off her back, and she left her car at her town house because she was going partying in New York with Carole to celebrate . . . and he'd seen you coming in and out upon occasion— he freaked and smashed up her car. That was the X-factor that she hadn't considered. The poor slob fell in love with her, and didn't care as much about the money as he wanted her.''

''Deep.''

''Very.''

Again silence fell between them, but not as frigid this time.

''Love will make a man do foolish things.''

''Yeah.''

''All of them are lucky, because none of the trucks had dropped shipments yet, so they'll do time, but not as much as they could have. The scam was botched before it went down, big-time.''

Adam rubbed his hands over his face. He needed to sit down as much as he needed to get outside into the fresh air.

"Look, man, I owe you one. Thanks . . . Where're Cecilia and Carole now?"

"Down at the roundhouse," Redfield said in a weary voice.

"I'm going to have to call my family . . . but this time I'm not bailing my cousin out, and bailing Carole out is not even on my mental radar."

"From a legal perspective, I wouldn't advise you to bail either of them out, family or old lover notwithstanding. And I'd stay as far away from them as possible. You coulda got snagged up real bad in this one, on a hummer."

"Yeah." Adam nodded, trying to think of what he could tell his mother and aunt. The truth, plain and simple, was the only thing that came to his mind. "I owe you one, man," he stated again, this time extending his hand to Byron Redfield. "I misjudged you, brother . . . my bad."

"Yeah, it's all good," Redfield said, accepting the handshake with a half smile. "I misjudged you, too, at first. Thought you were in on it, until the cops collared Dieter at his house, and the stupid bastard started blubbering and confessing . . . and when they picked up Carole and Cecilia, everybody started telling on everyone else."

Adam shook his head. "Why didn't you page me last night when all of this went down?"

"I had some, uh, other business to reconcile," Redfield said with a wry smile.

"I can dig it."

"But I need a character witness, so I'm going to call you on that."

"No problem. I can meet you down at the courthouse anytime—"

"Naw, man," Redfield said quickly. "Need you over at the salon. Victoria wouldn't speak to me or return phone calls. I had to have one of my brothers on the inside at the station literally flash his badge, pick her up, and take her downtown to show her, behind a two-way mirror, what was going down. Coulda cost my boy his pension, and I coulda been disbarred for that, if the wrong people had found out. Sneaked her in under the bogus claim that we needed somebody to identify who Cecilia was . . . but I had to get Victoria to trust me. She's a tough cookie.''

''Then why do you need me?'' Adam chuckled as he ran his hands through his hair. This was beyond crazy.

''Well, I used the last vial, I understand, that exists on the planet to, er, repair the fracture . . . uh, to be able to fully communicate with Ms. Jones. And, uh, there's nothing to take to the lab—but I'm still interested in investing in the establishment, even without a psychic or the elixir. They have a dynamite operation going on anyway . . . and one of the best stylists in the city connected to an up-and-coming design studio, so . . .''

''Yeah.'' Adam chuckled as he stared at Byron. ''But why do you need *me* to go by the salon?''

''Uh, Jo Jo . . . he's not convinced that my intentions are honorable . . . and Gail was unreachable by telephone, and Delores was unable to be located. And Nicole was skeptical . . . and, look, man, I want to—''

''Pass full family inspection. I can dig it.''

He watched Redfield's shoulders relax and drop two inches as he extended his hand to Adam again.

''I'm serious about her, you know, and I did not sleep with your cousin. I messed up the first marriage with career climbing, and I vowed never to go there again. But I'm at my apex and it's lonely at the top, so with Victoria, I wanted to give her something of her own, that she could depend on, and that would take care of her people. I don't care if I make any money on the joint . . . I've got more than I need, and more than one person can spend, but it's just not enjoyable spending it alone anymore. I had the papers all drawn up, she'd signed a set, and today we were supposed to get the other people a copy so they could review them with their own attorneys and sign on if they wanted in on the business. But Victoria got cold feet after she talked to Jo Jo, and . . . Can you hook a brother up?''

"Yeah, man. Don't know how much influence I have, but I can dig it.''

"Oh, so now you going to come in here and try to talk to me about my favorite girl, Miss Vic, huh?''

Adam summoned patience as he followed Jo Jo to the back room in the crowded salon.

"It's a madhouse out there. Mrs. Webster is burning up under the dryer, Victoria is upstairs in her condo stretched out, too damned tired and emotionally drained to deal, I have five new girls in here that don't know their shears from their—''

"Jo Jo, man, look, I just need a minute. Please, brother. It's important.''

Jo Jo leaned against the wall and shut the office door. "Everything is changing around here, and it could have been so good . . . so close.'' He swallowed hard and looked away. "The family is breaking up. Soon you'll be taking Nikki . . . Gail's already as good as gone—so is Dee . . . and Victoria, well, it's only a matter of time before Redfield wears her down—it ain't about the money! I have been a bartender, a cook, a caterer, a stylist, a designer, and some things I don't want to talk about.'' His eyes glittered with unshed tears as he thrust his chin up with pride. "I can make it.''

"I know you can,'' Adam said in a gentle tone.

"Well, I'm glad you do!'' Jo Jo folded his arms over his

chest and sucked in a huge gulp of air. "Because when *you all* break their hearts, and their mothers die away one by one, and their girlfriends are too focused on their own pain or joy to listen . . . and their kids are teenagers and too busy to care, *I will be here for them.*" Jo Jo leveled his gaze at Adam and pointed hard at his own chest. "I," he repeated in a shaky voice, "will be the brother they never had to look out for them, the one to take the bullet."

"Man, listen," Adam urged. "Nobody is in danger like that; there is no bullet—"

"No bullet! No bullet?" Jo Jo reared back and clasped his chest. "The silver bullet, brother! I take the silver bullet every time, and nobody ever realizes how much."

Adam was dumbstruck. For the first time in his life, he didn't know what to do. He couldn't process the image with the way the logic flowed in cryptograms. He furrowed his brow and opened his hands to gesture for clarity. *What bullet?*

"Just like a man," Jo Jo spat. "You are listening with your head instead of your heart."

"Guilty," Adam murmured. "I don't understand."

"The silver bullet that kills the spirit. When you all mess over these ladies, and you get up out of their beds and don't call, and you make them feel worthless and ugly—Jo Jo is always there. I make them feel loved, worthy, beautiful, make them laugh again, and share their pain. And I erase the damage of heartbreak right in my salon thrones. I, Joseph, love them without sex . . . without expectation that they do for me . . . without fathering their children . . . without competing with them. *I am their friend.* And when they go out there in that big, bad world, and get shot down by love, I am here to take the bullet out and put them back together again after you men shatter their dreams with one shot. So," he scoffed, turning on his heel to walk away, "what can you tell me about taking the bullet for somebody you love?"

"Wait, man," Adam whispered, touching Jo Jo's arm to stop his retreat. "You can tell *me* a lot about it . . . since I carry a gun. You're right to be concerned. If any of them were my sisters, I would be—Some of us don't know how to lock the gun cabinet and make it safe for women and children. I'm trying to hear what you've said."

Jo Jo turned and blinked back tears and sucked in a deep, steadying breath.

"I'm not going to hurt her, and if I do, I'm going to come to her big brother for advice."

The expression on Jo Jo's face softened as he studied Adam.

"You'd include me as family?"

Something in the sad tone in Jo Jo's voice drew Adam's spirit. Pain like that knew no gender or orientation. His arms opened as his heart did toward the good person before him, and he embraced Jo Jo warmly, the way family does when they haven't seen each other in a long time.

"I'm from down South . . ." Adam murmured as he pulled back, held Jo Jo by the upper arms, and looked at him squarely. "Where I come from, when you marry a woman, you marry her friends, her family, everybody—and you treat her children like they're your own, 'cause they are. Half the time you can't remember whose cousin belongs to which aunt. It's not important. We call it kin. The blood being thicker than the mud. And I hear tell Redfield's a good man—from North Carolina, or somethin' . . . and if he's plannin' on marrying Nikki's play sister, Miss Vic, well, then, that would be your and my brother-in-law."

"Are you saying what I think you're saying . . . about my Nikki?" Jo Jo covered his mouth with his hand.

Declining to clarify what was forming as a new concept in

his mind, Adam pressed on, trying to make Jo Jo understand. "And if I keep on down that path, then if the deacon makes the cut, then Miss Gail's Masonic-lodge dude gets folded into the mix . . . and if Delores works it out, whoever she brings to the table comes too. But none of us is going to make the cut unless their big brother Jo Jo gives the word— that's y'all's family law. Right?"

"You would invite me to your weddings, your homes, at family gatherings, picnics . . . holiday get-togethers, and let me be with all my nieces and nephews . . . you wouldn't just lock me away and try to act like I didn't exist because of—"

"C'mon, man. Cut that mess out. How you gonna lop off an arm of your family like that? My mother is a Christian woman, a tad unorthodox in some of her approaches, but she always said, 'Judge not, lest ye be judged.' Right?"

"It's happened so many times to me," Jo Jo whispered. "I just don't want to be extinguished, like I never existed. Once they marry, and the men come on the scene and can't deal . . . slowly but surely my girlfriends drift away . . . ."

"It happens to all of our friends, to a small degree. You link up with somebody, and when it's right, well . . . that spouse becomes the best friend. But that doesn't cut out family and joy and caring. That's why the holidays are so important, I guess," Adam murmured, dropping his hold on Jo Jo's arm as he thought about Easter and going home. "I guess that's why the old folks make such a fuss about it, because their houses get quiet and their loved ones move away . . . and they cherish the laughter."

"Sounds like you could use a dose of home, too, Adam."

"Yeah, I could, man. Hadn't realized that until I just said it. One day I ain't gonna have a momma or daddy to fuss with, and to heap big plates for me, and to get in my business . . . and that's going to be a very lonely day. That's why we have to keep adding and building good memories and good family—by blood or extension, you know what I mean?''

"Well," Jo Jo said, becoming revived as he issued Adam a sly wink. "I believe we should start building that business right away, putting up for a rainy day. But right now, hon, I have to get Mrs. Webster before her hair falls out and she sues us.''

Adam shook his head as Jo Jo flounced away from him and exited the office. He stood there for a moment collecting his thoughts, and then walked up to Jo Jo to say good-bye.

"She's coming over tonight for dinner. Just thought you should know . . . and—''

"Chile, that's old news," Jo Jo said with a wave of his hand to dismiss Adam. "I already knew. Who you think is baby-sitting?''

Chapter 22

His face still hurt from laughing when she'd told him about the potions and explained how truly interlocked their lives had been from the very start. When she got to the part about Gail's omissions of facts, and how his own god-mother's roots had sat on a kitchen shelf for ten years, he thought he was going to need paramedics. This crazy, fiery, petite ball of energy had come into his kitchen and taken over. She had told him to "get out the way, move, boy" so many times that he'd had to hold on to appliances to breathe because of laughing so hard.

And he'd especially loved the way she used a spatula to make a point while frying fish and how she'd fussed and stomped in her socks on the tile floor when he'd explained what Cecilia had done. It was exhilarating to have someone defend his honor, for once, and take exception to anyone messing with him. He liked the feeling of being claimed without mention. It was a subtle understanding that didn't require words. When a person just became shocked and then told you what they'd do if the offender crossed her path, you knew someone had claimed you—even if they were just venting.

But perhaps the part of her being in his kitchen that he liked the most was hearing the sound of her laughing with him. He knew he'd gotten to her too when he'd stopped her ability to fix red gravy midprocess. It was the explanation about why he'd no longer chew the sticks his mom always sent that had done her in.

He had to rescue the pan from flames as she screamed and bent over double, waving him away to make him stop telling her more. Oh, yes, this was a woman he wanted in his kitchen, one who shared good stories and made him forget about his day. One comfortable enough to take off her shoes while merrily admitting that she couldn't do a thing right with them on—that was who he'd always envisioned there.

And perhaps the best part of it all was that he had something to contribute, even though it paled against the delicate balance of offerings she'd made. But the homemade lemon butter pound cake dusted lightly with confectioner's sugar had been his undoing. It was all in the way she licked her fingers when she was finished, then pouted when he couldn't eat more.

"How about another glass of wine?"

"No, no, no, I cannot put another thing in my stomach," she said, laughing as they cleared the plates.

"Next time we do this, girl, I'm just going to wear sweatpants. I'm going to stop trying to be casually correct— the way you throw down, I have to loosen my belt."

"Compliment accepted. But I had to show you I had some skills," she said with an easy laugh.

"No, you didn't," he huffed as they went into the living

room to flop on the sofa. "I knew you was from down home."

"Yeah, but see, you might have thought I'd been in Philly too long . . . ooh, boy, I can't breathe myself. My belly is too full."

She sprawled in a lazy pose adjacent to him, and the action seemed so natural it was as though she'd lived there all her life. The soft light in the living room enveloped her and made it difficult to tell where her skin stopped and the fawn-colored mohair sweater she wore began. Even though she was casually dressed, looking at her made him wish that he'd put on something more than a pair of jeans and a Polo shirt to be in her company. She seemed so regal and relaxed, even in what she called casual attire, that he wondered how she mastered such composure and grace while he, on the other hand, was desperately struggling to maintain his.

It was as though she were sitting before him topless, save her faded denim jeans. Nothing was about her neck or wrists; there was no obstruction to that flawless skin. Her hair was loosely piled up high in a way that made him want to reach out and touch the delicate wisps of curls that had fallen from their hold, and he so wanted to kiss her earlobes, which teased him with a tiny glint of small dangling gold teardrops. Everything about her was soft, gentle. All of her was such a stark contrast to him.

He watched her sated expression and the way her eyes closed halfway while she took in and expelled long, deep breaths. He loved it and wished she would stay.

"You know they say that Philly is really a big down-South, and it is. People fall by your house without notice, and everybody knows somebody who knows somebody who knows you—which can be kinda good and kinda bad."

He laughed and nodded, almost too full to respond.

"Yeah, that's why I moved to Jersey. Wouldn't want them falling by tonight, though."

His truth made her blush and look at her hands in a way that he liked. She was the harmony he needed within the discordant life he'd been living. His mind repeated the hope like a bayou chant: *Please stay tonight, baby . . . stay here and make this a home.*

"I guess there are times when the closeness can become a little wearing," she said with an easy laugh.

"Not all the time . . . just sometimes," he murmured.

Again she smiled a demure smile and looked at her hands.

"But sometimes, even with all my friends here, I miss going home; you know what I mean?"

He did. "Been thinking about making a road trip down to New Orleans for Easter."

The concept of company was growing thick in his mind. It was just like watching her make that red gravy for the fish. It started out thin, but as she talked and stirred him, and watched him, but not too hard, and added a little of this and that, it became something spicy, rich, and good.

He waited as she rolled the concept around on her palate, tested it by dipping her finger into it, deciding if it needed something else.

"Yeah . . . I might go home myself," she murmured in a lazy, sexy tone. "Might be what the soul needs. Who knows?"

She'd taken a sip from the edge of the hot spoon he'd held out to her. Now it was his turn to decide if he needed something more.

"Think you might consider making it a double road trip?"

She cocked her head to the side and raised one eyebrow with a smile.

"Like maybe you and the baby could come see these

crazy people I hail from. Stay a day or two; then I'd drive you to Florida if you'd like."

"You're asking me to go *home* with you ... me and Lydia ... to meet your people? This soon?"

Too much pepper, and he needed to turn down the flame.

"You know what you know when you know, you know?"

She smiled. Yes, she did know.

"Last time we did this, you asked me if you could read some of the stuff I wrote."

He smiled. She'd turned the flame back up to keep the temperature even.

"Yeah, I did."

"Well, I started rummaging through all my old stuff, and all of it seemed so sad, or too journalistic ... clippings from articles, and stuff."

"And stuff?"

"Yeah," she said slowly, reaching into her pocket. "The old stuff was partial thoughts, or poems that no longer apply."

He looked at the piece of paper that she held in her hand and watched how her eyes no longer seemed to be able to meet his. He could tell that she was considering, thinking, deciding whether she wanted to flavor what was cooking with this ingredient.

"Would you read it to me?" he murmured, moving closer to be right next to her as she sat up. "Is this old, or new, or somewhere in between?"

"It's new, because it's how you've made me feel since we began doing this. It's old, because it draws on a comparison of everything I've felt in the past. And it's somewhere in between, because I'm not sure if I'm ready to read this to you yet ... even though I couldn't sleep last night and I stayed up late with it in my head."

"You stayed up at night to write something about what's going on between us?"

"Yeah." She laughed self-consciously. "Crazy, too sentimental too fast, don't you think?"

"No," he whispered, lifting her chin with one finger. "I am honored."

He wanted to kiss her so badly, but didn't want to spoil what she offered: a peek into her soul, laid bare as if she'd disrobed for him and was naked. No one had ever thought so much about him to give him such a tender gift, priceless beyond measure, and he watched her unfold the paper with reverent awe.

"Okay . . . but don't laugh this time, please."

"I wouldn't laugh at anything you had to give me from your heart, Nicole. I wouldn't; trust me."

He watched her take a deep breath, and he could see the paper trembling between her fingers. His arm found her shoulder as her head nestled against his chest. He closed his eyes as peace covered him and the sound of her unsteady voice arrested the rhythm in his heart. Oh, yes, most assuredly, he and God were on speaking terms again.

"'There's so much about you that's unfamiliar, new, frighteningly unlike me . . . '" she murmured, her writing coming alive as he visualized her words in his mind's eye.

"'But then you smile that lopsided smile of yours, and open your mouth, and I'm home. Your deep laughter becomes warm syrup over biscuits and grits. Filling, in a way that sticks with you, comfort . . . Carried on a familiar cadence of a slow drawl and reminiscent phrases, you transport me to all that is good, from where I blossomed and became a woman—not just a little girl. In your eyes I see back porches, and fireflies, and small gardens. Your gentle, easy manner pushing away concrete and broken glass . . . home training, church picnics—no, y'all, chivalry is not dead. And your touch becomes humid nights, sheets that cling from dampened bodies, where a fan and iced tea yield minor mercy . . . no escape from a heat that makes sleep impossible to claim.' "

Then she slowly folded the paper up and held it tightly before she tucked it away. "That's all I was doing, messing around, and—"

He touched his fingers to her lips. "Come home with me and sit on the back porch awhile, and laugh with me and my people, and let Lydia run in the yard catching fireflies in a mason jar. And promise me that you'll never stop writing, or ever hide this gift from me. Come home with me, baby. . . . It doesn't take a man that long to make up his mind."

He replaced his finger with his lips when he saw tears make her eyes sparkle, and he kissed them gently away from her cheeks as they ran down her face. And as her words burned in his mind, they ignited inside his soul, making him deepen their kiss to find her tongue and the traces of lemon butter pound cake that were left behind.

When her hands smoothed his shoulders, he covered one with his palm. "Come upstairs with me and let me show you what I hope you'll like . . . I tried to fix up a sanctuary and remember all of your specifications. But without your woman's touch, it will never be exactly right."

She followed him as he held her hand and led her. Her heart was beating fast, but she was not nervous or unsure. It felt so right, so peaceful . . . so natural to be with him this way, and as they neared the bedroom, a golden glow spilled out into the hall.

"I went up and lit these," he murmured, "while you were fixing supper. And I'd hoped that you'd come up and like a little bit of what I've done."

She traced her fingers over his jaw and soaked in the

anticipation that reflected in his eyes, and more tears rose to blur the beauty of the room that he'd changed just for her. Lush plants and potted flowers had turned the room into Eden. Tall, thick candles stood everywhere within sturdy wrought-iron holders. He'd lit a fire and cast a rug before it. And the leather chair and television had been exiled to another room. Thick goose down covered the bed, and pillows had been strewn in rich supply, and he led her past it all to the oasis he'd created in the adjoining bathroom.

He'd turned porcelain into paradise, lit with frankincense and myrrh, and scattered white rose petals in steaming water, with trees and plants enough to shame an arboretum—just for her. A carafe of wine with two long-stemmed flutes waited patiently for her to make a decision, while guarding a thin crystal vase of roses. Never in her life had a man redesigned his life to custom-fit her.

She breathed her appreciation into his mouth as she whispered, "Thank you." Her hands unbuttoned his shirt, to let him know her decision had been made. And as her palm covered the center of his bare chest, and her mouth landed a deep kiss behind it, his eyes closed and his head fell back. His grip tightened on her arms as she unfastened his belt and took her time with his zipper, telling him thank-you again as he took her mouth.

The delicate collarbone that he'd traced with just his finger, tonight he was allowed to trace with his tongue. And her granted permission shook him as she removed her sweater, and the form that he'd imagined beneath it was almost too perfect to ruin by touch. His lips, steadier now than his hands, paid homage to the skin she'd exposed. Short gasps came up from deep within her belly and brought him to his knees to caress her skin for the offense of making him wait so long.

And like the priceless gift that it was, he unwrapped the

rest of her body, carefully peeling away layers of clothing that swathed her until he could savor all that they had hidden from him before. In that moment, he could only look up at her, but being allowed to witness the expression on her face was the most sacred part of what she'd given.

He stood and revealed himself to her unashamed, standing so close without touching her that he could feel the soft hair on her skin brush his. When she touched his face and closed the seal, her full palm stroking his jaw, that was when he realized he'd never made love to a woman before.

The burn of anticipation was balanced so gingerly between immediate want and slow savor. Every light gasp she released summoned one from him in return. And her satin-smooth skin made him remember how much she liked strawberries; his mind soaked in everything she'd taught him about her.

Leading her from the tiled room, he decided to open that part of her gift later. He'd bathe her in petals, after he bathed her with his tongue.

He gently leaned her back on the bed and kissed her belly, then looked up at her—hoping to again see the urgent expression in her eyes. But instead she'd gifted him with a deeper intensity, by arching to his descending kisses with her lips slightly parted to breathe. And again, smooth chocolate eaten slowly from the tip of a ripe berry formed in his mind as he remembered what she'd shown him with her tongue.

Sweetest fragrance drew him down to find out where she hid her ripened fruit, and he was rewarded with a deep moan that told him he'd found exactly where it was.

Although the discovery made him want to rush to have more, he took his time to taste and savor this dessert. But each time she arched beneath his hold, and his tongue licked away the sweetness of her, his intent to remain unhurried

began to melt away in his mind. Her convulsions reminded
him that he'd been nearly starved. Awareness of his own
hunger cramped the muscles in his stomach. Primal memory
fused with instant need and brought him up to cover her—
he was only a fraction of chivalry away from being past
reaching out to the nightstand drawer.

And she transformed seconds into hours as he sheathed
himself to protect her. Her eyes and the short pants she
emitted while waiting turned his hands almost into stone.
Yet, as he returned to her, the touch of her hand against his
cheek steadied him, allowing him to again breathe as she
opened herself to him. Then he sank in hard and shuddered,
and held on to her under her waist, cradling her delicate
shoulders in the bend of his arm.

But it was impossible to keep kissing her when she found
his same rhythm, as though made for him, definitely from
his rib; his other half had sealed him to her.

What began in slow motion, a dance between perfectly
matched partners, became a chant of evenly matched breaths,
a concurrent harmony of voices . . . and that was when she
reminded him of who he was by repeating his name with
frenzied thrusts.

Again he could no longer keep his mouth to hers while
her supple spine worked her hips hard against him; her voice
and her skin and the smell of her fused to become one with
her name erupting with his spirit from the center of his chest.

Beneath him she lay breathing deeply through her mouth,
hair tousled, lips full and parted, tears streaming from the
corners of her closed eyes. Exquisite beauty lay in his grasp
as he sucked in life-sustaining air, arms trembling from
exertion and the realization of the fragile gift he held.

Kissing her eyelids, then the bridge of her nose and her
mouth, he summoned her to open her eyes so that his heart
could drink from their well. Tonight he'd bathe her in

affection; the bath would be just the start. Because this gift was so complex, yet so simple, and it had been so close to him, yet so far, it was not to be entered into irreverently, or unadvisedly. It was to be cherished forever ... as this gift called woman had been given to man from God.

"I've never felt like this," he murmured, "never so complete and never so sure. Come home with me, baby, meet my people, and one day soon let me meet yours."

Her mouth gave him her answer with a partial kiss shared by the simple word, "Okay."

Epilogue

Summertime in Jersey . . . two years later . . .

"Y'all watch out! Coming through with a hot platter of ribs!" Adam yelled. "Why is it that no matter how much space you have in the house, black folks always wind up congregating in the kitchen?" He'd asked the question with a laugh as he brought in a piping-hot tray and set it on the side counter next to the buttered stack of corn on the cob.

"You know that's where we meet," Delores fussed, leaning over to her husband to give him a peck on the cheek as he rubbed her rounded belly.

"Now you know Dee Dee was hanging back here waiting on a refill," Jo Jo teased. "That baby is going to come out looking like spare ribs if Delores don't stop."

Delores laughed as Jo Jo went over to assist Adam, dishing herself another helping of the potato salad that was in reach. "Just because Vikki and Byron are away in the islands on their honeymoon doesn't give you the right to start bossing me around while they're gone—even though they did give you an additional twenty percent of the business. We're still partners—equal partners, regardless of what the papers say."

Jo Jo flounced over to Delores, gave her husband a wink, and smiled. "The only reason I'm not going to read you is because you're carrying my namesake. But as soon as little Josephine gets out into the world, then it's on, girl. Me and you, like old times."

Delores threw her head back and laughed, which made Gail giggle.

"Aw, sookie, sookie, now! Don't y'all start a bunch of mess in Nicole's kitchen," Gail said with a mischievous grin. "Me and Deacon Rutherford might have to pray y'all straight."

"Hey, now, wait a minute," Adam jumped in, chuckling as he found a serving implement to stir the baked beans on the stove. "How, and since when, did this become only Nikki's kitchen? I cook, too, y'all—and everybody been wrapping their greasy lips around my food, so—"

"It became her kitchen when you married her, brother," Delores's husband said with a laugh. "Everything becomes theirs when you marry them."

"Yeah, I don't mind that a bit," Adam replied, casting his gaze toward his wife, who hadn't said much all day. In fact, she looked a little green around the gills. "Baby, you writing another book in your head again? I don't know how you do it with all these folks in here talking yang on kitchen stools."

"Nikki," Jo Jo exclaimed. "You're writing another book? I just told everybody I knew about the first one—which block-bustered, since you dedicated it to me, and all. Had to let them know to recognize . . . but thank you, sweetie. What's it about? Tell us; you cannot keep the scoop from me."

"I'm working on a story line, but have been so tired lately that I haven't been able to peck away at it with any speed."

Nicole peered out of the sliding glass doors that led to the screened-in porch and deck. Teenagers and young adults were laughing, playing cards, the music blaring, with her Lydia right in the center of the action. Homesickness immediately descended upon her, and she wanted to call her mother. Hot tears filled her eyes, and she tried desperately to swallow them away. What was wrong with her? This was what she'd always dreamed of, but at the moment the smell of the food was nauseating her, the laughter was grinding away her nerves, and she just wanted everyone to leave so that she could lie down.

"Baby . . . you all right?" Adam came to her side and put his hand on her back. "You want something to eat? How about some lemonade or iced tea or something? You haven't touched a plate all afternoon, not really, and I made the ribs extra spicy—"

"Please, Adam!" Nicole snapped. She covered her mouth and dry-heaved, and two big tears rolled down her cheeks. "I told you I wasn't hungry, okay?"

Silence hung in the air, and her friends all stared at her. Her husband's expression looked so wounded that it caused another torrent of tears to flow down her face. Then, to her surprise, she heard laughter.

"Ooooh, chile!" Gail squealed as she popped off a stool and rushed to Nicole's side. Then she took Nicole's face in her hands, studied it by cocking her head to the side with a wide grin, and made a clicking sound with her tongue. "That child is pregnant . . . look at her face, Deacon, and tell me I'm lying."

"Oh, Gail, go on," Nicole snapped, becoming peevish as a series of excited congratulations accosted her and Adam. "I can't be . . . I don't think."

"It's the 'I don't think' part," Delores said, giggling, "that gets you every time. Ask me how I know."

"For real? No, y'all, for real?" Adam said in amazement as he gathered Nicole in his arms. "Y'all don't play with me like that," he murmured against his wife's hair. "Oh, baby . . ."

"That's what got the girl in that condition in the first place. 'Oh . . . baby' . . . and puttin' your hands all over her," Jo Jo said with a wide grin. "Oh, I'm going to be an uncle again!"

"Wait, wait, wait, people," Nicole fussed, but smiling despite herself. "We don't know—-"

"Look, girl, I used to be a registered nurse. Don't argue with me. Your face is all round, you crying and actin' simple, and are passing up the best spicy ribs—"

Gail's mention of the ribs again made Nicole's stomach lurch. This time she knew it wasn't a false alarm as she fled the kitchen and went toward the powder room, bellows of laughter following her the whole way.

"Hey, Adam," Delores's husband asked, as Adam sat down very slowly on a stool. "What you put in these ribs? You have to give me your recipe."

"Yeah, dude," Gail's husband agreed. "No offense to my wife's cooking, as she's the best, but I think you got her on these ribs."

"If we weren't running an upscale restaurant, I'd allow Gail to put them on the menu—but I don't know of any way you can make ribs look gourmet . . . no matter how fantastic they are. It's just not haute cuisine . . . but Adam, seriously, you've got it going on. What's in the sauce? You must cut Jo Jo in on the secret ingredient." He laughed, giving Adam a wry chuckle in the process.

Adam looked down the hall toward the powder room, too stunned to immediately respond.

"Er, ah ... I need to call my mother and ask her what was in the spices she sent ... she promised me no more ... Oh, y'all ..."

The kitchen went still, and everyone cast a perplexed but knowing smile in Adam's direction. Then all of a sudden peals of laughter rang out in unison.

"It's a boy, if I know Miz Zelda!" Gail twirled around in the kitchen and laughed. "I'm so glad I got my tubes tied, or else I might be in the same condition, and Victoria would have a heart attack if she wound up this way! She and I are both in the clear on that one. We stopped meddling a *loooong* time ago, with surgery, chile."

"Girl, I've already been zapped." Delores laughed, taking a healthy bite from a rib. "Congrats, Adam," she added with a giggle. "You can't fight fate—or them old dolls down the way."

"Your mom did good," Jo Jo exclaimed with a clap of his hands. "Oh, give Miz Zelda my best regards!"

Slowly, as the concept poured over him, Adam smiled. "Yeah, my mom did do good, didn't she?"

The ringing phone made him stand quickly. He already knew who it was in an eerie sort of way. Without the technology of electronic panels to identify the caller, he knew as he picked up the telephone from its jack on the wall. "Hey, Mom," Adam said with a chuckle. "You've been misbehaving and meddling again."

When the warm Southern drawl connected with his senses and tried to offer him a denial, he laughed hard. "Nicole's pregnant—she's in the bathroom now. My poor wife is barfing, and couldn't eat my ribs. I love you, Momma."

"Pregnant? Oh, praise Jesus! That's so nice, son," his mother crooned in his ear. " 'Bout time. Miz Joleen and Maybell and I've been praying on a boy for y'all for a long time."

Dear Readers:

Within the heart of every human being, I believe there is a desire to love and to be loved. Also there is this elusive thing called hope, where we wish that a little magic might happen for us someday. We have all probably felt this at a point in our lives, and maybe we have even wished upon a star.

That's what LOVE POTIONS is all about—people with fragile inner hopes and dreams being brought together under the most magical of circumstances. Perhaps "magical" is the wrong term. Maybe "miraculous" is more correct . . . because there are miracles from the Divine source happening all around us daily, helping us and encouraging love to enter our lives.

Have fun with this romantic comedy. Have fun in life! And above all else, keep the faith! Dreams do come true.

Much love to you all,
Leslie Esdaile

ABOUT THE AUTHOR

Leslie Esdaile is a native Philadelphian and Dean's List graduate of the University of Pennsylvania, Wharton Undergraduate program. Upon completing her studies in 1980, she embarked upon a career in corporate marketing and sales. Her corporate tenure includes several Fortune 100 companies: Xerox, Hewlett Packard (HP), and ultimately Digital Equipment Corporation (DEC).

In 1991, after a decade of working in the corporate environment, Leslie shifted gears and began an independent consulting career, assisting small businesses and economic development agencies with marketing, grant writing, curriculum development, and workshop facilitation. In 2001 she was the recipient of the US Small Business Administration Minority Advocate of the Year Award (Eastern Region) as well as a City of Philadelphia Mayoral Tribute for Entrepreneurship, and she was nominated for a Golden Pen Award (Best Anthology) by the Black Writers Alliance.

Through technical writing, Leslie found a hidden talent—fiction writing—which has led her on a successful trajectory toward becoming one of the nation's premier African-American female romance and women's fiction authors. Successfully graduating in 1998 from Temple University's Masters of Fine Arts program with a degree in film and media arts, she adds the dimension of filmmaking and visual media to her artistic and business endeavors.

To contact Leslie, you can e-mail her at writerLE@aol.com or visit her Web site at www.esdailebooks.com.